In the Shadow of Time

Kevin Ansbro was born of Irish parents and has lived in Malaysia and Germany.

He is married and currently lives in Norwich, England.

BY THE SAME AUTHOR

Kinnara
(Paperback and eBook)

The Angel in my Well
(eBook)

The Fish That Climbed a Tree
(Paperback and eBook)

The Minotaur's Son
& other wild tales
(Paperback and eBook)

In the Shadow of Time

KEVIN ANSBRO

2QT Limited (Publishing)

2QT Limited Publishing
Settle
United Kingdom

Disclaimer

This is a work of fiction and any resemblance to any person living or dead is purely coincidental. With the exception of famous historical figures, all the characters in this book are fictitious. The place names mentioned are real but have no connection with the events in this book.

Cover image Copyright Kevin Ansbro
Cover Set by Charlotte Mouncey

Printed by IngramSpark UK Ltd

A CIP catalogue record for this book is available

from the British Library
ISBN 978-1-914083-22-8

Also available as an eBook
ISBN 978-1-914083-23-5

For Julie – my light at the end of the tunnel

Dear Holly

I hope that this book
leaves you with some very
happy memories!

Thank you for caring
for my lovely father-in-law.

~ Best regards, ☺
Kevin

"It sounds plausible enough tonight, but wait until tomorrow. Wait for the common sense of the morning."

H. G. Wells - The Time Machine

"Love is space and time measured by the heart."

Marcel Proust

CHAPTER ONE

Silkeborg Forest, Denmark, 1970

Poisoned by toxic waste and in excruciating pain, Måne and Stjerne swaddled their baby daughter in a rustic blanket of braided ivy and placed her in the hollow of an oak tree on the outer limits of their forest. It was their intention that the chalk-skinned infant would prove easy for a passer-by to spot, reminiscent perhaps of a religious icon looking down from a wall niche in a church.

With what little strength they had left, the baby's fabled parents kissed her tearfully for the last time and lay down at the base of the tree to die in each other's arms. As the last of the swallows flew south for winter, their dying wish was that a human, rather than a fox, would be the first creature to find their daughter.

CHAPTER TWO

England, 2020

From an upstairs window of their Surrey mansion, Dr Sofia Ustinova watched her murderous husband striding towards his chauffeur-driven Bentley, shoes crunching on a crust of dirty snow, and heaved a sigh of relief as the car disappeared from their driveway. Sofia, one of the world's leading physicists, had designs on leaving the evil bastard, but walking away from one of the Kremlin's most celebrated assassins carried a huge risk. Viktor would shortly be en-route to Heathrow Airport under the pretence of a business trip to Moscow, affording Sofia some respite from his volcanic temper and drunken insults.

"We shan't miss our dear lunatic, shall we, Copernicus?" she confided to her Siamese cat, who had leapt onto the windowsill to court some attention. "I hope to God they hit a sheet of black ice and skid headlong into a truck."

The British media was all over the story of the recent poisoning of the former Russian spy, Fyodor Oblonsky, in a London restaurant by means of a military-grade nerve agent. The Russian defector was swiftly admitted to a critical-care unit and had lost all of his hair within twenty-four hours. With his organs failing and only days to live, he was, in effect, a living murder victim. Though not privy to her husband's nefarious activities, Sofia instinctively felt that Viktor and his bodyguard were directly involved, and desperately hoped to find a way out of her marital predicament.

In celebration of her husband's departure, the scientist slipped into a silk kimono, bedded down on a nest of pillows and poured herself a lunchtime flute of Champagne as Vivaldi's *Soventi il Sole* patterned the air around her. She had just opened the pages of Carlos Fuentes' *The Old Gringo,* to feed her love for all things Mexican, and had settled down to read when an alarming noise screamed through the house, rattling it to its foundations and sending the cat scrambling for cover.

Terrified to her core, Sofia padded downstairs as the din bounced off walls and clattered her eardrums. In addition to it screeching like a rusty gate, there was a whirr to the noise which slowed to a menacing halt as she neared the cellar door.

Sofia reminded herself that the basement housed their central heating boiler and assumed that this was the cause of the disturbance. The door was protected by a digital keypad. She punched in the code, hit a light switch, and hoped that the noise wouldn't start up again while she was so close to it.

Having descended the cellar's concrete staircase, the physicist gasped out loud and stumbled back onto the steps, thunderstruck by a large and unanticipated object in front of her. It was a craft of some kind, of that she was certain. She wondered if she was having an out-of-body experience.

"What the hell?" she muttered, walking forward as if in a dream.

Without a shred of fear and mantled in its glow, she ran her hands over the machine's contours and marvelled at its resplendence. A Saturnian-style ring circled the vessel at low speed, though it bore no visible means of attachment and didn't create a draught.

As she struggled to come to terms with this perplexing occurrence, the air around her came alive with indistinct murmurings, leading Sofia to imagine that she was the subject of some far-off discussion. Almost as soon as it had begun, all discourse fell silent and an atmosphere of transcendental expectancy prevailed. Sofia felt the eyes of the universe upon her as she witnessed a dimming of the craft's luminosity until only a guiding blush of rectangular light remained on its lower flank.

Not needing a second invitation, and acting upon instinct, Dr Ustinova stepped up to the section indicated and passed through the skin of the vessel as easily as if she had walked through a cobweb. Allowing curiosity to override fear, and following her owner's lead, the cat also slunk into the vessel to see what was happening.

"Copernicus, my darling," said Sofia in her sultry Russian cadence. "Really, what are we to make of this? It is science fiction come to life, no?"

Her cat investigated the curvature of the craft's ovoid walls and sniffed the air, but offered very little by way of feedback.

A conspicuous handprint, reminiscent of those seen on primitive cave paintings, was the only motif visible on the wall of an otherwise bland interior. Sofia was surprised to discover that it exactly matched her own. So, led by scientific interest, she pressed her palm against it, prompting an illuminated hologrammatic control panel to manifest itself. The console had an intuitive interface and threw up a display of what appeared to be coordinates to some unknown destination.

Becalmed by unseen forces, and feeling that she had nothing to lose, Sofia prepared to take a leap of faith and shouted, "Forgive me for what I am about to do, Copernicus!" before gritting her teeth and touching the hologram's coordinates.

The ensuing clangour was enough to waken the dead and sent Copernicus scratching wildly at the craft's featureless walls. Sofia tried to gather him up but he was having none of it and squirmed free, terrified by the tumult that surrounded them. By the time the noise had whirred to a halt, Sofia was surprised to have not experienced motion of any kind. It was as if the machine had been standing still while it was making those hellish noises.

Sofia collected Copernicus in her arms and kissed his forehead. "I am so sorry, my darling. I don't know if there is more to come. We shall just have to wait and see."

After spending several minutes standing in irresolute silence, and becoming concerned that she was now trapped in what was effectively an airtight chamber, Sofia sought to extricate herself from the danger she had put herself in. Just as unease was about to give way to panic, the same reassuring rectangle of light reappeared on the inner wall of the craft.

With Copernicus still in her arms, the Russian stepped out into a room space she didn't recognise and tried to come to terms with the absurdity of her situation. "Dear God, where the hell are we?" she babbled, turning in a circle.

The air was warm and musty and, as far as Sofia could ascertain, they were in the confines of another basement. Her eyes were drawn to an aperture of light above her. An open door loitered at the top of a concrete staircase. She ascended the steps slowly, wary of what might be beyond the door, and stepped guardedly into a high-ceilinged hallway. "Hello! Hello! Is there anybody here?" she shouted in desperation.

Her cry was met by a deathly silence disturbed only by the tick-tock of a grandfather clock and the fluttering drone of electric fans overhead. The hallway was as spacious as her own but darker, with terracotta tiles and threadbare rugs underfoot. It boasted a bewildering succession of doors that led into an extravagance of rooms, one of which was a library puzzlingly bereft of books.

Sofia continued towards a shaft of powdery sunlight to the rear of the property and found that it emanated from a grilled window that overlooked a sunny courtyard with a fountain. The enclosure had a sense of personality and was replete with an array of tropical plants including poinsettia, bougainvillea and some broad-leaved banana trees.

What is this place? And who lives here? she wondered.

Shadowed by Copernicus, and still in her silk kimono, Dr Ustinova threw caution to the wind and paced the hallway with renewed vigour, shouting into palatial rooms at the top of her voice and then doing the same at the bottom of a grand staircase. She noticed an attaché case with its latches released positioned conspicuously on an antique side table. It seemed more than a coincidence that the case was embossed with her initials, so she dared to peek inside.

Finding that it was crammed with foreign banknotes of some description, she hastily closed it and jumped back in alarm. "What on earth?!" she sputtered, wishing she hadn't gone anywhere near it.

Becoming slightly hysterical, Sofia started to call out again with greater urgency. "Hell-o! Hell-o-o! Please, if anybody is here, I come in peace! I am a scientist and I really need to explain myself!"

The preposterousness of the situation was starting to get to her and she began to remonstrate with herself. "Oh, Sofia, for someone who is supposed to be so clever, you really are incredibly stupid. What *have* you got yourself into?"

Just as she was rueing the fact that she had left without her mobile phone and couldn't even call for a taxi, an antique doorbell above the front door jangled uproariously on its metal coil, sending shockwaves through her consciousness. In a high state of panic, at that moment Sofia wished she could make herself invisible. She fully appreciated the ridiculous sight she presented; one of the world's leading scientists cavorting around a stranger's house in a skimpy wrap-around with no reason for being there.

The Russian stood rooted to the spot in the wretched hope that the unseen visitor would simply go away, but this proved not to be the case. After each short lull, the brass bell jerked and clanged again until she could stand it no more. She grasped the nettle and rushed barefoot to receive someone at the front door of a house that wasn't even hers.

The door was a heavy colonial Spanish creation, an obstinate thing that initially refused to budge. Having wrestled it open, Sofia was met by a wall of brilliant light that forced her to shade her eyes. Directly before her, dressed in a tweed skirt suit and sensible shoes, stood a sturdy middle-aged lady with a kind face and Latina eyes, a woman of the sort Rubens loved to paint. "*Buenos días*, Madam," said the lady in a respectful tone. "Am I addressing señora Ustinova?"

Sofia, half-hidden by the door as she tried to preserve her modesty, was completely thrown by the greeting. "Why, yes. I am Doctor Ustinova, but how did you—?"

"My name is María Juanita Bravo," the lady declared with great pride. "I am here to interview for the vacancy of cook in your kitchen, señora.

"Vacancy?" replied Sofia, becoming even more confused by the day's startling turn of events.

"Yes, Madam. You advertised for a household cook with good spoken English. I worked as a cook for the former British Ambassador."

Sofia's head was spinning. "British Ambassador? Ambassador to where?"

María's face brightened. "To Mexico, of course!"

While they were talking, Sofia observed three vintage cars with whiplike aerials driving by on the sunlit road behind this mysterious lady. The pavements seemed foreign to her with their high, yellow-painted kerbs. The cogs of her brilliant mind were turning, and matters had begun to fall into place. "María, my apologies," she floundered. "I really have forgotten my manners. Please come inside."

María stepped onto the tiled floor and appraised her surroundings with a beatific smile on her plump face. "So very beautiful, Madam. You have a wonderful home."

Sofia wasn't really paying attention because she was still struggling to come to terms with this dreamlike reality. Putting her analytical skills to good use, she had arrived at an improbable hypothesis.

"María, I have two very strange questions to ask

you, but I would like them answered nonetheless."

The cook, thinking that the interview was already about to start, albeit in a large, dimly-lit hallway, steeled herself for the first question.

"María, which town or city are we in?"

A-ha! A trick question to begin with, thought María. "Madam, we are in Mexico City, the best city in the world."

Sofia took a sharp intake of breath and tried to contain her anticipation. "María, which year is this, please?"

A smile as wide as the Rio Grande broke across the cook's face. "I am loving these questions, señora. It is 1970, of course!"

CHAPTER THREE

England, 2020, one week later
– or fifty years later, depending on who you ask

Hugo Wilde, a nobleman by birth and an MI6 assassin by profession, stretched a black combat shirt over his athletic frame and slotted a loaded magazine into his Glock 22 handgun. Now in his mid-forties, the Eton and Sandhurst-educated Englishman was perhaps becoming too old for clandestine operations but found this line of work to be far easier than his army-officer tours of Kosovo and Afghanistan.

"My God, you are such a peacock," grinned Vincent O'Toole, Wilde's right-hand man and chief tormentor. "Do you deliberately order those shirts a size too small so you can show off your pretty-boy muscles?"

Hugo regarded his handsome face in a gilt-framed wall mirror. "Nothing wrong with taking pride in oneself, Vincent."

"Ah, but it is pride that changes angels into devils, Hugo, and it is humility that turns men into angels."

"That was rather profound, Vincent. Did you read it on the back of a cereal box?"

"It was said by Saint Augustine himself. A devout man who staunchly avoided the temptations of the flesh."

"He must have led a boring life then."

"Well, we can't all travel around the world killing people and bedding foreign beauties, can we, Hugo?"

"Oh, hark at you. You were hardly a babe in the woods back in the day."

"Here, let me help you with that," said O'Toole, assisting Wilde with his shoulder holster. "You're getting yourself in a tangle there, so you are."

Although the Englishman stood six feet tall, the Irishman towered over him like a redwood. Dublin's own Vincent O'Toole was a totem pole of a man who drank thirstily from the trough of life. He had a thickset brow, a strong jawline, a circus strongman's moustache and a nose like a wrung dishcloth. His only concession to vanity was the obvious toupée that graced his summit.

"Incredibly kind of you, Vincent. I don't know where I'd be without you."

"Dead in a ditch in Kosovo, that's where."

O'Toole, a former Irish Army Ranger, had been part of an international, NATO-led, peacekeeping force in Kosovo in 1999 when Wilde, his left leg bleeding profusely from a gunshot wound, broke cover and hobbled up to O'Toole's foot patrol on a remote country road seeking assistance. The Englishman was part of a covert British mission behind enemy lines that had become compromised, putting their lives in imminent danger. The Irishman had dined out on the story for years, regaling his army comrades with the anecdote about the privet hedge on the side of the road that suddenly started talking to him in a plummy accent.

The two had remained firm friends, leading to Wilde offering O'Toole the position of head gamekeeper on his Stoat Manor estate once the latter had retired from active duty. Theirs was never a master-servant relationship, and the Irishman lived rent-free in the east wing of the Englishman's seventeenth-century Jacobean manor house.

Vincent sat at Hugo's computer desk, his face bathed in the monitor's spectral glow, and scrolled through the details of tonight's assignment. "This Russian fella you're instructed to kill, I take it you've had a good look at his wife?"

"Briefly."

"Briefly, my arse. She's an absolute stunner."

Hugo continued with his pretence. "Can't say I noticed, Vincent."

O'Toole's eyes were as mischievous as a monkey's. "I knew it! She's beautiful and you've got an ego the size of a planet. I bet you can't wait to get your hands on her."

"The mission always comes first, Vincent."

"And your orders are to kill everyone in the house, including the delectable Mrs Ustinova if she poses a threat."

"May I remind you that you shouldn't be looking

at my stuff, you ape. You don't even work for MI6. It's for my eyes only."

The Irishman cocked an eyebrow. "So what's it to be with Mrs Ustinova then?"

Hugo returned to the mirror to attend to his already-neat head of hair. "The day I start murdering civilians is the day I lose my humanity, Vincent."

O'Toole typed 'Sofia Ustinova' into the search engine and read from her bio.

"Dr Sofia Ustinova is an astrophysicist and cosmologist," he began. "Also trained as a classical pianist… Too clever for you by far, Hugo. It says here that she's forty-five years old. It also says that she is the only Russian scientist to have appeared on the cover of *Vogue* twice—"

Hugo couldn't maintain his composure any longer. "Oh, I'll just take a quick peek then."

A photograph of the physicist, with her bee-stung lips and vivid green eyes, graced the screen. "Is she not a fine-looking woman?" raved Vincent, adjusting his toupée.

"I suppose," said Hugo, feigning nonchalance.

"Look at yourself now, trying to be all cool. Go on, admit it, you wolf."

A roguish smile broke across the Englishman's face. "Well, of course she's beautiful. It shouldn't even need to be said."

"So dab a little cologne behind your ears and try not to shoot her then."

"I'll do my best."

*

Under an inky sky, and in the harsh glare of a security floodlight, Wilde stood like a garden sculpture on the snow-covered rear lawn of Viktor Ustinov's[1] mansion. He had purposely activated the motion sensors knowing that the spy's personal bodyguard would come running from his gatehouse. As the brute appeared with his firearm drawn, Hugo greeted him with a wry smile and his arms behind his back.

"You make big mistake," snorted the Russian, his wintry breath caught in the security light's beam. "Put hands in air and turn around."

"Certainly," replied Hugo before calmly putting a bullet between the man's eyes and watching him faceplant into the snow.

Moving forward, he heard through his earpiece that the other two targets had remained *in situ*, one in an upstairs bedroom and the other in the downstairs living room.

Sofia Ustinova's reaction to witnessing the execution of her husband's bodyguard from a darkened living room was neither one of shock nor surprise. Then again, having recently travelled backwards and forwards in time, how many of life's revelations were likely to faze her?

---

1 The female form of Ustinov is Ustinova (i.e., Viktor Ustinov; Sofia Ustinova).

She saw that the intruder was dressed in black; British Secret Service, she assumed, and went about his business with practiced ease. Sofia observed the incident through French windows as if she were a spectator to a brightly-lit marionette show, one that was carefully choreographed and eerily silent. The suppressed gunshot that felled Sergei was little more than the sound of a nail being driven into a post and was unlikely to have roused her husband from his drunken slumber. It occurred to the physicist that instead of gawking like a fascinated deer she should perhaps be running from the hunter. Then, almost as if he had a sixth sense, the hitman looked directly at her and cast her a raffish wink. The very cheek of it! she thought, retreating into the shadows of the room.

Hugo forced the back door after receiving confirmation that the house's alarm system had been hacked into and disarmed. Holding his Glock in a two-handed grip, he stole through the house, moving like a cat, and appeared at the entrance to the living room as if he hadn't a care in the world.

Dr Ustinova, softly lit by a table lamp and dressed in a silk gown, had arranged herself elegantly in an art-deco armchair and was nursing a glass of Cognac. "I have been expecting you, Mr Bond," she said, arching one perfect eyebrow.

The Englishman, only too keen to reciprocate an instance of roleplay, replied, "The name's Wilde. Hugo Wilde."

"I don't actually care what your stupid name is, Mr Wilde," she scoffed, bursting his bubble and regarding him with disdain.

Hugo was taken aback but enjoyed her hostility nonetheless. "Well, I thought it only polite to introduce myself, Madam."

"You can go to hell, and my husband with you."

So enamoured was Hugo by this fiery Russian beauty that he had to remind himself he was on a mission. "You seem peculiarly unafraid, Doctor Ustinova. What makes you so sure that I'm not going to put a bullet in your brain as well?"

Sofia ran a manicured fingernail around the rim of her glass and maintained eye contact. "Because firing a gun isn't the first thing that men think of when they meet me."

The two shared an electric moment, from which the Englishman had to unplug himself. "Might we continue this conversation later? I do have an enemy agent to kill. I hope you don't mind."

"Not at all. The man is an abomination," Sofia said bitterly. "Turn right at the top of the stairs. His room is the second on the left. Just follow the snores."

"Thank you."

"And he keeps a gun in a drawer by his bed."

"Good to know."

As he turned to leave, Ustinova sized up the British secret agent with a mixture of admiration and contempt. Yes, he was handsome but God, didn't he know it! She imagined him as a roguish highwayman in a previous life and her an outraged countess in a velvet-upholstered carriage. How dare he come into her house acting as if he owned the place!

A congested walrus could not have snored any louder than Viktor Ustinov, and Hugo was in the man's room in no time at all. He shone his Glock's LED torch directly into Ustinov's flat-nosed face and enjoyed hearing him curse loudly in Russian as he sat upright in his monogrammed pyjamas and fumbled for his spectacles.

Scrunching his eyes against the light, Ustinov quickly adjusted to the truth of the matter and resigned himself to his fate with a gruff chuckle. "Step out of the shadows, my friend," he grinned. "Let me see the man who has been sent to kill me."

Hugo hit the light switch and theatrically announced himself. "Ta-dah!"

Ustinov laughed hoarsely and at the same time almost coughed up his lungs. "You are a very funny man. I like that. You are British, no doubt?"

"Undeniably."

"Your name?"

"Hugo."

"And Sergei, my bodyguard. He is dead, I assume?"

"Afraid so."

"I am sad to hear this. He was truly loyal. Do you have a friend who will lay down his life for you, Hugo?"

"I do, Viktor. A very dear friend."

"This is good. To have such a comrade is a rarity in this shitty world."

Ustinov looked at a half-finished vodka bottle and a shot glass that stood on his bedside dresser. "May I drink a toast to Sergei while I still have air in my lungs?"

A smile spread across Wilde's face. "Of course," he winked. "As long as you keep your hand away from that drawer."

"You are a smart man, my friend," Viktor nodded. "And if you are truly smart, you will get out while you can. Death follows assassins like a hungry dog."

"I plan to."

The Russian filled the glass to its brim and raised it to the ceiling. "To Sergei and to your dear comrade! May we always hold them in our hearts."

Without losing sight of the fact that the man was a sadistic psychopath, his salutation touched Hugo. "Thank you, Viktor. That was a kind gesture."

"Speaking of kind gestures," began the Russian, returning the empty glass, "perhaps you might extend me a professional courtesy?"

"Go on."

"You know, Hugo, that we have open caskets in Russia, yes?"

"I do."

"Well, if my body should ever make it back to Moscow, it would break my old mother's heart to see her son with his face repaired like some broken vase."

"Understood."

"So even though I do not deserve it, I would be grateful if you could shoot me only in the chest."

"Not a problem."

As Hugo levelled his handgun, Viktor ripped open his pyjama top and shouted, "Long live, *Rossiya!*"

The Englishman grouped four shots into the Russian's tattooed chest then checked the man's pulse as he lay on his back staring at the ceiling.

Viktor passed from this world, hoping to reunite with his father accompanied by a heavenly chorus. His last word was a froth of blood as death carried him away like blossom on the wind.

When Hugo reappeared in the living room, while at the same time texting Vincent O'Toole to inform him of the mission's success, Sofia was secretly relieved that it was he, and not her husband, who had survived their encounter. "You were upstairs a long time," she remarked. "I heard him shouting. Is he—?"

"Yes, he is."

"Good. It's no more than what the bastard deserves."

Wilde pocketed his phone, holstered the gun and stood before the scientist with hands on hips. "I see that you've poured a second glass of Cognac, Doctor Ustinova. Am I to understand that I'm joining you?"

Sofia offered him a glass while struggling to hold her gown together. "Don't read anything into it, Mr Wilde. You are far from being my knight in shining armour."

Grinning from ear to ear, Hugo declined the

Cognac. I'd much prefer to drink from *your* glass, if you don't mind? Old habits and all that." He sank into an armchair as if it were his own and made himself comfortable.

Sofia angrily returned his tumbler to her chairside table and shoved hers into his hand, spilling some of its contents in the process. "Really, are you always this insufferable, Mr English Spy?"

"Are you always such a perfect hostess, Mrs Russian Scientist?" he asked, raising the glass. "Cheers!"

A smile played at the corner of Sofia's lips as she settled back into her chair. *Damn, you are such a desirable bastard,* she thought as Hugo threw her a disreputable grin.

"So, are you one of the blunt instruments we so often hear about, Mr Wilde?" she asked, pulling the hem of her gown across bare legs. "One of those cold-hearted assassins who never settles down and always gets what he wants?"

"One does one's best for Queen and country," Hugo replied with a faint note of regret in his voice. "But of course no one gets all that they want in this world. Do you have children, Doctor Ustinova?"

A great sorrow descended upon the scientist. "I wanted children almost more than anything in the world, even if that meant having them by way of a cold-hearted sociopath. Sadly, infertility is a very unwelcome guest. One you think has come for a short visit but ends up staying a lifetime."

Sofia took a moment to gather herself. Wilde had

somehow unearthed her greatest heartache. "I endured five rounds of IVF before the doctor suggested that perhaps it wasn't meant to be. I could have punched him in the face for his insensitivity."

Her cat, with its oceanic eyes and ink-dipped paws, hurried into the room and made a beeline for the Englishman, winding in and out of his legs as it issued an emphysemic purr.

"Oh. Copernicus, he likes you," said Sofia with great surprise.

"Animals often do," Hugo replied, giving her pet the attention it craved.

"But he usually shies away from men. This is the first time I've seen him behave like this."

Hugo flashed his swashbuckling smile. "Perhaps Copernicus knows something that you don't?"

The scientist relaxed back into her chair, wearing her seductiveness like a catsuit. "Please, call me Sofia."

Wilde, while trying not to make it seem obvious that he was admiring her, replied in kind. "And you can call me Hugo."

A charged silence, fizzing with longing, existed between them but Sofia, knowing that she was once again allowing her heart to rule her head, snapped out of her reverie and dealt him a stare that would have extinguished a candle flame. "You are trying to win me over but I know just the type of man you are," she huffed. "And I suppose you think you can charm me into bed, you sexist pig."

"Not at all," Hugo demurred. "The thought hadn't

even entered my head."

The Russian had flicked an inner switch and was on a roll. "Are you really arrogant enough to believe that every beautiful woman you meet will fall into your arms, Mr Wilde? Do not think for one second that you can have your way with me. I would rather die."

Hugo took a sip of Cognac and chose to address her in fluent Russian. "Are you so conceited that you would class yourself as being beautiful?"

"You bastard," Sofia exclaimed. "You will never have me!"

"But I don't want to have you," said Hugo placidly.

The wind was taken out of the physicist's sails. "You don't?" She felt a pang of disappointment.

"You're as ugly as sin and that's as much as I'm going to say on the matter."

Incandescent with rage, Sofia sprang from her chair and slapped Wilde hard across his face. He didn't flinch and merely pointed to his glass as her handprint bloomed on his cheek. "I'm rather enjoying this Cognac," he grinned. "Any chance of a top up?"

Sofia employed a deep-breathing exercise that a yoga teacher had once taught her and returned to her chair. "Ah, yes. This is your famous British humour," she reminded herself with a wag of her finger. "Forgive me. Usually I like this tongue-in-cheek humour very much."

Hugo's eyes were full of mischief. "Then I shall endeavour to keep my tongue where it pleases you, Sofia."

As an involuntary gasp escaped her throat, Hugo returned to more important matters. "Thank you for the drink and the chat, Doctor Ustinova," he said, vacating his chair and stopping to smell a vase of freshly cut lilies. "With regard to the bodies, a team of chaps wearing ski masks will arrive later to clean everything up and spirit them away."

"Don't they trust you to do it yourself?"

"Me? Scrubbing blood from carpets? It would be like asking Nureyev to do the conga."

Sofia rolled her eyes. "It's obvious to me that you think far too highly of yourself."

Hugo adopted a more serious tone. "Important question. Do you have a place of safety you can go to?"

"Yes, I do, but—"

"That's good, because your husband's associates will be all over this. In their eyes, you know too much and pose a security risk. We will need to change your identity and give you a new life."

"Oh, so that's it then?" said Sofia glumly. "Just like that, you are leaving me."

"Yes, I'm leaving," he smiled. "But not before I've taken you in my arms and kissed your face off."

"Such arrogance! I would slap you again even harder if you were to try."

"We both know you wouldn't—" Barely had the words left Hugo's mouth than Sofia's hand was once again hurtling towards his cheek. This time he caught her wrist in mid-flight and held it in his iron grip. "I'll take that as a 'no' then?" he quipped.

"You can take it as a 'maybe'," she purred.

They rushed into a passionate kiss, their hands eagerly searching for skin and hidden contours. With her hair strewn fetchingly over one eye, the Russian undid Wilde's belt and slipped her fingers into his pants as he unclipped his shoulder holster.

"These people you know. When are they coming?" she asked breathlessly.

"In an hour or so."

Sofia led Hugo to a large sofa and allowed her silk gown to glide to the floor. The Englishman peeled off his combat shirt.

Her catlike eyes were fierce with desire. "Do it. Have your way with me, you bastard."

Sofia and Hugo were still rutting like animals when the MI6 black ops team appeared at the living room door with a medley of body bags and cleaning equipment. "Don't mind us, sir!" shouted one of the operatives, grinning splendidly through a hole in his ski mask. "We'll just carry on, shall we? You'll barely know we're here!"

"Very good!" said Wilde, grimacing over his bare shoulder.

As the crew trooped upstairs guffawing among themselves, the lovers disentangled themselves and retreated to a downstairs bathroom to continue their *amour* in the relative privacy of a shower cubicle. Sofia, in the throes of passion, had almost gasped out loud that she loved Hugo. The words had caught on the tip of her tongue, easy to summon but incredibly difficult to say.

*

After the clean-up team had driven off into what little remained of the night, Sofia lay in bed with her hair spilled across Hugo's chest. She thought his body was like that of a trapeze artist, albeit one vitiated by scars. The mood was transportive and poetic; they could just as easily have been drifting on a raft in the Indian Ocean.

Hugo shared with his lover that he had no family to speak of and that his mother and father had vanished, never to be seen again, while on a hiking trip in Denmark when he was a little boy. In his late teens, steeled with a burning desire to solve the puzzle, he had even returned to the area in which they disappeared. Regrettably, his enquiries with the local police had failed to cast any further light on the subject and their fate remained a mystery. It consoled him, though, to imagine his parents, watchful and vaporous, waiting patiently for him as they floated about in the ether.

"I too became an orphan," Sofia revealed with great sadness. "When I was only six years old, my parents both died in a terrible car crash on the outskirts of Moscow."

Hugo ran a hand through her hair. "I'm sorry to hear that."

"But maybe this is one of the reasons why the

universe has thrown us together," she brightened. "Perhaps you and I have so much more in common."

"Perhaps."

"I am worried that my husband's people will come looking for him today," Sofia said suddenly, her Russian consonants buzzing like flies.

"I think you'll be fine," replied Hugo, enjoying the scent of her shampoo. "My team will be keeping them distracted, responding to texts sent to his phone and so on. No doubt they'll also be driving his car all over the country. It'll be fun while it lasts."

"You must have wondered why I married such a person," she said, tracing Hugo's scars with her elegant fingers.

"It had crossed my mind, but I thought it impolite to ask."

"Viktor was truly charming at first. He wooed me with bouquets of flowers, jewellery in velvet boxes, the best seats at the Bolshoi. We had a whirlwind courtship until I realised too late what he was really like. You see, Hugo, I always allow my heart to rule my head."

Wilde, for the first time in his life, felt that he was falling into the same category, but kept his thoughts to himself. "Sofia, you mentioned earlier that you had a place of safety. How safe are we talking?"

The Russian could barely conceal her excitement and wondered if she should share her amazing secret with this wonderful man. "It is completely safe, actually," she enthused, sitting up on the bed and resting on her haunches.

"Nothing is ever completely safe," said Hugo, interlocking his hands behind his head.

Sofia's voice was full of mischief and promises. "But the place I'm talking about is," she beamed.

"Is it in England?"

"No. Try again."

"Russia?"

"Russia! Ha! After tonight, I may as well sign my own death warrant," she chuckled, bursting to unburden herself.

"Where then?" asked Hugo, totally captivated by the beautiful woman before him and hanging on her every word.

Because she had already secretly fallen for the Englishman, Sofia felt emboldened to confide in him. "It is in a different time and place."

"A fanciful idea."

"Not as fanciful as you might think," she teased, prodding him in the chest.

As patience wasn't one of Hugo's virtues, he capitulated. "I give up, Sofia, where exactly is this fabled destination?"

"Mexico City!"

"I went there once," he declared. "Wonderful place."

"On vacation?"

"Not quite."

Sofia wrestled with her thoughts as she gazed into Hugo's eyes and saw a nobility therein. "Darling man, if you could truly get away from all of this and start a new life in another time, another place, would you?"

Wilde noted her earnestness and treated the question with the sincerity it deserved. "In all honesty, if I had the opportunity to do such a thing with you, Sofia, I would seize it with both hands."

Sofia could have wept tears of joy at that moment but kept her emotions in check to prepare for her revelatory announcement. She took a deep breath and steadied herself. "Hugo, I'm going to share a secret with you that I have not shared with anyone."

"Share away," he replied, plumping up his pillow. "I'm good at keeping secrets."

"And you promise not to make fun of me?"

"Scout's honour."

Holding Hugo's gaze, Sofia began her recital. "I have a house in Mexico City. One which Viktor knew nothing about. I took ownership of it only last week."

The Englishman's eyebrows almost leapt from his forehead. "You did well to keep that from your husband, especially as Russian intelligence has eyes everywhere."

Sofia continued, her tone measured. "He was away last week. A so-called business trip to Moscow. I left for Mexico and returned the same day holding a set of keys to my new house."

"The same day?" Hugo frowned. "You must have been a diaphanous blur."

The Russian bit on her lower lip. "Please listen carefully, darling. What I am about to tell you will sound completely crazy, but thankfully I have the evidence to back it up." She stood up from the bed and slipped into her robe. Expecting to be mocked, she folded her arms defensively. "Are you really ready for the truth?" she asked, narrowing her eyes.

"I'm totally ready for the truth," said Hugo compliantly. "You're not going to slap me across the face again, are you?"

Sofia took the leap of faith, her words tumbling at twice their usual speed. "I was in Mexico City for three months, and yet returned to England on the same day that I left. There! I've said it. Make of it what you will."

Rendered speechless by the nonsense coming from Sofia's mouth, Hugo sat up cross-legged on the bed and stared at her in disbelief.

"Really, darling. You look completely gormless," she huffed. "Put your clothes on and follow me. I have something to show you."

CHAPTER FOUR

Silkeborg Forest, Denmark, 1970

With the cold morning air smoking from their ragged breath, Leif Hartvigsen and his faithful gundog were on a track at the edge of the forest, heading home to their remote log cabin. It had been a successful shoot; Hartvigsen's twelve-bore shotgun was unlocked as it hung in the crook of his arm, and a trinity of dead pheasants were still warm in his canvas shoulder bag.

Picking up a scent, the dog suddenly raced off into the undergrowth and stood immobile at the base of an oak tree with its tail erect.

"What have you found there, Odin?" asked his master, tramping through ground cover. Odin, caught in two minds as to where he should point his nose, stood on hind legs. Stretching against the tree trunk, he gazed upwards.

To Leif's utmost surprise, staring directly down at him from a hollow in the tree, propped up with willow sticks and swaddled in ivy leaves, was an infant girl with a shock of white hair. By his feet, tight in each other's arms on a bed of ferns, were the child's deceased parents. He knew the alabaster-skinned couple only by the fleeting glimpses he had caught of them and through local folklore; they were said to be non-human forest dwellers with mystical powers who lived in trees and knew how to live off the land.

Hartvigsen, knowing that the authorities would treat such a child as a curiosity to be passed around from one scientist to another, decided there and then that he would raise the little girl as his own.

CHAPTER FIVE

England, 2020

Hugo had previously imagined he'd experienced everything there was to experience in this crazy world, but what Sofia had just shown him in her cellar was beyond earthly belief.

After the great reveal, they sat together in her living room sharing a pot of Earl Grey accompanied by warm buttered croissants and apricot conserve. Relieved to have at last shared her secret with someone, Sofia wore a triumphant smile as she prepared to answer Hugo's questions.

Quite understandably, he was still in a daze. "So that *thing* definitely wasn't built by you and your rocket scientist friends?" he enquired.

Sofia took great pleasure in being the one in control. "As I said, Hugo, no human is capable of building such a machine." Here she paused for dramatic effect. "Let's just say that it was gifted to me."

"Gifted? Gifted by whom?"

Sofia pointed skyward inasmuch as anyone is able to point skyward whilst remaining indoors. "It would seem that my scientific theories are also appreciated much further afield. It was Thomas Edison's belief that the spirits of the dead, along with every word spoken, exist among us."

She paused to pull open a croissant. "But it is my belief that extraterrestrial voices exist among us too. They are, in effect, whistling in the wind, hoping to be heard." Allowing her words to hang in the air between them, Sofia took a sip of tea and watched Hugo over the rim of her cup.

He scratched his head and considered his reply. "So, what you're saying is that these extraterrestrials are rewarding you for somehow being on their wavelength?"

"Yes! Precisely that. Thank God, a man with a brain! Though we are able to print calendars and manufacture clocks, we humans have no control over time. Only those with an intelligence far beyond ours can achieve that."

Had Hugo not seen the craft with his own eyes, he would have passed this off as an outpouring of deluded claptrap, but he understood enough about human psychology to recognise the sincerity in Sofia's voice.

"Yes, it's absurd," she continued, "but nature is also absurd, no?"

Hugo saw the hope in Sofia's eyes that he would have the ingenuity to believe her story. That he might be able to think the unthinkable.

"And you *actually* travelled back in time?" he asked

for the third time in as many minutes.

Sofia touched his arm. "Yes, I travelled back in time. Would it help you to understand the science fiction if I gave you some science fact?"

"I don't disbelieve what you say," said Hugo. "It's just a lot to take in all at once. A dose of pragmatism is needed – and perhaps I need to take a ride in the blessed thing. Tell you what. Let's see if it can whisk us off to Mexico, shall we?"

Sofia's face lit up. "You would really do that?" she asked, almost tearful with joy. "I would love to take you to Mexico, darling. And if the place doesn't suit, I could have you back in your house before the milk in your fridge has had time to curdle."

"Splendid," said Hugo throwing her a playful smile. "Could my good friend Vincent tag along too? He'd never forgive me if I didn't cut him in on the trip of a lifetime."

Sofia pursed her lips. "Can he be trusted?"

"Absolutely. To all intents and purposes Vincent is my right-hand man, my confidant, my bodyguard and, above all else, my very best friend."

"Is he likely to get on my nerves?"

"Not at all," said Hugo, allowing himself a little white lie. "You two will get on famously. I'm sure of it."

*

Vincent O'Toole, though he wouldn't have admitted it, was mightily relieved when Hugo phoned. Seven hours had elapsed since his friend last texted him and he had begun to worry.

"Good morning, Hugo, you dirty stop-out," he quipped. "Stayed on to offer the wife of the deceased some bereavement counselling, did you?"

"I might possibly be in love, Vincent," Hugo answered.

It was not quite the reply that the Irishman was expecting. "After one brief encounter? You can't be serious," Vincent snorted. "Jesus, you've gone soft in the head, you goon."

"I think not," Hugo continued. "This spectacular woman has stolen my heart. I'm utterly bewitched."

O'Toole's face was a picture.

Meanwhile, Hugo was talking nineteen to the dozen, his words galloping between their phones. "Vincent, listen up. We have much to talk about but very little time. Here's the thing. Would you like to travel to Mexico with me today?"

Vincent held his phone at arm's length and stared at it as if he had never seen it before. "Hugo, did one of those Russians clatter you over the fecking head with a shovel?"

The Englishman's tone was insistent. "Vincent, Vincent, please listen to me. You have an opportunity to accompany me to Mexico today. Come on over to Doctor Ustinova's place as soon as you can and I'll furnish you with all the details."

"Christ alive, Hugo. We're in the grip of a global pandemic and you expect me to board a plane that is filled to the gills with filthy people coughing up their lungs?"

"We'll be flying privately, Vincent."

"Ah, now you're talking. I'll grab my passport, pack an overnight bag and jump into a taxi."

"You won't need your passport."

"Don't talk nonsense. I'm bringing it anyway. Yours too, if I can remember the code to your safe."

"Oh, and Vincent?"

"Yes?"

"You know my suitcase, the one that I'd already packed for my trip to Florence next week?"

"I do."

"Would you be so kind as to bring that too?"

"Consider it done, fair Romeo."

*

"So why Mexico City?" asked Hugo as he and Sofia awaited the arrival of Vincent O'Toole.

Sofia, sitting at her Steinway piano, having played the theme from Tchaikovsky's *Swan Lake*, considered the question. "Actually, that decision was already made by entities unknown. I'm guessing that, through my research on time dilation, I must have touched on something that was previously unfathomable to the scientific community. In recognition of that, the unimaginables awarded me a time machine. Crazy, yes?"

"Most right-minded people would think it was crazy," Hugo conceded. "And you were happy there?"

37

"Darling, I was happier there than I have ever been in my entire life," she said shutting the piano lid. "It was always my dream to travel to Mexico and the extraterrestrials must have known that. And I own the house outright, even though foreigners, back then, weren't allowed to own a house in Mexico. My friends in high places have seen to it that I am a Mexican citizen, even to the extent that I have documentation to prove it."

"So, why did you come back?"

"Because all my research papers and dissertations are here. I wanted to take at least some of them with me."

Hugo, not one to allow a paucity of knowledge to stop him from engaging in a discussion that was almost entirely out of his depth, sailed into Sofia's waters. "But isn't it a commonly held precept that you can't go back in time to alter events that have already happened?"

"It is," replied Sofia looking suitably impressed.

"Well, that being the case, surely you won't be able to retrospectively use your expertise and knowledge to affect the course of science?"

Ustinova's reaction was one of unbridled delight. "Hugo! Not only are you a bad boy, you are also a very clever one. On top of that, you can speak Russian. Really, this is a dream package for me."

Looking rather pleased with himself, the Englishman soaked up her compliment as readily as a sponge absorbs water. "So my question remains the same. Is it possible to go back in time and alter that which has already happened?"

"Hugo, if you had asked me this question before my journey into the past, I would have said with all certainty that you cannot alter the course of history. In fact, if any of my colleagues had argued to the contrary, I would have thought them quite stupid—"

"I can see that there's a 'but' coming," smiled Hugo.

"There is." Sofia reached for her laptop. "But maybe it is better if I show you."

She pulled up Google Earth onto her screen and zoomed in on an aerial shot of a park. "You see this?" she asked, pointing to a fully-grown coconut tree. "I planted that as a sapling last week in Mexico City. And now look at it, a fifty-year-old tree."

Hugo could barely believe what he was hearing and seeing. "Incredible, just incredible."

Sofia was thankful that the Englishman hadn't poured scorn on her revelation. "I did it purely as an experiment without expecting it to succeed. Really, I was shocked to see this on my return."

"So you *can* effect changes? That tree obviously would not have existed, in either era, a week ago."

"Sadly, this tree was possibly my only success," sighed Sofia with a shrug of her shoulders. "Whilst I was in Mexico, I posted anonymous letters to the world's leading research institutions outlining present-day findings that would have greatly accelerated their scientific and technological advancements. I half-expected the media to be alive with excitement but nothing came of it. It was as if I had never sent them at all."

"And yet your tree experiment succeeded against all expectations," said Hugo, trying to make sense of something that appeared to be nonsensical.

"The past is already written," declared Sofia despondently. "The moment in which you first picked up that teacup has already passed, and the future doesn't exist until we actually reach it."

"Ah, but wasn't it Nietzsche who believed that the future influences the present just as much as the past?" said Hugo, much to Sofia's amazement.

"My darling, you are so insightful! I cannot imagine why you chose the life of an assassin."

"It was either that or join the circus," he grinned.

CHAPTER SIX

Mexico City, 1970

As he had each morning since her death, Gerardo Quiroz, who suffered as much from loneliness as he did from constipation, brought a cup of black coffee to the bedroom shrine he had created in his wife's honour. "Good morning, my darling Rosa. Did you sleep well?" he asked her photograph. "I've added cinnamon and sugar, just as you like it."

Gerardo, identifiable by his short stature and white Van Dyke beard, shared a tenement apartment in a wretched part of town with Pablo, his sixteen-year-old son. Each worked together to eke out a simple existence, Gerardo by playing his trumpet on the streets and in the public areas of the Centro Histórico, Pablo by shining shoes in the same locale.

The diminutive musician looked considerably older than his fifty-seven years, having withered on life's vine since losing his job at the tequila factory in Jalisco ten years earlier and then losing his beloved wife only six months ago. His sleek-haired son, in addition to being a humble shoeshine boy, was a self-taught artist of considerable talent. Inspired by Frida Kahlo and Antonio M Ruíz, his colourful paintings adorned every wall of the apartment.

After lighting a candle to his wife and whispering a small prayer, Quiroz kissed her well-thumbed face. "I cherished you, my one true love," he said tearfully. "You were the cadenza to my song and I will love you for all eternity."

Outside, above the bark of neighbourhood dogs, the enchilada vendor was already calling out to anyone who might be interested in his wares. Gerardo's meagre breakfast amounted to little more than stale tortillas and refried beans but he appreciated the fact that Pablo, to spare his honour, always enthused about what he was given. True to form, his pride and joy appeared wet-haired from the bathroom and made a beeline for the simple plate of food Gerardo had set aside, thanking him profusely. Though Quiroz couldn't hope to give Pablo the kind of life enjoyed by princes and movie stars, he had ensured his boy had a decent grasp of the English language and that he understood the value of good manners.

Gerardo helped the teenager to slip into the shoulder straps attached to a lightweight kitchen chair which hung against his slender back. As well as his trumpet case, the musician carried a small packing crate filled with Pablo's shoe polishing equipment, which also doubled as a foot rest.

"Reach for the stars, my beautiful son," said Gerardo. "And one day, in the place of this chair, you will grow wings to take you there."

They opened their apartment door to a city alive with the thrum of traffic noise and distant car horns. In addition to his crumpled suit and kipper tie, Gerardo wore a brown trilby adorned with a hen feather. Pablo was dressed in plaid trousers and a white short-sleeved shirt. As they set off, women in the surrounding buildings walloped clouds of dust from rugs draped over clothes lines and called out morning greetings to one another.

No sooner had father and son broken cover at the foot of the communal stairway than they were accosted by the food vendor who hastened into a hopeful gallop shouting, "I have warm enchiladas, señores!" only for Gerardo and Pablo to politely decline his exhortation.

They proceeded for three miles through a cheerless part of town that God had long since turned his back on. Brimming with optimism, the duo threaded through a labyrinth of street markets and fruit stalls until the city ascended, grey yet majestic, from the chaos. They arrived at the wide-open spaces and colonial architecture of the Centro Histórico, where uniformed police officers were out in force checking street permits and banishing a bowler-hatted Bolivian balloon seller who trundled off in her brightly-coloured dress, knowing that she had no chance of fading into the background. Gerardo suggested to his son that they hang back, hoping that the police would become tired of harassing people and move on to pastures new.

Their old friend, Jesús the organ grinder, once a very famous wrestler, approached. He was cranking up a jangling cacophony on his badly-tuned barrel organ, murdering *Cielito Lindo* for the millionth time.

"Good morning, Gerardo! Good morning, Pablo!" he greeted, waving a straw cowboy hat above his head. "Too many policemen about today. How are we talented musicians supposed to earn an honest living, hey? It is the pickpockets who have it easy."

Gerardo chuckled and shook Jesús warmly by the hand. "I believe that the worst of the pickpockets are in the government, my friend."

"How true!" replied the ex-wrestler, running a sleeve across his sweaty forehead and replacing his hat. "Hey! The football World Cup is starting in just two months' time. Do you think our boys can win?"

"One can only hope," said Gerardo. "But I think that Brazil has the best team."

Jesús shrugged his shoulders in acquiescence. "True, but long live Mexico, yes?"

"Long live Mexico!" cheered father and son proudly.

With another wave of his hat, the organ grinder bade his friends farewell and clumped off in the direction of the Metropolitan Cathedral, bringing with him a caterwaul of noise.

Gerardo, who once had dreams of somehow being able to earn enough money from his love of music to be able to build an orphanage, stroked his son's black hair and looked sorrowfully into his trusting eyes. "This is not the life that I wanted for you, Pablo. Hiding from the police and scraping a living. My dreams were once iron towers and mighty oaks. Now they are just rust and dust."

"Don't say that, Papá," his son protested. "I love my life and I am happy as long as I have you by my side."

The musician saw in his boy a sparkle of infinite happiness that almost broke his heart. "No man could be prouder of a son," he said, holding back tears.

"And no son could be prouder of a father," said Pablo.

In due course, Pablo set up his shoeshine station in a shaded corner of the vast Zócalo Plaza, his vinyl chair seat ready for the backsides of local businessmen and tourists alike. In front of the chair, he placed the upturned packing crate upon which his customers could rest their feet. Adjacent to this, on the plaza's flagstone surface, he arranged an orderly line of brushes, polishes and rags. With a sunshine smile on his face, Pablo sat on the crate from which the tools of his trade were emptied and waited for his clientele to appear.

Gerardo, meanwhile, had unlatched his black leather case and withdrawn a trumpet that was very dear to him, the one his parents in Puebla had sold their cow for so that he would have enough money to pay for it. It was therefore important to him that he played it every day in their memory.

He stood with his upended hat by his feet at the north end of the square, hoping to catch the eyes and ears of the tourists who stood in line for the Metropolitan Cathedral. Once the trumpet was pressed to the maestro's lips, most of them forgot they were even in a queue as his melodic fluency began to brighten their day. Some of the sightseers ignored him completely for reasons only known to themselves, but others listened to his soaring notes with tears in their eyes.

Gerardo, as ever, allowed his emotions to speak through his music and by late afternoon his trilby was heavy with coins. Pablo's takings were also of a sufficiency to swell their modest savings and to at least put some food in their stomachs.

But their day's good fortune hadn't gone unnoticed. Rubén Cuevas, a backstreet gangster and full-time thief, watched slyly as the musician pressed banknotes into his wallet and poured coins into a cloth money bag.

"I have seen them around. They live in our neighbourhood," said Diego Dosdedos, one of Cuevas' cohorts, a man who had cultivated a moustache that would have given Zapata a run for his money.

Cuevas, a powerful man capable of extreme brutality, scratched his scrub of bristles and produced a sharklike smile. "Then maybe we will follow them home."

With the instincts of hyenas, Rubén and Diego shadowed the musician and his son from an inconspicuous distance, leaving the historical centre behind and tracking them through the bustling street markets. They hung back as Gerardo and Pablo drank ice-cold *horchata* at a sidewalk stall and saw them buying corn tortillas and other provisions with the money that they themselves coveted.

"There will be nothing left for us if they keep spending it," whined Diego, his voice like that of a petulant tomcat.

"Trust me, they have plenty," said Rubén, rolling gum around his mouth.

As they proceeded onto a quiet sidewalk, father and son were suddenly jolted from their cheery conversation by the two thugs, who had cornered them in a pincer movement.

"How are you today, my friends?" asked Rubén. Though his smile was expansive, his beetle-black eyes were filled with menace.

"Very well, señor," replied Gerardo nervously. He knew the man only by reputation: a neighbourhood thief with a predilection for violence.

The brute continued to smile and at the same time lifted the hem of his shirt to reveal a switchblade knife attached to his belt. "It is as simple as this," he explained. "I want your money."

The musician begged for leniency. "Please, señor, we have barely enough to live on as it is. I would consider it an act of kindness if you simply allowed us to continue on our way."

"All of the money, *cabrón*, or I will gut you like a fish."

The musician looked around, hoping that some

brave soul would come to their rescue, but this was evidently a street of forgotten obligations and unseeing eyes.

Pablo blazed with righteous indignation and stuck out his chest as if bracing himself for an incoming wave. "My father will never give you the money, you savage! It is not yours to have!"

Gerardo sought to diffuse his son's anger. "Pablo, remember how I advised you that it is never wise to resist bandits—?"

"Who are you calling bandits?" snarled Diego, slapping the musician's hat from his head.

"But, Papá, we worked hard for that money."

Rubén pinched the boy's cheek, causing him to yelp. "You would do well to listen to your father, you little sissy."

"Here, take the bag," said Gerardo, wishing that Jesús the organ grinder was on hand to vanquish these two with his wrestling skills. "Just please don't hurt my son."

"And the rest of it," growled Rubén, relieving the musician of his wallet while Diego hissed at the few locals who had stopped to voice their disapproval.

Rubén prodded Gerardo's leather case with his shoe. "What do you have in there?"

"Just my trumpet, señor. You have all of our money. I swear."

The thug spat his chewing gum at the musician, his signature gambit, and abruptly seized the case. "I'll be the judge of that."

"No!" screamed Pablo as he tried to wrestle it from Rubén's grip, only to suffer a sharp backhander across his face for his valour.

"You animal!" shouted Gerardo, swinging a feeble punch that barely troubled the brute's chin. Rubén's immediate response was to fell the musician with one decisive blow.

"Papá!" shrieked Pablo, throwing himself onto his father's prone body, hoping to shield him from further harm. Rubén unlatched the case and shook the instrument onto the sidewalk.

"Any money in it?" asked Diego.

"Just foam padding," grunted Rubén.

Gerardo hauled himself onto his knees and begged the thug not to damage his prized trumpet. He may just as well have waved a red rag at a bull because Rubén snatched the instrument from the ground and swung it ferociously against a wall, putting a large dent in it.

In the meantime, galvanised by word of mouth, a group of honourable citizens had gathered and started marching towards the two thieves, intent on giving them a taste of their own medicine. Seeing that the odds were stacked against them, Rubén and Diego held onto their spoils, gave the finger to the incoming vigilantes and scurried off like cockroaches.

CHAPTER SEVEN

England, 2020

As his taxi driver sped off to another destination and more snow began to fall, O'Toole heralded his arrival at Dr Ustinova's mansion by simultaneously sounding the doorbell and rat-a-tat-tatting the brass knocker.

Wilde checked the CCTV monitor and opened the door. Carrying a suitcase in each ginormous hand, the Irishman stood with a cheery grin on his moustachioed face and a Covid mask dangling from one ear. A sudden gust of snowy wind caught him by surprise and flipped his toupée upwards like the lid of a pedal bin.

"Hoist the mainsail!" cheered Hugo.

"Feck it!" cursed O'Toole.

"I'd say you need a little more glue on that monstrosity, Vincent."

"I'd glue a cow bell to your pecker given half a chance," growled O'Toole, ducking under the door frame, setting the suitcases down and brushing snow from his shoulders. "That way the ladies will at least be given fair warning that you've walked into a room."

Hugo took charge of the suitcases and ferried them to the cellar door. His shoulder holster, gun and ammunition pouch were already stored in a holdall. "It really is good to see you, Vincent. Don't worry about the facemask. Come along and meet Sofia."

The physicist, who had changed into burgundy leather trousers and a white roll-neck top, approached O'Toole with a cashmere coat stylishly draped across her shoulders. "Vincent, delighted to meet you," she said, offering a hand.

"Likewise," replied the Irishman, bending his knees to receive a kiss on each cheek. "Now aren't you a treat for the nose, Sofia? Honest to God, you smell divine."

"Thank you," she beamed, liking him instantly. "Hugo tells me that you're his most trusted friend."

"Did he also tell you that he was hiding in a hedge when I first clapped eyes on him?"

"He did not," said Sofia, casting Hugo a glittering smile.

At that moment O'Toole saw in his friend's face the unconcealed and irrational love he had for this woman. "Ah, now would you look at the handsome devil?" he said with a twinkle in his eye. "Sure, if Hugo was made of chocolate, he'd eat himself."

Sofia linked arms with the Irishman. "You and I are going to get along splendidly, Vincent."

"I believe we will," he replied smoothing the tips of his moustache.

With introductions over, Hugo clapped his hands

together and directed his friend's attention to the matter in hand. "So, are you ready to have your mind blown, Vincent? We have something pretty amazing to show you."

"Hey now, wait a minute. Aren't we off to sunny Mexico?" enquired O'Toole, narrowing his eyes. "Jesus, Hugo, I just knew you were up to something."

"We *are* going to Mexico," Sofia interjected. "But let's just say that our mode of transport might not be one that you're familiar with."

"Go on," said Vincent, grinding his teeth.

Sofia gathered Copernicus in her arms. "Just relax. I will show you. This way, gentlemen."

She walked to the cellar door and punched in the security code while Hugo and Vincent stood behind her. The former was bursting with excitement, the latter was wondering what on earth Hugo had roped him into.

Sofia patted their suitcases after opening the door. "Could you please take those with you?"

At the bottom of the cellar stairs, she and Hugo stood aside to allow O'Toole to gaze at what awaited him. Instead of being blown away, he studied the craft with no more curiosity than a horse would have for a washing machine. "So what's this when it's at home?" he sighed. "A fancy art installation that probably cost an arm and a leg?" Realisation had dawned in Vincent's mind that their promise of a trip to Mexico was evidently just a masquerade to involve him in something much less exciting.

Sofia placed her hand on the small of the Irishman's back and urged him to look closer. "Touch it, Vincent. Use your instincts."

Sensing he was the subject of some ridiculous prank, O'Toole gave Hugo the evil eye and stepped forward, ducking under the phosphorescent ring that orbited the installation. When he put his hand on it, the surface of the craft produced a ringing noise reminiscent of a wet finger being run around the rim of a wine glass. "God in Heaven!" he shouted, almost jumping out of his skin. "What sort of trick are you two playing on me?"

"It's a time machine," Sofia announced without fanfare, leading Hugo to groan loudly and bury his head in his hands.

Disappointment was writ large on Vincent's face and his nostrils had begun to flare. "A time machine, you say? A fecking time machine? My name's O'Toole, not O'Fool, you prize eejits. And to think I gave up a pub lunch for this nonsense."

"Vincent, this is not what you think," said his friend.

"I'm quite entitled to my opinion, Hugo. And you know as much about quantum physics as I do about flower arranging."

Sofia gently held one of the Irishman's big hands and placed it against the opalescent skin of the craft. "Please, Vincent. This is not a trick. Touch it again. Tell me what you think it is made of. Really, it is like nothing on Earth."

"Jesus, I don't know," he grumbled, giving the surface a cursory rub, not knowing if it was vegetable or mineral.

"And listen to this," she continued, rapping the machine's flank with her knuckles, creating a melodious reverberation that continued in waves.

"Perhaps it might help if he could see inside?" suggested Hugo.

"See inside? The damn thing hasn't even got any hatches," Vincent grumbled. "And your new girlfriend, beautiful though she is, is entirely crazy if you want my opinion."

"Careful, Vincent. She's also something of a wildcat," Hugo chuckled.

The physicist gazed up into Irishman's eyes, seeking to win his trust. With an angel's grace, she ushered him towards the rectangular light that had appeared before them. "Free your mind, Vincent, and don't be afraid."

"Afraid? I'm not in the least bit afraid," Vincent grunted as Sofia led him through the wall of the craft before he had the chance to think. "Whoa! Jesus Christ Almighty! What the feck?"

"So, what do you think now?" asked Sofia as Hugo and the cat joined them on the inside.

"W-what the hell just happened?" stuttered Vincent, his jaw hanging like a sporran. Hugo patted his friend's wide shoulders as the Irishman looked around in wonderment.

Sofia's gentle smile would have becalmed a cornered

tiger. "I know that it's a lot to process, but truthfully this is a time machine. And if you still want to travel to Mexico, Vincent, we can go there right now."

"For feck's sake, you pair of lunatics. There is no such thing as a time machine and there is no such thing as time travel," said O'Toole, gesticulating wildly. "It's the stuff of fantasy."

"I totally understand that," said the scientist, resisting the urge to slap some sense into him. "But please allow me to present a scenario. As we speak, are people in Australia sitting down to an evening meal?"

Not wanting to fall into some type of theoretical trap, Vincent considered his answer carefully. "Yes, I guess so—"

"And can you see them?"

"Well, no—"

"Just because you're not able to see them doesn't mean that they don't exist in another time and place, does it?"

Vincent rubbed his chin and eyed her with suspicion. "Er, you've got me there, so you have."

"Nature's abstractions are endless," continued Sofia. "And it's only recently that I've come to believe in the existence of multiple universes and higher beings."

Seeing that his friend was wavering, Hugo drew O'Toole's attention to what was around him. "As you can see, Vincent, none of this is make-believe."

Even though Vincent had begun to imagine that there must be an element of truth in their madness, he continued to survey his modest surroundings with a degree of scepticism. At the very least he would have expected a console room bedecked with a bewildering array of switches, monitors and lava-lamp columns. Moreover, apart from Sofia's stack of files and a small collection of her suitcases, there was scarcely enough room for three persons and a cat. But then Vincent considered the weird barrier that he had just walked through, and wondered how that was even possible.

"Jesus, it's hardly the Tardis," he quipped, using humour to disguise his unease. His interest was drawn to a solitary handprint that adorned the craft's bare walls.

"No! Don't touch that!" yelled Sofia, causing him to jump back as if jabbed with a cattle prod. "Biometrics, Vincent. It's modelled to recognise only my hand. If you would like to be of some use, perhaps you could slip back through the skin of the machine and fetch your luggage."

After first tentatively putting his arm through the wall of the craft and seeing it disappear, O'Toole dutifully did as he was asked and returned with the suitcases. He was becoming increasingly bewildered by the unearthliness of what he was experiencing. As he set the cases to one side, a tinnitus of unearthly mutterings filled the air around them. Vincent and Hugo stared at each other with mutual uncertainty.

"Christ alive! What in God's name is that satanic babble?" Vincent squawked, grabbing hold of Hugo's arm. The two of them looked to the physicist for reassurance.

"Relax. You've merely woken them up," explained Sofia. "They're just having an intergalactic conference call."

"*Them?*" said Vincent with a look of horror on his face. "Don't tell me we've got aliens for company?"

"Not in the physical sense," she replied. "They're several galaxies away."

"That's reassuring, isn't it, Vincent?" said Wilde, enjoying his friend's nervousness.

"Oh, sure. It's just grand."

Hugo, suddenly struck by a matter of unstated importance, patted his pockets as if looking for spare change. "Money," he remarked. "Has anyone thought to bring money?"

"I've brought a couple of grand in cash," said Vincent. "I knew you wouldn't have anything on you."

"Now, here's a great idea," grinned Hugo, as if the gods had suddenly granted him a rare genius. "Knowing what the future holds, we should invest in the stock market when we get there."

"And there it is!" said Sofia, rewarding him with a sarcastic handclap. "The first thing anyone thinks of when considering a time-travel hypothesis. How very original."

"So what did you do to accrue money when you were last there?" asked the Englishman. "Our modern-day currency and credit cards couldn't have been of any use."

"Of course I played the stock market," she beamed. "I might be bound by ethics, but I'm not actually stupid."

"Well, I'll be damned," grinned Hugo.

A control panel appeared before Sofia, illuminating her face. "Are we ready to travel back in time, gentlemen?"

Hugo was thrilled; this was the magic-carpet ride he'd dreamt of in his youth. Meanwhile Vincent crossed himself and looped his surgical mask over his ears.

"You won't be needing that where we're going," said Sofia, thinking the Irishman's ears were big enough to hang umbrellas from. "Covid doesn't exist in the distant past."

"Shouldn't we at least be strapped in?" he asked, his eyes wild with panic as the machine began to screech.

"What a big baby you are!" shouted Sofia above the din. "Relax, it won't take long!"

As promised, the noise swiftly ground to a halt, yielding to an immaculate silence that brought Copernicus out from behind the suitcases. Vincent looked to Sofia in the way that a nervous flyer looks to a flight attendant in the event of extreme turbulence. "What's going to happen now?" he asked, his moustache drooping and his face ashen.

Sofia wore her tranquility with aplomb. "Nothing else is going to happen," she smiled, remaining cool as an autumn mist. "Welcome to Mexico City, fellow travellers! The year is 1970!"

Because Dr Ustinova had already blown each of his preconceptions out of the water Vincent had no reason to doubt her, even though it seemed perfectly clear to him that the infernal machine hadn't moved an inch. He also saw that Hugo was champing at the bit, an adult about to realise one of his childhood dreams.

Sofia stood beside the portal, barely able to contain her excitement. "Shall we?"

"Go on, let's do this," said O'Toole, suddenly remembering that he was once a fearless soldier.

"That's the spirit," said Hugo. "Only by venturing beyond reality do we find the truth."

Vincent shot him a quizzical look as they prepared to follow Sofia and her cat through the skin of the craft. "What in God's name are you babbling on about?"

The two friends, relieved to find that the journey appeared to have had no appreciable effect on them, stepped into a musty cellar that smelled strongly of stored onions. With Copernicus streaking ahead of her, Sofia click-clacked up a flight of concrete steps and unlocked a door. The men followed on in a state of wonderment and stood in an expansive hallway while Sofia locked the door behind them. She then led the way, strolling past a sweeping staircase of polished wood and painted tiles prior to slipping into a kitchen that smelled of fresh-baked bread and chicken stew. Before they were able to catch up with her, Hugo and Vincent heard a velvety voice emanate from within.

"*Buenas*, Sofia!" greeted María, wiping her hands on an apron. "Such a noise just now! Another small earthquake, I should imagine. Did you enjoy your morning stroll?"

"I did," replied Dr Ustinova, her face beaming. "María, allow me to introduce two very good friends of mine, señor Hugo Wilde and señor Vincent O'Toole. They will be staying with us for a while."

As the trio were getting to know each another, Sofia unlatched a stable door that opened out onto the fountain courtyard. How beautiful was her little corner of Paradise, she thought; how wonderful it was to have this Garden of Eden on her doorstep. She closed her eyes to listen to the ripple of falling water and raised her chin to the Mexican sun. There she stood in salutation, arms by her side, stretching up from her toes to her neck, a human incarnation of a carved maiden at the front of a Spanish galleon.

"Thank you, whoever you are!" she called out to the Universe with joy on her face and love in her heart. "It feels good to be home."

CHAPTER EIGHT

Mexico City, 1970

In the unseeing darkness of their bedroom, Hugo was awakened by the pluck of Copernicus's paws on his chest and the rattle of the cat's breath in his ear. As if in the grip of an hallucination, his consciousness was arrested by the sudden realisation that he had woken up in a different time and place. Hugo considered the preposterousness of it all and found it hard to reconcile the fact that he was now living in an era that had existed before he was even born.

Sofia, sensing his restlessness, surfaced from an ocean of dreams. "Go back to sleep, darling. You really are such a fidget."

Hugo illuminated the face of his wristwatch: it read 5.18 a.m. As he was not yet suited to the time difference – it was already approaching noon in England – he decided that an early morning jog would be a better use of his time.

Taking care not to disturb Sofia, he pulled on a pair of briefs. Quietly unzipping his suitcase in the dark, he gathered shorts, a vest top and running shoes then slipped from their bedroom and dressed on the landing. The colonial mansion in which he now resided, apparently the oldest and the grandest on the block, reminded the Englishman of his own manor house. It was imposing and generously proportioned, and he mused that if its walls could speak, their scandalous stories might make a sailor blush.

After descending the wide staircase, Hugo padded along the hallway and left a note for Sofia on an antique console table before picking up a house key reminiscent of the type used by the Count of Monte Cristo's jailers. Apart from the tireless tick-tock of a grandfather clock and the murmur of ceiling fans, there wasn't a sound to be heard in the house.

Before leaving, he couldn't resist the nostalgic thrill of winding a number on the hall's rotary phone to the finger stop and watching it whirr back again, something he had enjoyed doing as a little boy. Thwarting his best efforts to maintain the quietude, the front door opened with a pained groan and closed in a similar fashion. He locked it behind him and stepped out into a world where dial telephones and typewriters weren't yet anachronisms and where any suggestions of a virus being able to bring the world to its knees were broadly hypothetical.

The vastness of Mexico City stretched out beneath the Englishman's soles. He ran at a brisk pace, pounding the sidewalks of tree-lined avenues in the glow of streetlamps, his shadow dancing around him. How freeing it was, he realised, to be able to step outside without having to be in a perpetual state of vigilance.

He marvelled at the diverse architecture; no two houses the same and each with a story to tell. This was an elegant neighbourhood where stately art-nouveau mansions and well-maintained art-deco apartment buildings stood cheek by jowl with nondescript edifices that only their soulless architects could love. On every available wall space, bullfight posters were being usurped by Mexico 1970 Football World Cup ones, and Hugo was immediately excited at the prospect of attending an iconic event that he had only hitherto seen in grainy TV documentaries.

He raced past a beautiful park that slumbered in the dark and made a mental note of the many cafeterias and restaurants he would like to try. Both he and Vincent had considered themselves extremely fortunate to have feasted on the scrumptious food prepared by María the previous evening, and he was looking forward to more of the same for breakfast.

As the metropolis woke to the sorcery of dawn, the air became alive with birdsong and the roads began to fill with the lazy growl of traffic. Hugo acknowledged a road sweeper, who was brushing up the detritus of the previous day with a broom made from birch twigs, and returned the wave of an elderly gentleman who was sitting reading a newspaper on his balcony dressed only in a pair of baggy Y-fronts.

By the time he had completed his circuit, having earlier consigned to memory that Sofia's mansion was situated on Avenida Destino, the sun had announced itself and more and more people were out on the streets. As well as the ubiquitous Volkswagen Beetles, he passed a great many classic American cars from the 1960s, namely Corvettes, Buicks and Mustangs, chrome-trimmed and bat-winged with whitewall tyres.

Hugo stopped to admire the stately mansion from the opposite side of the road as he jogged on the spot while waiting for a dusty pineapple truck to chug past. The house stared back at him with all the hauteur of a conquistador, its grand façade a thing of beauty with its wrought-iron window grilles and decorative stone mouldings. As the Mexican sun slanted through the trees and glinted on car mirrors, the Englishman could not have been happier with his new-found sense of freedom.

He opened the monastery-style front door with its hefty key and stepped into a hallway now suffused with the wonderful aroma of cooked food. Led by his nose, Hugo followed the ambrosial trail in the way a bear tracks the scent of salmon. "*Buenos días,* María!" he said, poking his head around the kitchen door. "Mmm, smells so good."

The cook's dimpled smile would have lit up the dullest of days. "*Buenos días,* Hugo. Would you like some *chilaquiles* served with eggs and beans?"

"I don't know what they are, María, but count me in. Allow me fifteen minutes to shower and change and I'll be right down."

"Very good, señor."

Hugo was joined by Sofia and Vincent. Breakfast, which included some of the previous night's leftovers, was eaten informally at a rustic kitchen table that groaned under a supply of fried tortilla triangles that were first bathed in salsa then topped with leftover chicken, diced onions, cilantro and grated cheese. These were served with eggs cooked to order, accompanied by beans, sour cream and fresh guacamole.

"I was only expecting bacon with my eggs," said Vincent, "but I could happily tuck into this every day of the week."

"Any time you would like some bacon, you just ask," said María with a wink, refilling the Irishman's coffee cup from a stainless-steel pot.

With appetites well and truly sated, the three time travellers helped the cook to clear the table of crockery despite her protests. While she was wholly oblivious to the facts surrounding the trio's extraordinary circumstances, there existed a flush of unspoken excitement between the diners. In this instance, the metaphor of 'the elephant in the room' was perfectly appropriate for the time machine that remained hidden in the cellar.

Sofia had scheduled a 10.30 appointment with a city stockbroker whom she had previously come to trust and set off promptly, attaché case in hand, in a coral-coloured taxi. Hugo, looking every inch a character in a Somerset Maugham story, had dressed in a cream linen suit paired with a pale blue shirt and silk cravat.

It had earlier dawned on him that he'd travelled without his toiletry bag and he felt that this oversight should be his number one priority. In pursuance of this purpose, and with his pockets stuffed with the Mexican banknotes that Sofia had given him, he asked María for directions to the nearest department store. True to her obliging nature she went the extra mile by sketching him a map while singing along to a Latin ballad that was playing on the radio.

Through the kitchen window, Hugo spied a lady's bicycle propped against a sunny wall in the courtyard. "Whose bike is that?" he enquired.

"It is mine, señor."

"May I borrow it? That little beauty will get me to the department store in no time."

"Of course, señor, but I think maybe it is too small for you. Look, my legs are like little tree trunks."

"María, it will be just the job. And whilst I'm in the store, I shall buy you something nice for your trouble."

O'Toole lumbered into the kitchen pulling on a giant-sized Ireland rugby shirt and wearing shorts that revealed his squid-white legs to the world. Wilde's dapper appearance was just too much for him to ignore. "Hey, look – it's our man in Havana," he chuckled. "Saints alive, Hugo, you look as if you should be hobnobbing with Inspector Poirot on the Orient Express."

"Every Englishman abroad likes to consider himself

a traveller and not a tourist," said Hugo, paraphrasing Evelyn Waugh.

María stepped forward to put the finishing touches to his cravat. "Do not listen to him, señor Wilde. I think you look very stylish."

Vincent rolled his eyes. "Sainted Jesus. Is there a woman alive who isn't beguiled by your dubious charm, Hugo?"

"*Dios mío!*" yelped María suddenly as she rushed to attend to a saucepan that was threatening to boil over.

"And what are your plans for today, Vincent?" asked Hugo, thinking the Irish marvel was unsuitably dressed for anything other than cleaning out a chicken coop.

"My only plan is to find the nearest bar. Yours?"

"I need to buy a few essentials and then I intend familiarising myself with some of the city's cultural sights."

O'Toole leaned in. "And I intend to drink myself silly. I barely slept a wink last night, thinking about you-know-what."

Hugo nodded in sympathy, then directed his friend's gaze towards the sunlit bicycle. "Look, Vincent, my chariot awaits."

"Surely to God you're not going out on *that*?"

"I most certainly am."

To observe Hugo astride María's cramped pushbike was akin to seeing a praying mantis balancing on a tiny leaf. His knees were almost level with the handlebars, and he had to lean back in the saddle to allow himself enough legroom. He nevertheless enjoyed pedalling along the sidewalks and roads of Mexico City on a contraption that came equipped with a sturdy wicker basket and a chrome bell.

From its exterior the department store didn't appear to be quite as grand as Hugo had hoped, but nevertheless he was excited to venture inside. Of course there were items he had left behind in England that couldn't be replaced, most notably the small gilt-framed photograph of his parents that he liked to keep by his bedside. Then there were the personal effects that would seem inconsequential to the casual observer but meant a great deal to him: objects that had become a part of his daily routine, such as the badger-fur shaving brush he'd bought at Sotheby's and his favourite Wedgwood teacup and saucer.

Hugo pushed the bicycle into a metal rack on the edge of the sidewalk and secured it with a lock that María had provided. Then, straightening his suit jacket and returning the salute of a uniformed commissionaire who held open the door for him, he strode briskly into the store's atrium.

The emporium's interior was plusher than he had anticipated and cheery muzak tickled the senses of all who trod its shiny floors. He passed a Jackie Onassis lookalike who was demonstrating the benefits of an electric carving knife to an eager audience of housewives, then rode an escalator up to a level whose sign included words he loosely understood such as

'*Regalos*' and '*Accesorios.*'

Seeing a flamboyance of bouffant-haired female assistants attired in mini-skirted uniforms and chiffon scarves immediately gave Hugo an idea for the thank-you gift he had promised María.

"*Buenos días*," he said across a brightly-lit glass counter as a version of 'Raindrops Keep Falling on my Head' played in the background.

"*Buenos días*, señor!" replied three assistants, bunching together.

Though Wilde was fluent in four languages, Spanish wasn't one of them. He directed his question to the ladies collectively. "*Habla Inglés?*"

"Yes, I speak English," said one, pushing herself front and centre.

"Me too," said another.

"I speak a little also," added a third.

"I would like to look at some of these, if I may." He pointed to a selection of silk scarves.

The ladies jostled to remove the drawers from their glass tomb and spread a selection of the scarves along the countertop. "For your wife?" asked one, folding her arms and narrowing her eyes.

"No, for a friend, actually," he replied, comparing the patterns.

"For a friend!" they chorused, beaming at each other.

Hugo decided on an Yves Saint Laurent neckerchief that had caught his eye. "Yes, this one please," he confirmed with a broad smile. "Oh, and this one too."

Leaving the ladies in a dizzy state of longing, he proceeded to a nearby display that hosted an array of masculine aftershaves. Among the offerings he was delighted to see a ceramic bottle of Old Spice cologne, complete with its inky drawing of a three-masted boat.

"Well, I never! My grandfather used to splash this all over his face," he remarked to a young male assistant, who was then too embarrassed to admit to wearing it on a daily basis. "Granted it's not Christian Dior, but I shall buy it in his memory."

Hugo left the store wearing his flamboyance like a cape. He stopped at the bicycle rack and loaded María's basket with a bag that held his aftershave and two gift-wrapped scarves, one for the cook and the other for Sofia. He found room for a second carrier bag, which was crammed with a double-edged safety razor, a canister of shaving foam, an aerosol deodorant, and a tin of hair pomade smelling of lemon floor cleaner.

Hugo couldn't resist removing the cap of the Old Spice bottle to sniff its contents. It had an overpowering nutmeg and star-anise scent that immediately elicited happy memories of the grandfather who had brought him up. He patted a generous amount onto his face to keep that evocation alive for the rest of the day.

The roads were heaving with traffic and the air was thick with the sound of motorists honking their horns incessantly in the mistaken belief that this was a surefire way to get things moving. Wilde weaved merrily in and out of vehicles, adding the ringing of his bicycle bell to the general cacophony. A uniformed officer, wearing a glossy-peaked cap, directed the chaos as best he could while the continuing orchestra of car horns competed with the constant shrill of his whistle.

As Hugo cut through side streets, whose uneven pavements were tentacled with tree roots, he happened upon a large park which welcomed him with open arms. He stopped to allow a man to hurry by with a tray of maize balanced on his head and walked María's pushbike through one of the park's entrances. Verdant and recuperative, he felt that the calm restraint of the gardens was the perfect antidote to the chaos beyond its wrought-iron railings.

Soon the traffic noise was a distant thrum and Hugo had put aside any thoughts of the people back home who, under normal circumstances, would be wondering where he was. Among them would be his stable master, the stable hands, his housekeeper, the gardeners, the head gamekeeper's assistants and, not least, his handlers at MI6. As difficult as it was to wrap his head around the absurdity of his present circumstance, he offset any feelings of discomfort by recalling Sofia's promise that, no matter how lengthy his absence, she could return him to his house before the milk in his fridge had time to curdle.

Sofia, Sofia, Sofia, Hugo mused, enjoying the memory of the previous night. She had once more given herself to him and he'd responded by making love to her like a satyr. His world had become a better place and he again conceded that he had fallen hard for the Russian.

The air was filled with music thanks largely to an accordion player, who moved with a jester's gait, and a trilby-hatted trumpeter. All along the park's borders, broad-leaved plants danced to their cheerful tunes.

On an intersection where six pathways converged, there stood a large circular fountain whose centrepiece was a bronze statue of Neptune seeing off a sea monster with his trident. No sooner had Wilde sat upon a bench to admire the scene than a cheerful boy, slight in frame and short in stature, hailed him. "*Hola*, señor! Would you like that I shine your shoes?"

Hugo was immediately taken by the lad's exuberance and effortless smile. "Yes, I would like that very much, my good fellow. Shine away."

The Englishman lifted his right knee and rested a tan Oxford brogue on a wooden box that the teenager had provided. "What is your name, young sir?"

"My name is Pablo, señor. Pablo Quiroz."

CHAPTER NINE

Silkeborg Forest, Denmark, 1980

Leif Hartvigsen was still hurting from the death of his beloved gundog when he set out on the first Monday in September to hunt for something other than woodland creatures. Formerly the sole heir to his father's food manufacturing empire, Leif's self-imposed seclusion from the outside world and his tendency to forgo medication had further worsened his troubled state of mind. Moreover, his only sounding board was a ten-year-old girl.

Within an hour he had found his prey in a large forest clearing fringed by brambles: two hikers, one male, one female who, by the sound of their voices, hailed from England. Hartvigsen had come armed with a traditional longbow strapped to his back and a large hunting knife tucked into his belt. With the zinc-bright surface of Thorsø Lake glimmering in the distance he edged closer.

The snap of a small branch under his boot alerted the couple to his presence. Visoring his eyes against the sun, the male rambler was the first to speak. "I say, old chap, I wonder if you could help us? I'm afraid we've strayed from the hiking trail and have lost our bearings."

Hartvigsen, haloed by the sun as it broke through the trees, refrained from speaking and instead responded to the Englishman's request with a menacing glare.

"Let's just move along, Roger," suggested the man's wife, sensing that conviviality wasn't the local's strongest suit.

Her husband, though, was irked by the woodsman's inhospitality. "Cat got your tongue, sir?" he said, putting hands to hips. "Usually, when one is asked a question, it is common courtesy to respond."

The hunter's dark intentions soon became horribly clear to both hikers when he calmly gripped his bow and fixed an arrow onto its string. The Englishman, swift to react, rushed the man with every intention to kill or maim, only for Hartvigsen to fire the arrow deep into his chest and stop him in his tracks. Despite this, his quarry continued to march forward, wild-eyed and determined, hands outstretched. Alas, the rambler's fortitude was in vain. The Dane calmly withdrew another arrow from his quiver and released it into the Englishman's throat, causing him to slump to his knees with a strangled gasp.

Almost paralysed with fear, but trying to remain calm, the man's wife pleaded with the maniac to spare her life. "I have a son... His name is Hugo," she faltered. "Only five years old. Please think about that, would you?"

Hartvigsen remained impassive and, with the eyes of the forest upon him, loaded a second arrow. Seeing that there was no hope of salvation, Octavia Wilde drew her shoulders back and met her end with valiant defiance.

CHAPTER TEN

Gerardo and Pablo were disheartened to spot the contemptible Rubén Cuevas watching their every move at the Zócalo Plaza the day after being robbed.

Gerardo, sporting two black eyes, felt it best that they retreat to the leafy refuge of Alameda Central Park. "There are not so many tourists, but it will make a welcome change," he explained. "Also, I seem to remember that you like the ice creams there, Pablo."

Ice cream or no ice cream, the boy was inflamed by the unfairness of it all. "Why should we live in fear of bullies, Papá? I hate him! I really hate him!"

The musician placed a hand on his son's shoulder. "Hate is such a wasted emotion," he replied. "A very wise man once said that holding onto one's anger is like drinking poison in the hope that the other person will die. Let go of it, my darling Pablo."

Despite being forced to decamp, the two were all smiles by the time they arrived at the park. Gerardo purchased ice-cream cones from a canopied trailer near the entrance while Pablo relieved his sore shoulders by unstrapping the chair from his back.

"I feel bad that you don't have a need for the chair today," his father remarked as Pablo smoothed the edges of his ice cream with his tongue. "They have so many benches in this park. Tell you what, Pablo, if things go well here we could make this our regular spot."

With their ice creams polished off, they elected to split up, Gerardo playing his trumpet under the shade of a chestnut tree and Pablo establishing himself near the cool spray of the Fuente de Neptuno.

Despite it suffering a sizeable dent, courtesy of Rubén Cuevas, the trumpet delighted the musician by continuing to deliver a beautiful tune. Meanwhile, his son spotted a dapper foreigner sitting on one of the curved benches that faced the fountain. With his paraphernalia clattering about him, Pablo hastened to the man and seized the moment. "*Hola*, señor! Would you like that I shine your shoes?"

He noted that the gringo had a kind face, an easy smile and was clouded in a most heavenly smell. The two struck up an immediate rapport and the man even took the trouble to ask Pablo for his name. His handmade shoes were finer than any the boy had ever seen, so he took extra care in his endeavour.

Pablo learned that his client's name was Hugo, but couldn't quite place his cultured accent. "Americano?" he enquired, sitting on his haunches and buffing the man's brogues with gusto.

"English," was the response.

"I love the English!" the boy enthused. "Shakespeare, Bobby Charlton, Queen Elizabeth, The Beatles, Lawrence of the Arabia—"

"And do you have family, Pablo?"

"Only my father, señor. My mother, she die six month ago. My father is so sad and he cry every day."

"And is he good to you?"

Pablo dabbed his brush into a tin of tan polish. "Yes, he is good to me. My father is the best in all of Mexico. Why do you ask me this?"

From the outset, Hugo had noticed a purple bruise around one of the boy's eyes and a cut on the bridge of his nose. "So, how did this happen?" he asked, indicating the damage.

Pablo's shoulders slumped and he heaved a despondent sigh. "Really, it is nothing, sir. A bad man. He yesterday hit me and also my father. Then he stolen our money."

The Englishman clenched his jaw and hardened his tone. "Where would one find such a man?"

Pablo wagged his brush. "This is not a man you would want to find, señor. He is—" As if arrested by a sixth sense, he stopped mid-sentence and glanced fearfully behind him. His heart skipped a beat because, sitting on the rim of the fountain and grinning like a chimpanzee, was Rubén Cuevas.

"Is he the man who hit you?" Wilde enquired, seeing trepidation in the boy's eyes.

"Yes," said Pablo, trembling like a candle flame.

"Do not look to his face, señor. He will hurt us both and take our money."

"This is very important, Pablo. Does he carry a weapon?"

"He has a knife, señor. He keep it in his belt."

"And what is his name?

A look of heightened alarm had blossomed on Pablo's face. "His name is Rubén Cuevas, sir. But please, you must not—"

Before the boy could finish his sentence, the Englishman had grabbed María's little pushbike and was setting off in the lowlife's direction. "Hang back and watch this, Pablo!" he shouted over his shoulder.

"*Por Dios!*" the boy wailed.

Wilde cycled up to the Mexican, sounding his bell with a cheery tringg-tringg and shooting him a flirtatious wink. Cuevas' expression immediately went from one of self-assured delight to one of complete confusion. With the smell of Old Spice wafting into his nostrils, the Englishman went on to circle the fountain, and each time a circuit was completed he winked at the bully and rang his bell.

After three laps, the Mexican was puce with rage. He slid down from the water's edge, hitched up his pants, tucked his gold chain into his vest and waited for the gringo asshole to round the bend.

Seeing that Cuevas had risen to the bait, Hugo lifted his backside from the saddle to pedal faster and crashed straight into him. "I am so sorry!" he apologised, clinging to the burly Mexican, his hands

KEVIN ANSBRO

all over him and getting into an unnecessary tangle while the bicycle lay on the ground, its wheels still spinning.

Rubén gave Hugo a hefty shove and spat a wad of gum in his face. "You want to play games, huh, gringo?"

The Englishman took a step back and tidied his cravat. "What I would like, Rubén, is for you to leave Pablo and his father alone."

The Mexican threw back his head and laughed like a villain in a Bollywood movie. "Be very careful, *cabrón*. You are the cockroach who has come to a chicken dance."

Though he hadn't shown it, Rubén was slightly unnerved by Hugo's casual air. In his experience, such men were either lambs to the slaughter or entirely unpredictable. "So, why are you so interested in this boy?" he asked puffing out his chest and cracking his knuckles. "Maybe you want him as your little *polluelo,* huh?"

With lightning speed, Hugo punched Cuevas hard in the solar plexus, leaving him doubled up with pain and honking like a seal. "Easy now, try to breathe, there's a good chap," he soothed, patting the Mexican's back and helping him to shuffle back towards the fountain's edge. Some of the park's visitors had stopped to gawk, unsure as to what was going on, but the Englishman sent them on their way with his genial smile and a few well-chosen words.

Rubén, now propped up against the stone rim

of the centrepiece, caught his breath and felt for his knife. "Looking for this?" grinned Hugo, opening his suit jacket.

"Son of a bitch!" rasped the Mexican.

The Englishman also produced a snakeskin wallet that was falling apart at the seams. "And you can have this back," he said, entirely relieving it of its banknotes.

The fountain came to life and jets of water erupted behind the thief's miserable head. It would have been easy to imagine Neptune striding through the water and dispatching Cuevas with his trident in the same way that he had the sea serpent.

"So, Rubén, have we come to an agreement that you will leave my friends alone?"

Cuevas, known as 'Rubén the Bull' to his sycophants, nodded reluctantly. "Yes, I will leave them alone, gringo. But if I ever see you again, I will kill you."

Hugo patted him on the shoulder. "We all have dreams, Rubén."

When he picked up the bicycle to pedal back to Pablo, Hugo saw that the boy was accompanied by a trilby-hatted gentleman whom he assumed to be his father. Both stood with mouths agape, their bruised eyes like headlamps.

"Hi, I'm Hugo. And you must be Pablo's father," he said breezily, offering his hand and following up with "*Cómo estás?*"

"*Muy bien, muy bien,*" replied the wonderstruck musician, clasping the Englishman's hand with both of his. "You speak Spanish, Hugo?"

"Barely, I'm afraid."

Gerardo watched incredulously as Cuevas clumped off with a wretched look on his face and his tail between his legs. "Señor, you have the heart of a lion. How can my son and I ever thank you?"

"No need to thank me," said Hugo, pressing a fat wad of Rubén's ill-gotten banknotes into the musician's palm. "And if that isn't enough to reimburse you for the money you've lost, I shall make up the difference."

Gerardo thumbed through the bills with eyebrows raised. "Señor, there is too much here. We must go after him and pay some of it back—"

"You need do nothing of the sort," Hugo declared. "Hopefully, he has learned a valuable lesson today."

Pablo gazed up at the Englishman with a reverence usually reserved for deities. "Sir, you do not know this man. The next time he sees us, he will beat us and steal our money again."

Hugo plucked a *Visconti* fountain pen and a small notepad from his jacket pocket. "If he gives you any more trouble, you can find me at this address." He went on to congratulate the musician for the way in which he and his late wife had raised such a well-mannered young man and complimented him on his and his son's command of the English language.

"Oh, thank you, Hugo," replied the father with great pride. "I do what I can because they did not teach it at his school. My son, he is also a great artist and, as you can see, he is not afraid of hard work."

"If you do not work hard for something," said Pablo brightly, "it will never be truly yours."

Hugo couldn't escape the feeling that he had heard the name Pablo Quiroz before and sensed that the boy had a bright future. "Gentlemen, I don't know what your plans are, but could I treat you both to a late lunch?"

Wilde and his two guests dined outside a cafetería in a touristy part of town. They sat at a round metal table whose steadiness was improved by the introduction of a folded serviette to the underside of one of its legs. Hugo went along with their recommendations and the trio enjoyed a spicy sweetcorn soup, followed by a tomatoey rice dish with chicken. Father and son initiated the Englishman into the thirst-quenching welcome of an *agua fresca de limón* – essentially a fresh limeade – and soon he was hooked on the stuff, ordering them at will. Then, as if his day couldn't be any more immersive, a mariachi band, wearing embroidered sombreros and red neck ties, struck up a symphonious bombast of guitars, violins and trumpets, and sang *Guantanamera* at the top of their lungs. Just as the Englishman was dwelling on the fact that such a day was a rarity, he was further delighted by the sight of Gerardo grabbing his trusty trumpet and getting up to jam with the band.

Later, after Hugo had tipped the musicians and settled the restaurant bill, the newly acquainted friends prepared to go their separate ways. Gerardo doffed his hat to the Englishman with a musketeer's flourish and shook his hand warmly. "Hugo, you are a true English gentleman, very much like the ones I have seen in the movies. We thank you from the bottom of our hearts for the kindness you have shown us, and we hope to see you again."

With a look that might have tugged at Ebenezer Scrooge's heartstrings, Pablo added, "I think that my heart will hurt if I never see you again, señor."

Hugo patted his pockets for a phone that wasn't there. This was the first of many instances where he would come to realise how future societies will readily take technology for granted. "Guys, I would love to give you my home telephone number but I'm afraid I don't have it to hand just yet," he apologised.

"It is fine, my friend," Gerardo replied, his kind eyes twinkling. "We do not have the luxury of a telephone in our apartment anyway."

Hugo produced his notepad and pen. "Could you jot down your address just in case you misplace mine? I would love to stay in touch because you two are great company."

The musician scribbled his full name and address on the pad and handed it back to the Englishman who studied it carefully. "Well, señor Quiroz, and Pablo the Wonder Boy, it has been a true pleasure getting to know you. This won't be the last you see of me."

The three hugged and said their goodbyes before the Englishman rode off on his miniature pushbike with its cargo of shopping bags.

"Hugo is no ordinary man, Pablo," said the father watching him disappear up the road. "I wonder if he is an angel sent to us."

"I wonder too, Papá."

Upon his return to the mansion house, Wilde unlocked the wrought-iron gate that guarded the peaceful courtyard to the rear of the property. Catching the late afternoon sun, the yard, with its pageant of tropical plants, hand-painted tiles and leafy borders, was as pretty as a picture and would have had Monet dashing off to fetch his paintbrushes.

Alerted to Hugo's presence, a lizard scuttered up the braided trunk of a money tree and the two-tiered fountain spritzed him with a cooling mist as he wheeled María's bicycle back to where he'd found it. He stole into the kitchen where the contents of several copper pots spurted and bubbled like molten lava, but señora Bravo was nowhere to be seen. He followed the burr of a reverberating sound that emanated from the library and there she was, lost in concentration, busily vibrating a polishing machine from side to side across the parquet floor.

The air smelled strongly of beeswax and Hugo had to shout above the din. "María! I have a little something for you!"

"Oh, *buenas tardes,* Hugo," she said, cutting power to the machine. "What did you say, sir?"

"I said that I have a little gift for you, María. A token of my appreciation for lending me your bike."

"For me?" she enthused, ripping open the crêpe wrapping paper and running the scarf through her pudgy hands. "Oh, sir, it is so beautiful!"

"You like it?"

"I love it!"

"Good, I'm pleased. It's the least I could do."

"Sir, is it bad etiquette to give you a hug?"

"Of course it's not bad etiquette," he replied, spreading his arms. "Bring it in, Miss Mexico."

Sofia appeared, floating down the curved staircase wearing a boho peasant dress and sandals. "Seriously, you two, get a room," she chuckled.

"Miss Moscow!" cheered Hugo, producing a scarf from its wrapping and swishing it in the manner of a stage magician. "I also have a present for you, gorgeous lady."

"Darling, how thoughtful," said Sofia, planting a kiss on his lips and then pausing to sniff the air around him. "Hugo, unless it's the floor polish, you smell very much like my grandfather did when I was a little girl."

At that moment, O'Toole barrelled through the front door with eyes glazed and his rugby shirt on back to front. "Ladies and gentleman, you are looking at the local arm-wrestling champion! Three cheers for me!"

"Found a watering hole then, Vincent?" Hugo chuckled.

"Indeed I did, my fine friend. And like Kerouac before me, I have found saints amongst the sinners."

"Seems as if you had a good time," said the

Englishman.

"I did. These Mexican fellas are marvellous. Took me into their hearts like I was their long-lost cousin. And the place was thick with cigarette smoke, so it was. Picture that, Hugo. People smoking indoors like they did in the good old days—"

María unplugged the polish machine and toddled off to the kitchen to attend to her pots and pans. Sofia followed, intent on fixing the Irishman a mug of strong coffee.

"But these *are* the good old days, Vincent," Hugo prompted. "Hence the reason why everyone was smoking indoors and why you smell like an ashtray."

"Of course, of course," said O'Toole tapping his nose. "Anyway, a grand bunch they were, and they asked me to do a bit of the old Irish dancing after I'd sung them a few songs."

"And is that how you ripped your shorts?"

"It is."

Sofia returned with a steaming hot mug of coffee which Vincent was grateful to receive "Hey, guess what," he said, lowering his voice in a conspiratorial manner. "I've only been here a day and already I've found someone who can provide us with fake resident visas, ID cards, passports—"

"That won't be necessary," Sofia interjected, her expression one of pent-up jubilation. "All of the documentation that you two could ever need was waiting for me in the time machine when I returned from the stockbroker."

*

In the early evening, having returned home to drop off their equipment, Gerardo and Pablo bought loaves of bread, blocks of cheese and bottles of Coca-Cola from a minimart and headed to La Ciudadela Park. On the rare occasions that they were blessed with good fortune, they liked to share some of it with those who had none.

A tented community of children and teenagers, left destitute by abandonment or the death of their impoverished parents, existed on the fringes of the park. These waifs, the flotsam and jetsam of society, were easy targets for predatory males and trusted only each other. Many inhaled solvents to escape from their nightmarish existence. Most had lost all hope.

As they approached the park, Gerardo elucidated with the flair of a great orator. "We must always remember how fortunate we are, Pablo. Though we are not rich by any means, these unfortunates have nothing at all. We live in a bizarre world where the only people who can make money are those who don't need it. Our government would charge the poor an admission fee just to gaze up at the sky if they could only find a way of owning it."

Pablo squeezed his father's hand. "As long as I have you, Papá, I am rich. Without you, I would be just like these kids. We must give what we can."

CHAPTER ELEVEN

Silkeborg Forest, Denmark, 1986

As Leif Hartvigsen lay on his deathbed, riddled with the most pernicious of cancers, the day outside was a joyous one, as resplendent as any that could be found in a poetry book. A gentle breeze drifted languidly through an open window, carrying with it the chirrup of distant birds.

The white-haired girl, now aged sixteen, listened with great sorrow to the rattle of his lungs. Though she had foreseen his demise in a premonition, she nonetheless found it to be quite harrowing.

Apart from the dogs he had owned, the porcelain-skinned girl was the only thing in this world that Leif had ever cared for. Even now, as death sniffed at his diseased body, her welfare was the only thing on his mind.

Hartvigsen murmured to her, as if in the midst of an unsettled dream, "Luna, forgive me, but I have committed the most unspeakable acts. My dying wish is that you put me in the ground without telling a soul that I am dead."

The girl knew that the old man was ill-tempered and sometimes deranged but had no knowledge of the unspeakable acts he was alluding to. Her voice was like the whistling of wind. "What terrible things did you do, Father?"

"You do not want to know what I did, girl," he snapped, suddenly glaring at her through one rheumy eye. "And you certainly wouldn't want to know what the government scientists will do to you if they ever find out what you are."

The girl's irises swirled like gasoline on water. "Why? What would they do?"

"They would cut you open, Luna," he wheezed, "and drop little pieces of you into jars. You will be better off on your own."

To settle her nerves, Luna took a cigar from the old man's box, snipped off one end and lit the other against a candle flame. She filled her mouth with smoke and puffed until the cigar could breathe on its own. Veiled by a milky cloud that smelled vaguely of burnt coffee and roasted almonds, she ruminated on what her guardian had just said. "So, what am I to tell the Magnussens when I collect the mail and provisions from their store? They always ask about you."

Leif's words were nearing the end of their spool. "Just tell them … that I'm getting old," he coughed. "No one can know."

Death wrapped Hartvigsen tightly in its skeletal wings, causing the woodsman's mouth to open with an eruptive gasp. Though the old man was unable to utter Luna's name one last time, he at least left this world secure in the knowledge that he had done right by her.

CHAPTER TWELVE

In the months that followed, and with the benefit of future hindsight, Sofia stepped up her investment strategy, defying all odds by purchasing high-risk stocks in a failing market and going on to reap huge rewards. Such was the astonishing reliability of her clairvoyance that even Carlos, her usually cautious stockbroker, was emboldened to follow her lead.

As word of her pecuniary success spread, the Russian, without once mentioning that she was actually an acclaimed scientist with a master's degree and a PhD in physics, was warmly welcomed into the inner circles of Mexico City's movers and shakers. She lunched with bankers, industrialists, architects and attorneys, and was invited to lively parties held at the homes of ambassadors, musicians, actresses, poets and artists.

Realising that it was unfair to expect María to continue to prepare meals and also be responsible for the cleaning of the house, Sofia took on a housekeeper. Verónica Guadalupe Valdez was a nervous but diligent young lady whose nose suffered from a rabbit's twitch.

She came to the mansion house each day of the working week while María continued in her role as a live-in cook, happily ensconced in her own private quarters.

For his part, Hugo improved the household security by fitting new mortice locks on the front and back doors and installing outside lights. He also converted part of the cellar into a matted dojo where he and Vincent could practice Brazilian jiu-jitsu in private.

After María had offered a prayer to Saint Juan Diego, the patron saint of indigenous Mexicans, that he may continue to bless this house, Hugo and Vincent set to work on restoring its faded elegance, painting the burnt sienna walls with a profusion of white emulsion to brighten the place up.

The Irishman, who was extremely good at persuading people to do things against their will, roped in his rogue's gallery of drinking buddies with the lure of hot meals and free beer. He continued to fight a losing battle with the Spanish language and it amused Hugo greatly to see his friend rallying the troops using mostly sign language and the art of mime. Whatever the enticement, O'Toole's wheedling worked like a dream. Despite their seeming to get more paint on themselves than on the walls, his team raced along with a determination that would have impressed the pharaohs.

One of the workers, a coarse fellow with gold teeth and mournful eyes, wondered out loud if they had tripped themselves up by finishing two days ahead of schedule. "Hey, María! Does this mean that we have stupidly kissed goodbye to two more days of your delicious food?" he whimpered.

"Not at all, señor," she replied, tightening the strings of her apron. "A deal is a deal. You can come back tomorrow and the next day too. I have saved the best for last."

Sofia commissioned her artist friends to produce flamboyant paintings that prettified the bare walls. In addition to hanging a selection of Diego Rivera and Frida Kahlo prints, she laid Aztec rugs in almost all of the bedrooms. Handwoven Turkish carpets were imported from Istanbul, silk screens from Tokyo, Tiffany lamps from New York and chandeliers from Marrakesh. Along with a truckload of fashionable furniture, the scientist took delivery of a state-of-the-art colour television set, complete with its own wooden surround. A more prestigious addition, a Steinway piano with elegant curves and a gloss-black finish, was accommodated in the library. Large planters filled with rubber plants and indoor palms added the finishing touches. Before long, the elegant house had become a beautiful home suffused with a splendid atmosphere of *joie de vivre*.

With a shared sense of belonging and togetherness, Sofia and Hugo settled back one afternoon and took tea in the drawing room. Because he was a principled man, and a wealthy one at that, Hugo had increasingly felt ill at ease with the fact that he wasn't contributing to any of the household's running costs. "It's against my nature not to pitch in," he remarked. "But with my funds tied up in a different point in time, I have very little choice in the matter."

Sofia mocked him by pulling a pouty face. "Darling, I know that this puts a dent in your precious machismo, but I really don't have a problem with it. And anyway, I'm not exactly obtaining the money by fair means myself, now am I?"

"True," nodded Hugo, feeling slightly less of a freeloader.

The Russian lay back in her seat and shrugged like a Sicilian. "So, in reality, the money is not mine to keep. It belongs to you and to anyone else who deserves it. Have you got that, lover boy?"

"Loud and clear, darling."

In the course of getting to know one another, the couple had each shed their natural scepticism and concluded that their crossing of paths must have come as a result of some type of cosmic intervention. The hypothesis had become impossible to ignore, given the startling coincidences in their lives. It transpired that they were both born on the same day in the same year, that they were each orphaned at a very young age and, moreover, that the intensity of their instant attraction was something neither had hitherto experienced.

In the first days of their relationship, Sofia had told Hugo about the grandmother who died before she was born, the one with whom she had always felt a spiritual connection even though they had never met.

"My maternal grandmother was a prima ballerina with the Kirov Ballet company," she clarified. "And my grandfather was a respected architect who was permitted to travel to the west. They were flying home to Moscow from Havana in mid-June, 1970 and, twenty minutes after taking off, sploosh! Their plane crashed into the Atlantic."

At the time, Hugo, because he was still new to the convoluted rules of time travel, had rashly suggested that she telephone her grandmother long-distance, adding that it would prove to be a wonderful experience for them both.

"As we speak, they are both still alive, Sofia. Unless I've got my dates muddled up, they haven't yet flown to Havana."

The venomous stare that ensued was likely to remain in his memory forever. "Hugo, darling," she had started in a clipped tone. "For a supposedly intelligent man, you sometimes say the most stupid things. Imagine how you would react to a phone call from a granddaughter who is not yet born. Really, you should process the thoughts that pop into your head before you say them out loud."

*

With the house now dressed up to the nines, and because she couldn't play any part in correcting the outdated scientific research of the time, Sofia was keen to channel her energy into hosting dinner parties and charitable social events. In consideration of this, she suggested to Hugo that they employ a butler on an ad hoc basis. Though not entirely sold on the idea – he had less than happy memories of the starchy manservants of his youth – the Englishman agreed that it would indeed add a dash of grandeur to any special occasion.

"I know it's all rather pompous and ostentatious," said Sofia. "But it will only be on a part-time basis, and Verónica has already said that she would be happy to help out when the need should arise."

They had placed an advertisement in the local newspaper asking for a trained butler with a good understanding of conversational English; one who would be able to oversee the setting of tables and the serving of food and drinks. The advertisement clearly stated that the position was not a permanent one and would therefore only suit someone prepared to work flexible hours on a sporadic basis. Having sifted through the many résumés sent to them, they felt that only one applicant had the right credentials.

On the morning of the interview, Sofia and Hugo were sitting in a shaded area of their courtyard jotting down the questions they would like to ask, when the famous Mexican opera singer, Madame Díaz-Zorita, appeared on her neighbouring balcony to loosen her vocal cords with a stirring aria. She sang out loud with exquisite *pianissimo* and afterwards milked the applause of her audience of pedestrians, construction workers and neighbours as if she were performing at the Palacio de Bellas Artes.

"What a wonderful way to start the day," said Hugo, breaking away from his standing ovation as the sound of the doorbell jangled through the house. He dashed the length of the hallway with effortless strides to reach the front door.

On the other side of it, clutching a leather briefcase in both hands, stood a cadaverous fellow with a pencil moustache. As if to emphasise his professional credentials, he had come dressed in an actual butler's uniform. The man's lips were thin as sliced ham and words leaked through them like a poisonous gas. "I am Severiano Salazar, señor," he said unctuously. "At your service."

Wilde shook the butler's limp hand and immediately likened it to grabbing a dead fish. The Mexican did look the part though; his appearance implying the high level of fastidiousness expected for the role. He wore a stiff wing-collared shirt over a black tie and his shoes had been shone until he could see his weaselly face in them. His greying hair was brilliantined to his scalp and parted in the middle like the pages of a book.

Hugo stood aside and beckoned the man in with a matador's flourish. "Good morning, Mr Salazar. I'm Mr Wilde. Do come in."

The Mexican thanked the Englishman with an oily smile. Sofia, who had walked in from the courtyard clutching a clipboard of notes, intercepted them in the hallway.

"Sofia, this is Severiano Salazar," said Hugo breezily.

"Mr Salazar, may I introduce Doctor Ustinova?"

She shook the man's clammy hand and instantly wondered if he resided in a damp basement. "Good morning, señor Salazar."

"Good morning, Madam," he murmured in a reedy voice. "But I prefer to be addressed as 'Mr', if you would be so kind. It adds an international flavour, don't you think?"

"If you say so," replied Sofia.

The Mexican, although he had a simpering way about him, abruptly fixed them with a beady stare, his pupils moving from side to side. "Am I to understand that you two are not married?"

"We're not," said Hugo firmly. "Is that a problem?"

"Oh, no, sir," replied the butler lowering his gaze. "I am willing to move with the times."

"Let us step into the library," Sofia instructed in a business-like fashion. With head held high, she click-clacked through to a Louis XV desk that they had set up earlier. She filled a glass tumbler with iced water from a jug and offered it to the interviewee. "Please, take a seat, Mr Salazar."

The interview went well. The butler demonstrated good listening skills and remained cool, calm and collected throughout. He mentioned stints at some of Mexico City's finest houses, including being drafted in to serve at presidential banquets. His enunciation was flawless, with barely a hint of an accent, and he claimed to know how to manage a wine cellar.

"Our cellar is kept locked, I'm afraid," Sofia interjected. "But just ask either one of us, and we can go down there to fetch bottles when they're needed."

"Very good, Madam."

Though he had a glum look about him and reminded Hugo of a goldfish that he'd once won at a fairground, the Englishman felt that Salazar was the right man for the job. To convey this he discreetly tapped Sofia on the knee – a prearranged secret signal of approval.

The Mexican sat rigid as a violin case. "I would like to assure you that I steer a tight ship," he said imperiously, only for Copernicus to spring up onto the desk and hiss fishy cat breath into his cheerless face before he could utter another word.

"Really, there is no need for authoritarianism in this house, Mr Salazar," said Sofia, returning the cat to the floor. "We are all fairly relaxed and get along like one happy family."

The butler bowed his head obsequiously. "As you wish, Madam."

"We emphasised that the position is not a full-time one," Sofia continued. "With that in mind, would you be happy to be held on a retainer and only turn up when required?"

"More than happy, Madam," Salazar replied with a thin smile that barely troubled his lips. "Working part time suits me at my time of life."

Before announcing her decision, Sofia looked to Hugo. He, despite having some reservations, reaffirmed his approval with a smile and a nod. "We pay our staff handsomely, Mr Salazar," she declared, offering a typed agreement for him to read and sign. "And we would very much like to offer you the job."

CHAPTER THIRTEEN

Silkeborg Forest, Denmark, 1986

Goose-white and spectral, the girl worked by moonlight, the smoke of her breath phosphorescent in the damp forest air. The night had already sent birds to their nests and painted the trees as silhouettes. Overhead, a splendour of stars spangled the sky, reminding Luna that her parents were still out there somewhere in the Universe. In her formative years, they had visited her in hollow-voiced dreams, their features as indiscernible as ripples on the surface of a lake. Though they spoke in a language she didn't understand, they had left her with an overwhelming sense of hope for the future.

Having raked away a layer of leaf mulch, Luna attacked the ground near to her cabin with a hefty pickaxe that she was barely able to swing. Digging proved even harder for one so slight and her palms, though gloved, were soon ragged with blisters. Luna, however, was born of an indomitable lineage and stuck to the gruesome task with unyielding determination.

The girl toiled through the night and, having

reached a point where she could barely reach the rim of the hole, knew that she had excavated to a depth of six feet. She lobbed the spade onto the ground above her head and scaled the dirt wall with a squirrel's ease. The mud had stuck to her boots in clods, so she scraped them on the shoulders of the spade and stood back to admire her handiwork. Meanwhile, a dawn cluster of blackbirds, who were perfectly relaxed with her kind, had been feasting on worms in the loose earth that hemmed the edges of the grave.

Luna returned to the cabin, looped a length of rope under the old man's armpits and secured it across his chest with a bowline knot. She wrapped the trailing end around herself and heaved his corpse from the bed, wincing as it hit the floor with a thud – a fumble she apologised for, even though it was too late for any harm to be done. The teenager hauled Hartvigsen's stiff body with all the strength that she had, dragging it through the cabin like a sled, lugging it down the decking steps with a bumpety-bump and across leafy ground. Once she had bundled his cadaver into the hole, she began the process of returning the displaced soil from whence it came.

If a group of devout pilgrims had stumbled across this astonishing scene, they could have been forgiven for imagining that an angel had been sent by God to reclaim a lost soul. The girl, with her white hair cut straight across in a fringe and her face the smooth marble of a Michelangelo sculpture, was peering into the grave, arms extended behind her as if she might take flight. Luna had shed a year's worth of tears in the past twenty-four hours but, because she only believed in the divinity of nature, there would be no prayers for her *de facto* father, just the recurring swoosh of shovel into mud and the raining down of soil and stones as she buried him in the ground along with his murderous secrets.

Later, perhaps because the old man's presence was now smothered six feet under, a prior apparition, that of a black-haired boy in a far-off land, returned to her consciousness.

CHAPTER FOURTEEN

The winged horses of fate rode into Mexico City on the morning of Saturday, the 13th of June, 1970. As if answering a siren's call, Hugo stopped what he was doing and traipsed along the hallway with the cellar key in hand and a faraway look in his eyes. In a daze, he passed Verónica without saying a word to her as she vacuumed the tiled floor. Ignoring her salutations, he unlocked the cellar door and then secured it from the inside. He then descended the steps without being fully aware of his actions and passed through the skin of the time machine, unconsciously heeding the extraterrestrial whispers that surrounded him.

A dark handprint, exactly matching his own, presented itself. Hugo pressed his palm against it and activated a string of pre-set coordinates as soon as they appeared. The ensuing screech of the craft abruptly woke him from his stupor and he immediately wondered where on Earth he was headed.

*

Unaware that her beau had recently passed through in a trance, Sofia greeted Verónica in the hallway. The young housekeeper was singing like a lark and in a dizzy state of rapture as she ran a brand-new upright Hoover vacuum cleaner over terracotta tiles and handwoven rugs.

"You seem especially happy in your work, Verónica," Sofia called out, watching the machine's dust bag billow like a sail.

"Madam, I am happy as the birds in the trees with this expensy new cleaner that you have bought. It have so much power and I cannot imagine how they can ever make these any better."

"Really, I think they will," said Sofia reliving childhood memories of her paternal grandmother using exactly the same model. "Would you like a cup of tea or coffee, Verónica?"

"Please and thank you, Madam. The coffee is my favourite more than the tea."

"One coffee it is then."

No sooner had Sofia turned on her heels than a familiar noise tore through the house, juddering the walls and rattling crockery.

Verónica crouched on the floor and wrapped her arms around her head. "*Madre mía! Madre mía!*" she wailed, her voice storm tossed and frantic. "It is the end of the world! We are all going to die!"

The noise stopped almost as soon as it had begun. Filled with dread, Sofia got down on her haunches and seized the housekeeper by her shoulders. "Verónica!

Verónica! Listen to me. Have you seen señor Wilde?"

The housekeeper's nose twitch had gone into overdrive. "Yes, Madam. I–I see him walk past me just five minutes ago. He go to the basement."

*

Not knowing what to expect, Hugo stepped guardedly from the craft into the cool of an unfamiliar forest that was alive with birdsong. A vapour percolated up from the earth, fragrant with the scent of bracken and myrtle. He turned 360 degrees, scanning the trees in his line of vision, and saw nothing but forest aisles, lush and majestic, untracked and boundless.

He wondered what century this was and wished he had his gun to hand in the event of being ambushed by medieval bandits. Unsure what to do next, but at the same time intrigued, he advanced through the forest, instinct driving him forward.

Most unexpectedly, through the trees there came a cheery shout. "Over here, Hugo!"

The voice was male, unmistakably polished, and enunciated in the Queen's English. Hugo wondered at that moment if he was dreaming, or if he was part of someone else's dream.

He headed in the direction whence the shout had originated and arrived at a large clearing in which stood a log cabin. In advance of the cabin, sitting on a fallen tree trunk and dressed in clothes suited to an English country estate, were a youthful man and woman who greeted him with radiant smiles and a high degree of familiarity.

The woman, who wore tan jodhpurs and glossy riding boots, was the first to speak. "Come closer, darling, that we might get a better look at you."

Hugo took stock of their beaming faces as they stood to receive him. Miraculously, theirs were the same two faces that had smiled out at him from a framed photograph for the past forty years.

"Mother! Father!" he cried out, rushing into their arms and feeling like a five year old again.

"God, we've missed you, son," said his father as the three held each other tightly and shared kisses.

Hugo choked on his words. "A day hasn't gone by when I haven't thought of you both. How can this be? Are you alive? Are you dead?"

His mother wiped his tears with a handkerchief. "Unquestionably dead, my lovely darling boy," she said, gazing deep into his eyes. "Please sit with us, dear. We have much to discuss but very little time."

Mr Wilde senior brushed scraps of loose bark from the fallen trunk. "Park your backside here, dear boy."

Hugo sat between his parents and tried to reconcile himself with this inconceivable state of affairs. As outlandish as it was to be conversing with his dead parents, it was also difficult for him to process the fact that they were younger than he.

Mother aligned her legs in a duchess slant, while his fresh-faced father leant forward with elbows on knees.

"Please forgive me, but I'm utterly at a loss for words," said Hugo, turning from one parent to another. "Are you okay? You both look well—"

Mr Wilde senior tugged on the cuffs of his Highland tweed jacket. "We are both fine, Hugo. Tickety-boo, in fact."

"And what is this place?" Hugo asked, seeing nothing but trees and a mackerel-skinned sky.

"We're in Denmark," said his mother, her smile like the breaking of dawn. "And the year is 1986."

Hugo's lips moved in silence as if he were rehearsing something in his head.

Father clasped his shoulder. "And I guess the question on the tip of your tongue must be along the lines of 'what the blazes happened to us'?"

"Of course. It's a question that has plagued me for most of my life," Hugo admitted.

His father furrowed his brow, not knowing quite where to begin. "The long and the short of it is that we were murdered in cold blood. Not many miles from this very spot, as a matter of fact."

"Murdered?" said Hugo. "I'd always imagined that you'd lost your way somewhere secluded and died from exposure."

"Not so. Your mother and I were enjoying a brisk walk off the beaten track when this bloody maniac appeared from nowhere brandishing a bow and arrow. I was intent on strangling the sick bastard – either that or gouging his eyes out. But he shot me through the chest and throat before I had the opportunity."

"And he dispatched me in much the same way," Mother added. "Then he returned with a spade to bury us whilst we watched him from the treetops."

"Do you know the name of this man?" asked Hugo. "I'll see to it that he faces justice, in the courts or otherwise."

"Rather late for that, I'm afraid," said his father. "The creature died peacefully in his bed only two months ago."

"And that brings us to the real reason you're here," Mother interjected, gesturing vaguely to the log cabin behind them. "Our killer has left behind a most remarkable teenager, one who has found herself orphaned and with no one to turn to."

"His daughter?"

"Not as such, though he brought her up as his own."

Hugo's father placed a hand on his son's knee. "We would like you to take this exceptional young lady under your wing, dear boy. Welcome her into your home and give her the upbringing she deserves."

"She's sixteen," Hugo's mother explained. "Living alone in a forest in the middle of nowhere is no place for one so young."

"Nor for one so gifted," Father reiterated, his eyes sparkling.

"But why should I be the one to step in," enquired Hugo. "Haven't social services become involved?"

"They've already turned up at her doorstep," said his father, "but she was resourceful enough to stall them."

"I'm not sure I follow," said Hugo.

His father looked him directly in the eye. "It won't be long before they return with police officers and warrants. It is imperative, absolutely imperative, that this girl doesn't fall into the hands of the authorities."

Mother also shuffled closer.

"The Universe sometimes throws together a unique collection of interactions, dear Hugo. Please be aware that none of what has happened to you lately has been purely by chance."

His father, who was fond of talking in metaphors, elucidated further. "Imagine for one second, Hugo, that you have lived your entire life in a vast human zoo. The zookeepers, in this case, have trusted you to step out of your enclosure."

Hugo was starstruck by his parents and entirely convinced by their powers of persuasion. "So, what makes this girl so special?"

"We shall allow you to find out for yourself, dear." His mother smiled. "Take note. She is exceptionally bright, so you will need to keep your wits about you."

Wishing he could pause the passing of time, Hugo couldn't stop gawping at his parents. The love he had for them was so deeply felt and so achingly raw as to be both celebratory and wounding at the same time. "I cannot get over how young you both look," he remarked with a shake of his head.

"Ah, yes, our eternal youth," said Mother. "What you lose in one life, you gain in another."

Father stood up and offered his hand. "Sadly, Hugo, the time has come for us to leave. Though we don't particularly approve of your choice of profession, your mother and I have followed your life path with the greatest of pride. It goes without saying that we love you very much."

Hugo stood to shake his father's hand. "You're going?" he gasped.

"We have to, Hugo darling," said his mother, kissing him on each cheek. "Moments such as these are always fleeting."

"You, on the other hand, still have much of your life to live, dear Hugo," said Father, ruffling his son's hair. "I'm sorry we weren't there for you as you grew from a boy into a man, but I am the proudest father in the cosmos."

"And I'm the proudest mother. Our love for you is immeasurable, Hugo."

"Oh, and please tell Sofia that we love her too," said Father.

"Very much so," agreed Mother, her eyes lighting up. "That remarkable lady will prove to be the love of your life, Hugo."

"I believe she already is," he grinned.

"Now listen up, darling. The girl's name is Luna," said his mother hurriedly as her form and that of her husband started to blur. "The girl in the cabin, her name is Luna—"

Despite Hugo wishing he could keep hold of them forever, his parents rushed their goodbyes and vanished in a scattering of mist.

Stoic as ever, Wilde tried to push his feelings of sorrow aside and headed for the cabin, keen to fulfil his parents' wishes. All was quiet, save for the rat-a-tat of distant woodpeckers and the flutey cries of blackbirds. Spotlighted by a column of powdery sunlight that sifted through the canopy, the dark shack sat brooding as if it were a living thing. Despite being supported on robust stilts, it stood at an uncertain angle and could be heard creaking like a pirate ship.

Hugo noted obvious signs of life: a plume of white smoke drifted lazily from a stone chimney, and an amber glow burnished the windows from within. Alongside the structure, there existed a rough-and-ready log store and a small allotment, in which fruit and vegetables grew in tidy rows.

With the day's events still uppermost in his mind, the Englishman absently scuffed through a carpet of dead leaves, failing to notice a taut rope that pulled hard on a sharply bent tree branch. He trod on a hidden trigger stick that whiplashed the branch and gathered the net around him, propelling him into the air in a flurry of twigs and leaves. Squirrels scurried for safety and crows were raucous in the trees.

"Wrro-oghh!" he yelped, his cry sending the forest girl rushing out onto the veranda with a loaded shotgun in her arms.

"*Hvem er det?! Hvad vil du her?!*" she called out, aiming her weapon as Hugo bounced about in mid-air with one leg dangling through the net.

"Luna! It's a pleasure to meet you!" he yelled, spitting a centipede from his mouth. "I'm afraid that I don't speak any Danish!"

Barefoot, and wearing a folksy apron dress, the girl descended three wooden steps and walked underneath the Englishman, gun still pointing towards him. "Who are you? What do you want here?"

"I come in peace," said Hugo, finding his predicament hilarious. "If you would be so kind as to cut me down, I will prove to you that I am here with the very best of intentions."

He had a clear view of the girl. She stood almost five feet in height, had bowl-cut hair, skin the colour of rice paper and dainty hands.

Mistrust smouldered in Luna's falsetto voice. "Who do you work for?"

"I work for no one and am here solely to extend you a kindness."

"I doubt that, mister. And how do you know my name?"

"My mother and father mentioned you. They have your best interests at heart and want me to protect you from the local authorities."

She looked at him askance. "Who are your mother and father? How do they know me?"

"As is the case with your father, they are no longer with us, Luna."

A spark of alarm flashed in the girl's eyes. "How do you know about my father? Nobody knows this."

"Questions, questions," said Hugo, shifting himself into a more comfortable position. "So here's my proposition, Luna. How about you ease me down from here so you can listen to what I have to say? If I should step out of line, you can let me have it with both barrels. How does that sound?"

"I am not at all afraid to shoot you, mister."

"I can see that, Luna. A very sensible approach, in my opinion."

The wind, which was the girl's secret sweetheart, suddenly picked up and swirled about her ears to impart some celestial truths. She cocked her head and listened intently, keeping her eyes and aim on Hugo as he treated the net as a hammock. "You have my trust, for now," she announced abruptly, making the shotgun safe by opening it at its hinge pin. "But that could change at any time."

Lifting the hem of her dress from the mulchy ground, Luna scampered off to the cabin. She returned with a large hunting knife and scrabbled up the tree with practised ease. "Are you ready, mister? You will come down fast."

"I'm ready," said Hugo, bracing himself.

She sawed through the rope and the Englishman came crashing to the ground with one leg still tangled in the net. "Ha! I'm alive!" he chuckled, freeing himself from the knotted ropes and brushing leaves from his clothes.

A wild fox emerged from the cabin and wondered whether it should stay to watch or skulk back inside.

"Keep your distance at all times," Luna instructed from the base of the tree, brandishing the knife in her dainty grasp.

Hugo adopted a placatory stance and spoke calmly. "Perhaps we might talk inside?"

Luna looked back at the fox as if to secure a second opinion, but the creature wasn't very forthcoming and just stared back with a woebegone look in its eyes. Other than the old man and herself, no one else had ever set foot inside the cabin.

"Assuming you are not a deviant, I see no reason why not," Luna said stoutly, gathering the fox as if it were a toy poodle. "By the sound of your voice, you are English, yes?"

"I am."

"Then I must make you a cup of tea."

"Extraordinarily kind of you. I would love one."

Luna carried the fox under one arm and waved the knife so as to remind Hugo that she was the one in charge.

"Knife duly noted," said Hugo, thinking what an amusing little thing she was. "After you, young lady."

As Wilde had envisaged, the interior of the cabin was rustic but warm and welcoming, with kerosene lanterns augmenting the lack of natural light. Small logs spat and crackled in the windowed blaze of a black cast-iron fire, and an aromatic stew bubbled frantically on the kitchen stove. There was a proliferation of books, either packed shoulder to shoulder on bookshelves or squished into cardboard boxes. Others were simply piled high on dressers.

Hugo noticed that the girl had an inborn grace and moved about the place like a Geisha. Her translucent skin bore a patina of grime, and tiny leaves dotted her white hair. It struck him that she had something of the hedgerow about her.

Luna returned the fox to the floor so she could concentrate on making the tea, and it slunk under an oak dresser to hide. She set a scorched kettle on a gas stove. Not yet certain of his motives, every few seconds she paused to give her uninvited visitor the evil eye.

Hugo settled into a rocking chair and pushed to one side a Nordic folk blanket that was criss-crossed with silver snail trails. "Just how far is this place from civilisation?" he asked.

The pint-sized curiosity stood on a stool to grab a teapot from a shelf. "Oh, about fifteen kilometres," she replied. "As you have seen, there are no roads in or out."

"I neither drove nor walked to this place," he remarked, intending to pique her interest. His words seemed to have had the desired effect as Luna stopped what she was doing and stared at him with renewed curiosity. The brilliance of her eyes disarmed him slightly; they were crystal blue and fringed by white eyelashes.

As the kettle began to whistle she regarded him as a cat watches a canary. "What is your name?" she asked, spooning loose leaf Darjeeling into the teapot.

"Hugo."

"There is something unusual about you, Hugo," she said, staring at him as if she could see into his soul.

"Is there now?"

Luna tapped the blade of her hunting knife against the teapot and gave her visitor further consideration. Her voice was warbling, almost tuneful. "I have it!" she said triumphantly. "You are from the future!"

Hugo was lost for words. His parents had alluded to the fact that the girl possessed many gifts, but he hadn't bargained on clairvoyance being one of them.

Luna saw that he was dumbfounded and seized upon it. "I am correct, am I not?" she postulated.

Wilde couldn't quite understand how he, a British secret agent at the top of his game, had allowed a teenage girl to run rings around him. She possessed the rare ability to seem young and old all at the same time.

His reply was measured, each word enunciated slowly. "I have indeed come from the future, Luna, but I know nothing about *your* future. Nor do I know anything about your past."

"You knew about my father's death," she reasoned.

"Only that he had died in his bed a couple of months ago—"

He sensed that the girl was unaware of her father's proclivity for murder and kept the particulars of his parents' double homicide to himself.

Luna seemed to brush off the news of her guest's time-travelling ability as if it were no big thing. She poured his tea through a strainer. "Do you take milk and sugar?"

"A dash of milk, please. No sugar"

Hugo could see that the girl's barriers were coming down and that she no longer considered him a threat. The shotgun leaned idly against the dresser next to her. She offered him his brew and at the same time waggled the hunting knife at him with a peculiar look on her face.

"Ooh, I'm scared," he grinned, accepting the tea.

"You should be," she replied, setting the knife down and preparing a cigar for herself.

"You smoke cigars?" Hugo asked.

"I do. What of it?" she huffed.

"Nothing."

"Would you like one?"

"No, thanks."

"So shut up then."

"Okay."

Luna drew on her cigar and blew out a succession of smoke rings. "Tell me how you are able to time travel, Hugo. Are you a quantum physicist?"

"You seem to be extremely well informed for a hermit," said the Englishman.

"I know a great deal about a great many things, Hugo," she declared, her eyes bright as stars. "I know that Sudan has more pyramids than Egypt. I know that our planet is a giant magnet. I know that an octopus has three hearts and nine brains."

"Are you sure about that last one?" Hugo enquired.

"Perfectly sure." The girl was on a roll. "I can speak three languages fluently: Danish, German and English." Here she paused for optimum effect. "And I also know that we are being lied to by government scientists who are keen to tell us that the Earth is not flat—"

Hugo stared at her with incredulity. She had greatly impressed him up until that point. "Hey, steady on. I was with you every step of the way, genius girl, until you began spouting nonsense about the Earth being flat."

Luna blew cigar smoke over her shoulder and glared at him. "So are you one of those fools who doesn't realise that the world is flat?"

"How could the world be flat? If it were, the sea would cascade violently off the edges, taking ships and whales with it. Just think about it."

An uneasy silence ensued, in which Luna looked at her houseguest contemptuously for several seconds before breaking into an unexpected smile. "Just look at your face, Hugo! Of course I don't think that the world is flat. This is what my father taught me to believe, but he was crazy in the head."

Hugo, shamefaced by a gullibility he didn't know he possessed, chuckled so hard that he slopped tea over the brim of his cup. "Oh, Luna, if my friend Vincent were here, you'd have totally made his day."

The girl had a self-satisfied look on her face. It surprised her greatly that she was enjoying the company of this genial Englishman. "You didn't reply when I asked if you were a scientist, Hugo."

"I'm not a scientist, but my girlfriend Sofia is. She's the one who can answer all of your time-travel questions. You two would get along."

"And do you have a time-travelling machine?" Luna asked. "I did not see one."

"It's a short walk though the trees. God, I hope it's still there."

"Could you take me to this machine?"

"I could. In fact, I was rather hoping you would come with me and live as a guest at our house. You'll be safe there. I'm given to understand that you don't want to be taken into the care of the local authorities—"

"I do not! They came here recently with their cameras and ID cards. The Magnussens at the provisions store must have tipped them off. I told them my father was out hunting and wouldn't return until nightfall. They said that they would be back soon."

Hugo sought to calm her anxiety. "You do know that they are acting in your best interests, don't you, Luna?"

She stubbed her cigar out forcefully in an ashtray. "I don't have birth or adoption certificates. I have nothing to prove I even exist. They will look deeper, starting with fingerprints and moving on to blood tests. They will find out what I am—"

Hugo thought this an odd way for Luna to refer to herself. "And what *are* you exactly?"

"You don't already know?"

"No."

"Then cover your ears."

"Why?"

"You will see."

As Hugo put hands to ears, Luna took a step back, rose to her full height, drew a gallon of air into her lungs and let rip a blood-curdling scream. Vases exploded, lids flew from saucepans and the fox scarpered to the back of the cabin.

Hugo was rooted to the rocking chair, his eyeballs and lips the only parts of him that remained in motion. "That … was … interesting."

Luna placed her hands on her hips in a told-you-so fashion. "Now you know why the authorities must not know what I am."

"Are you an extraterrestrial?" asked Hugo, saying the first thing that came into his head.

"I don't quite know what I am," she said despondently. She felt that this considerate stranger might be her only hope. "But please take me to England with you. I have not travelled beyond this forest and would very much like to see your castles and drink tea with your Queen."

"Sorry to dampen your enthusiasm, Luna, but I now reside in Mexico—"

"Mexico!" she shrilled, her eyes as wide as tortillas. "I love Mexico even more than I love England! Mayan temples, the Day of the Dead celebrations, turquoise oceans, Frida Kahlo. Oh, and those wonderful sombreros—"

Hugo's heart melted at the sight of this extraordinary

little lady as she continued to wax lyrical about all things Mexican, from the Rio Grande through to Pancho Villa. She even went so far as to point out the bookshelf she had reserved for her Mexican history and travel books. Her zeal was infectious and the Englishman came to understand what his mother had meant when she said that the Universe throws together a unique collection of interactions. This was one such interaction, and it made him feel good to be a part of it.

He stood up from the rocking chair and placed his empty teacup on the kitchen table. "If you are serious about wanting to travel to Mexico, I suggest you gather some of your clothes and a few belongings."

Quick to seize the opportunity, Luna set off to fetch a large trunk. Without any further need to hide what she was, she hovered an inch above the floor and glided about the cabin as if on roller skates.

"That's a neat trick," said Hugo, surprised at how easily he had become accustomed to phenomena in all their guises.

"I cannot do it for long," said Luna, seemingly embarrassed by the inadequacy of her superpowers.

"Regardless of what you can and can't do, Luna, it might be a good idea to keep your skills hidden when you venture out into the real world," advised Hugo.

The teenager shot him a glare that might have curdled milk. "I already know that," she snapped.

"Yes, I imagine you do," he grinned.

Luna set about stuffing clothes, books and bedding

into tea chests. Hugo helped her by ferrying any filled containers to the front porch. She zealously filled bags and cardboard boxes with personal effects including shoes, sewing kits, batteries, a one-eyed teddy bear, a favourite mug, art posters, a flashlight, a cassette tape recorder and a transistor radio. Despite the Englishman advising her that she wouldn't need certain items – most notably snow boots, a compass, boxes of matches and an axe – she ignored him and packed them anyway.

Hugo was astonished by the number of books in her possession and tried to impress upon her that they wouldn't all fit into the time machine.

"We introverts find our friends in books," she explained, unbowed by his misgivings. "I want to bring as many as I can." From a very young age, reading had been Luna's addiction. Hartvigsen, mindful of the importance of his own private education, had sated her thirst for knowledge by ordering books through catalogues and having them delivered to the Magnussen's convenience store. The alphabets of the world had in the meantime roosted in her brilliant mind, hoping for their chance to fly.

"There are more books here than in my local library," quipped Hugo, dragging a tea chest filled with volumes of *Encyclopaedia Britannica* out to the decking. He reflected upon his own boyhood relationship with books, remembering how they had once led him to imagine that his destiny was to rescue maidens from draughty towers. Now, to all intents and purposes, he was doing just that. However, the rescue of this particular maiden wasn't going as fast as he would have liked and the girl only listened when she felt like it.

Just when he thought that Luna was nearing the end of her preparations, she disappeared into the dark bowels of an enormous closet for a vigorous rummage. "If you come out of that wardrobe with a lion and a witch in tow, I'm leaving you behind," he joked.

Night had descended on the forest by the time Luna had gathered her chattels together. The trees were more watchful than usual, sad in the knowledge that they might not set their bark-rimmed eyes on the girl again. Under a dark, oceanic sky, Luna and Hugo lugged the chests, bags and boxes to the time machine. On each trip, the forest girl stopped to marvel at its splendid luminosity and the phosphorescent ring that orbited it.

Once her belongings were stowed on board, Luna returned to the cabin for the last time, extinguished the kerosene lanterns and wedged open the front door so the fox could come and go as it pleased. She felt intuitively that her rescuer would have no interest in her adoptive father's large steel safe, nor the fortune it held, so neglected to mention it. The teenager had witnessed the fall of the old man's dilapidated empire; now that he was in the ground being stripped to the bone by worms, she felt that nothing more needed to be said about the life of Leif Hartvigsen.

Walking to the time machine, Luna considered the most cherished things she would leave behind: the cold snap of frost on crisped leaves; the dewy gilt of morning cobwebs; the tittle-tattle of trees, and the companionship of forest creatures. At peace with her decision, and without fear or trepidation, she waved goodbye to the forest, blew a kiss to the moon and followed Hugo into the craft.

Inside the vessel, they barely had room to stand with Luna's worldly goods stacked around them.

"Prepare for lift-off," said Hugo. He turned to put his palm to the biometric handprint on the wall, only to discover that it had shrunk to half the size it was previously. "Ah, it seems that you are currently the master of this ship, Luna," he said, inviting her to do the honours.

Luna, whose only adventures in life had come from the pageantry found in books, was exhilarated now. Upon her command, the machine screeched through the corridors of time and swiftly rematerialised in a Mexican basement.

Hugo removed a twig from his jacket pocket and smiled at his charge. "Luna, I would like to welcome you to Mexico City in the year 1970."

The girl's eyes brightened. "1970?"

"Yes. Unless I'm very much mistaken—"

"1970 is the year in which I was born!"

"Well, your life can start again, can't it?"

"I think so!"

*

Sofia, who had tried her best to calm Verónica, ran upstairs to fetch a spare key to the basement. No sooner had she returned to the hallway than the machine launched its hellish din again.

The young housekeeper was once more down on the floor with her hands wrapped around her head and nose twitching like a telegraphist's finger. "*Dios Santo!* It is the devil noise again!" she shouted, crossing herself several times. "Do not go to the basement, Madam! He wait there to kill you!"

As the clangour gave way to a meditative silence, María poked her head around the kitchen doorway. "Was it another earthquake, Sofia?" she asked, while continuing calmly to peel an apple.

"I think it's just an airlock in the hot-water pipes in the cellar," Sofia fibbed. "I'll go down to have a look."

"Hey, Verónica! Get up on your feet!" María scolded. "You heard señora Ustinova. It is only the hot-water pipes making the noise."

Verónica, preferring to put her faith in higher powers, pressed her palms together and murmured a frantic prayer to the blessed Virgin of Guadalupe.

Sofia had unlocked the cellar door and was about to descend the steps when she saw Hugo and a white-haired teenage girl looking up at her. The youngster was an arresting sight – barefoot, short in stature and with eyes that seemed slightly too big for her porcelain face. She was dressed in a traditional Nordic costume.

"And who is this pretty girl?" asked the Russian warmly.

Hugo pointed to the heavens. "Your friends in high places have sent us an extraordinary young lady who is in need of our help and support. Her name is Luna."

Sofia's expression was one of unbridled joy. "Luna, you are very welcome, darling. I'm not sure if Hugo has already told you who I am, but my name is Sofia."

Luna, who had never experienced a hug before, nevertheless enjoyed being wrapped in the arms of the Russian. She so wanted to trust this nice lady but had a burning question to ask. "You are a scientist, Sofia?" she said guardedly.

"I am indeed. An astrophysicist and cosmologist, to be precise."

"So are you one of the scientists who cuts people up and puts pieces of them in jars?"

Sofia, though taken aback, managed to retain her beautiful smile. "Oh, sweet darling. I am not that kind of scientist. I'm one of the good ones."

"Then perhaps we shall be friends," said Luna.

*

Sofia and Hugo cobbled together a cover story in which Luna was purportedly a girl sent to live with them by an international adoption agency. It was agreed that she would take on Hugo's family name. Only Vincent was told the truth of the matter, while María and Verónica immediately took the orphaned youngster under their wings and into their hearts.

Though she was offered a spacious bedroom off the main landing, Luna asked to be billeted in a poky attic room whose only access was via a rickety staircase, stating that she preferred to sleep nearer to the stars. Hugo and Vincent heaved most of the girl's personal effects up to her garret, but her substantial book collection had to be stored on the library floor until such time that they could be put onto shelves.

It transpired that Luna was vegetarian and María rose to the challenge by preparing her sweet-potato burritos for lunch.

Several hours elapsed before Sofia and Hugo were able to spend any private time together. Naturally he was as keen to tell her about his incredible exploits as she was to hear them. Later, when the Englishman went to their bedroom to shower and change, the gilt-framed photograph of his parents that he had left behind in England was standing on his bedside cabinet.

CHAPTER FIFTEEN

The 14th day of June, 1970 was one in which optimistic smiles would be shared and fifty-one million hopes would be dashed. The whole of Mexico was in a fevered state of excitement as the host nation prepared to play Italy in the quarter finals of the FIFA World Cup football championship, a match that would be broadcast live around the world.

The temperature in the city centre was hot as Hades as Pablo took a break from shining shoes to enjoy an ice cream that melted faster than he could eat it. A good friend of his, Magic Miguel, a snub-nosed street urchin with trousers too long for his legs, appeared from nowhere, the fierce sun putting a shine on his chubby face. Had Charles Dickens been born in Mexico, Miguel was precisely the type of scamp he would have written about: an illiterate boy who lived by his wits and who was immune to the sharp rebukes meted out to him a thousand times each day.

"Pablo! How's it going?" the boy said, scratching his back passage through his trousers. "Hey, that ice cream looks so tasty on a hot day."

"Hi, Miguel. Would you like my ice cream, by any chance? Your tongue is hanging so low I could almost tuck it into your shirt."

Miguel wiped his grimy hands on his equally grimy trousers in anticipation of his friend giving him the cone. "I would accept it only if you have had enough, yourself," he said, licking his lips and rocking on his heels.

"Here, take it," said Pablo. "I cannot bear to see you suffer any longer."

They sat together in a shaded corner of the Zócalo, Pablo with his glossy hair almost blue-black and Miguel's as dusty as camel fur.

The urchin was forever coming up with new ways to persuade tourists to part with their money and today was no exception. "Turn away for one moment," he said, with ice cream all around his mouth and a glint in his rascally eyes. "You will be the first person to see my latest magic trick."

Pablo averted his gaze while his friend rummaged in the canvas bag that he was carrying. A few moments later, Miguel was ready and tapped his friend on the shoulder. "Pablo, would you like to fee an amafing magic trick?" he said with a lisp that wasn't there previously.

"You're talking funny," Pablo observed.

"Mo, I am mot. And you will luff this trick."

Pablo couldn't help but notice that drool was trickling from the corners of his friend's mouth; nevertheless he feigned interest in the unpromising magic trick that Miguel was about to foist upon him.

The scamp wiped his mouth with a handkerchief. "Señor, I can turn a coin into a pebble before your very eyes."

"You're getting better at this," chuckled Pablo.

"Pleef could you gif me a fen-peso coin, sir?" Miguel continued, slobbering down his chin.

Pablo fished a ten-peso coin from his pocket and handed it to the shabby magician who held it up to an imaginary audience. "Behold, fadies and fentlemen," he said theatrically. "A fen-peso coin." He pretended to chew on it, his eyes rolling in their sockets as if he had fallen into a mystical trance. It was a veritable pantomime to the eye.

After a brief display of facial gymnastics, the boy produced a saliva-wet pebble from his mouth. In a sonorous voice he announced, "Look what has happened to your coin, sir."

Pablo, unable to hide his disenchantment, stared at the pebble, then regarded Miguel's eager expression, then stared back at the pebble. "That's it? That's your amazing trick?"

"Do you like it?" Miguel grinned. "The punters are going to be so impressed that they will let me keep the coin."

"I am lost for words," said Pablo.

"I knew you would be."

There followed a conversation where Pablo brought his friend up to speed with the latest occurrences in his life, detailing how señor Wilde had continued to act as a benefactor to his father and him by paying off their debts and giving them money to spend in any way they wished.

Miguel looked as glum as a fish. "I wish you could send him my way, Pablo. I could use some charity."

Pablo produced a twenty-peso note and pressed it into his friend's hand. "Take this, Miguel. You can keep it, along with the ten-peso coin that is still in your mouth."

"I forgot it was there," his friend fibbed. "Thank you, Pablo. You are the kindest boy I know."

"You will think I am even kinder when I take you to my home to watch the big football game today. On a colour television, too!"

By the expression on his face, a passer-by might have imagined that Miguel had just witnessed the resurrection of Jesus. "A colour TV, Pablo? You have such a thing?"

"We do. Señor Wilde bought it for us so we could watch the World Cup in style."

"Pablo, stay there. I am going to buy you an ice cream, my friend."

*

At precisely the same time that Pablo, Gerardo and a bevy of excited guests were huddled around a colour television set watching the Mexican national team taking on Italy, Hugo and Sofia were among the crowd at the USSR versus Uruguay game in the Aztec Stadium. The match was played in sweltering heat and, to Sofia's disappointment, because she had no future idea as to the outcome, Uruguay won by a single goal scored in extra time.

As the couple filed out of the stadium, an elegant lady, who bore more than a passing resemblance to Grace Kelly, glided effortlessly through the throng wearing a silk headscarf and large sunglasses. The woman was chatting in Russian to someone Sofia assumed to be her husband.

As she was keen to speak to someone in her native tongue for the first time in months, the scientist offered some passing words of consolation. "We played extremely well, despite losing the game, don't you think?"

The lady removed her sunglasses. Her smile was warm and there was a Cartier sparkle in her eyes. "We did play well. How wonderful to meet another Russian so far from home. I'm Anastasia and this is my husband, Leonid."

Handshakes were exchanged. "I'm Sofia, and this is my boyfriend, Hugo."

"Pleasure to meet you both," said Hugo, understanding every word.

"An Englishman," said Anastasia with a catlike smile. "You must watch out for this one, Sofia."

A grim-faced man accompanying the couple – a KGB handler, Sofia guessed – enjoined them to keep moving. Time seemed to stand still for an instant as the two women locked eyes and shared a moment of electrifying familiarity; a synchronicity preserved in

134

the catacombs of time.

"I'm afraid we must go," said Anastasia with a sadness that she couldn't quite comprehend. "It was so lovely to meet you, Sofia, if only for the briefest of moments."

"Likewise," said Sofia, dazed by a sense of déjà vu.

"You see, we have a flight to Havana tonight," added Leonid over his shoulder as the handler shepherded them towards an exit. "And another to Moscow in the morning."

"A charming couple," said Hugo, waving them off as they disappeared in a tide of straw hats and white shirts. "As a matter of fact, she reminds me of you."

Sofia wasn't listening; she was standing with a faraway look on her face.

"Penny for your thoughts?" asked Hugo.

"I know those people," she said distantly. "I know them in my heart."

"You do? How?"

"Anastasia and Leonid… Of course! You silly, silly girl—"

"What is it?"

"They were my grandparents, the ones I dream about. The ones I have never met."

"Oh, God. Really? Should we run after them?"

"No, I don't think so. Today I was given my moment and for that I'm extremely grateful." A tear rolled down her cheek. "And tomorrow is the fateful flight—"

"Ah, yes. Of course. I'm so sorry."

"No need to be sorry. I know them now, and they know me. This is all that matters."

*

On a day that was hot enough to melt road surfaces and buckle rail tracks, Magic Miguel headed back to the tin-roofed hovel he shared with his prostitute mother. Though his team had been knocked out of the World Cup, having been soundly beaten by Italy, he'd spent the afternoon in the convivial company of friends which, in itself, was good reason to celebrate. Moreover, there were the thirty pesos he had kept hidden in his underpants.

As the setting sun dipped behind rooftops and buildings gasped for air, he trudged down a dusty street that smelled of charcoal smoke and open sewers. Mexican cover versions of Elvis Presley songs blared out from a ramshackle bar frequented by local villains. A few of them, gold-chained, tattooed and wearing cotton vests, had congregated outside to catcall passing women, smoke cigarettes and drink Corona beer. One of the goons was entirely missing one ear, the consequence of a knife fight in his youth. In its place was a neat orifice resembling a dolphin's blowhole.

The teenager habitually avoided making eye contact with such men but an all-too-familiar voice, gruff in its tone, rang out from their ranks. "Hey, Miguel, you son of a whore! Where have you been lately?"

The youngster stiffened as he caught sight of Rubén Cuevas' loathsome face grinning back at him.

He was all too aware that an encounter with Rubén the Bull often meant a slap across the face and the loss of earnings. "Señor Cuevas!" he quavered. "Always a pleasure to see you!"

"Never mind the pleasantries, you little shit," growled Rubén, stepping forward and spitting his gum on the ground. "Hand over the money."

"What money?"

"The money that you've no doubt hidden in your shoes or stuffed down your underpants. If you don't give it to me, I will strip you naked."

"Please, señor. What little I have I give to my mother—"

"Your mother is nothing but a slut, you worthless runt. So hand it over."

Miguel reached down the back of his pants and produced a ten-peso coin that was wrapped in a twenty-peso note. "There is nothing else, señor. You are a wicked man to take money from someone who has none."

"Blah, blah, blah, you whiny little bitch. I guess I will have to say a few Hail Marys on Sunday to make my peace with God."

Cuevas patted down the boy and made him remove his shoes while his toothless drinking buddies belched like frogs and cackled like witches from the sidelines.

"Please just let me go home, señor," said Miguel wretchedly. "You have stolen my money and you have taken my dignity."

"I haven't finished with you yet. Where have you

just come from?"

"I was watching the football game on TV with friends. In colour too, a sight I will never forget."

Rubén's sly curiosity was kindled. "You have friends who have enough money for a colour TV?"

"Yes, señor. Do you know Gerardo the trumpet player? He—" The words died on Miguel's tongue as he abruptly realised his terrible indiscretion.

"Gerardo, the fucking trumpet player," rasped Cuevas. "Tell me where he lives."

CHAPTER SIXTEEN

As midnight approached, Luna changed into cotton pyjamas, enjoyed a cigar in the dark and reflected upon her first day in a foreign land. Considering that she had little in common with Hugo, much less the world at large, the forest girl knew that she had taken a huge leap of faith. The Englishman had assured her that, other than himself, only Sofia and Vincent would be privy to her secrets.

With regard to O'Toole, he had told her this: "The man has an executioner's stare and a handshake that could crush a coconut. But scratch beneath the surface, Luna, and you will find the most loyal friend."

Her cramped attic room, into which a rectangle of moonlight had crept, was the least prestigious of all that the house had to offer but she loved it nonetheless. As far as she was concerned, the whole house was like Aladdin's Palace and her room its one unfinished adornment.

In addition to a dead yucca plant, the garret accommodated a miscellany of old furniture and a large bed whose installation must have necessitated an undertaking of great ingenuity. When left to her own devices, Luna had created a comforting familiarity for herself by attaching art posters to walls and scattering her accoutrements about the room, including a cymbal-clashing clockwork monkey. She had also set aside three bedside books: *On the Origin of Species,* by Charles Darwin, *The Diary of a Young Girl,* by Anne Frank, and Hans Christian Andersen's *The Snow Queen,* a book she'd first read at the age of four but kept returning to at different points in her life.

The room, with its lingering evocations of secret trysts and tears shed into pillows, enchanted Luna by whispering sweet nothings into her ear and drawing her attention to an official-looking slip of paper that had magically appeared at the foot of her bed. Typed in the Danish language and flamboyantly signed in black ink, it was a counterfeit birth certificate that bore her new name: Luna Wilde. She noticed, moreover, that her date of birth had been amended to read 1954 instead of 1970. As excitement gave way to tiredness, she snuggled up to Kai, her one-eyed teddy bear, and drifted into a dreamless sleep.

*

Unused to the rumble of vehicular noise and the ringing of handbells, Luna rose earlier than usual. She grabbed the only chair in the room and rushed excitedly to her small dormer window. Standing on the chair to look outside, she sniffed the air and imagined herself the keeper of her own watchtower, reassured that the sky above Mexico City was every bit as infinite as the one above Silkeborg Forest.

Because she had already found the creak of the rickety staircase outside her room somewhat irksome, Luna checked that the coast was clear and floated to the bottom step in the manner of a descending angel. Sofia and Hugo had reserved a bathroom at the foot of her stairs solely for her use, and the teenager entered it clutching the same tide-marked washbag she'd owned as a child.

Unaccustomed to bathing in hot water, Luna filled the bathtub from its cold tap and lathered herself with carbolic soap. She then proceeded to clean her skin with a scouring sponge that was designed to scrub pots and pans. After using the toilet and washing her hands in the bidet, she came down to breakfast barefoot wearing the Danish national costume she had travelled in.

Vincent was sitting at the kitchen dining table with the others. Knowing that Sofia would slap him across the back of his head for his playfulness, he resisted the impulse to break into a chorus of *The Hills are Alive* and instead greeted the peculiar youngster with the propriety she deserved. "Good morning, fair Luna!" he shouted with all the pomp of a medieval herald. "I trust you slept well."

Unused to good cheer in the morning, the girl responded with a scowl. "I slept very well, thank you."

In truth, Luna would have preferred to eat alone in her room but knew she would have to adapt quickly to this brave new world of companionship and conversation. Sofia, whose maternal instincts had kicked in the moment she set eyes on the diminutive teenager, rose from the breakfast table to wish Luna a good morning and planted a kiss on each of her alabaster cheeks.

While this was happening, María put a hand to her chest and vented an impassioned sigh. Luna had already caused her big heart to melt several times since she had first seen her. Smelling of coffee beans and the avocado oil she routinely combed through her hair to make it shine, the cook gambolled over to smother the forest girl in her bosomy embrace. "*Buenos días,* Luna. Specially for you, I have prepared breakfast burritos," she bubbled. "They are nice and spicy, stuffed with rice, refried beans, cabbage and mushrooms. How does that sound?"

"They sound very delicious," replied Luna, a faint smile curling the corners of her lips. Being cosseted was a new experience and a part of her wondered if she should be wary of the warmth and kindness of these people. Then there were the hugs and kisses lavished upon her; though difficult to become accustomed to, she considered them preferable to the scowls and grunts she had hitherto endured in her young life.

As Luna took her place at the table, Copernicus sprang onto her lap and stretched up to whisper in her ear that all was exactly as it seemed and that everything would be fine.

Hugo filled the girl's tumbler with freshly squeezed

orange juice and proposed a toast. "Could we all please raise our cups, mugs and glasses to welcome Luna, not only into our home but also into our hearts... To Luna!"

"To Luna!" they all cried.

Not knowing what to do or say, the girl covered her face with her little white hands and choked on an eruption of tears.

"This is your home now, Luna," said Sofia hugging her tightly. "And it will be your home for as long as you want it to be."

Sofia, Hugo and Luna convened in the library where the teenager's books stood in teetering columns on the parquet floor. Because it was overcast outside, Sofia approached a bank of switches that lit up chandeliers, table lamps and a pop-art print of Marilyn Monroe fixed above the fireplace.

Books had always been Luna's escape, her flung-open windows to the universe; without them her life would have been intolerably lonely. In the solitude of her childhood and adolescence she had picked the brains of Einstein and Darwin and learned almost all there is to know about relativity and evolution. She had sat with Charles Dickens, Victor Hugo and Scheherazade, revelling in their exuberant capacity to tell a story. Along the way, she had become friends with Tom Sawyer, Scout Finch, Bilbo Baggins, Tintin, Mary Poppins and Quasimodo. Last, but not least, were Hassan from *The Kite Runner*, and Pip from

Great Expectations.

The adults set themselves the task of helping Luna to arrange her collection into some kind of thematic or systematic order. Before this day, most of the library shelves had lay bare except Sofia's, scantly supplemented by Hugo's three holiday reads.

He was the first to pitch in with a suggestion. "How about exhibiting the books in alphabetical order?"

"By author or by title?" asked Sofia.

"Author, of course."

The scientist scrunched up her face. "Oh, no! I really couldn't put Curie next to Cervantes, or Galileo alongside Goethe."

"Then I think that the decision should rest with their owner," said Hugo. "Your thoughts, Luna?"

The seven colours of the spectrum seemed to pass through the girl's prismatic eyes as she deliberated. "I think that it makes sense to display each genre separately and then arrange the author surnames alphabetically within those categories," she concluded.

Sofia and Hugo, as impressed with Luna's command of the English language as they were with her brainpower, agreed that this was the way forward. The trio worked well as a team, and within the hour Scott Fitzgerald was rubbing dust-jacketed shoulders with Gustave Flaubert; Shirley Jackson was cosying up to Henry James, and William Shakespeare had struck up a bromance with George Bernard Shaw.

"Hugo told me you were quite the bibliophile," said Sofia, astonished by Luna's literary intellect. "But really, darling, you have left me speechless. You are undoubtedly well-read and well-informed."

Vincent stepped into the room to announce that he would soon be heading off to his favourite watering hole. In the past few months he had become a much-loved sight in the neighbourhood and many of the locals referred to him as *el gigante Irlandés* – the giant Irishman.

"Hugo, it's hot enough to melt the Devil's hooves out there. What d'you say to a few cold ones at Benito's? Or is today the one you usually set aside to tidy your cravat drawer?"

Sofia had stated earlier that she was taking Luna out to shop for clothes and shoes, so Hugo knew that his day was free to do as he pleased. "Vincent, I will join you for a few drinks on one condition," he replied. "First you must accompany me to a local bookshop. The three paperbacks I packed for my trip to Florence now look rather pitiful set against Luna's magnificent collection."

"Deal!" said the Irishman rubbing his enormous hands together. "Don't go wearing anything too fancy – Benito's isn't one of your Martini bars in Mayfair."

In keeping with the fashion of the time, but mostly to horrify Vincent, Hugo changed into a pair of flared trousers and a tight paisley shirt. Completing the look was a baggy corduroy cap worn at a jaunty angle, and a flamboyant neckerchief. Looking forward to the afternoon ahead, he hastened down the staircase and into the hallway where Verónica was vigorously discharging noxious bursts of insecticide from a metal spray pump that she wielded like a machine gun.

The vaporous droplets settled into the back of his throat and stung his eyes. "Whoa, Verónica. Shouldn't you be wearing a mask for that?" he coughed.

"It is okay, señor Wilde. It only kill the insect, not the human, so is very safe. I use this all the time from when I am a little girl."

O'Toole emerged from the kitchen, where María had been feeding him cinnamon doughnuts for the past fifteen minutes. "Christ Almighty!" he spluttered, walking into a carcinogenic cloud and immediately wafting his hands about his face. "Has there been a toxic chemical spill of some kind?"

"Verónica has been spraying the house with insecticide," explained Hugo.

Vincent did a double take when he saw what his friend was wearing. "Holy Mother of God. What have you come as?"

"It's the latest fashion."

"Jesus, Hugo. The very sight of you is hurting my eyes more than the bug spray."

María came running from the kitchen, clutching a paper bag filled with sugar-dusted fritters. "Some *buñuelos* for you, Vincent," she said coyly. "A lion of a man such as you should keep his strength up."

"*Muchas gracias,* María," he replied smoothly, drawing on his limited reserve of Spanish phrases.

"Oh, you speak Spanish so nice, señor," she cooed,

fanning herself with her fingers.

Hugo took a moment to process what he was witnessing but then pretended to be oblivious to it. "María, you are just the person I need," he interjected. "Would you be so kind as to tell me where the nearest bookstore is? And it must be one that sells books that are printed in English."

"Yes, señor, I know just the place," the cook enthused. "If you turn left at the door and walk straight ahead for—" here she counted in her head "—for five blocks, you will come to Avenida Serenidad. Turn left there and keep walking for twenty minutes. You cannot miss it. The bookseller, he is Eduardo Volante, a very lovely man. And the name of his shop is Utopía del Libro."

"Thank you, María. Most kind," said Hugo, turning briskly for the front door, flares swirling about his ankles. "*Hasta luego*, Verónica! Hurry along, Vincent. Time and tide wait for no man."

"One more thing, señores," added María as the two friends stepped out into an oven of midday heat. "If you are lost, do not ask a Mexican man for directions. When Mexican men do not know the way, they will pretend to know rather than lose face. And then you will be even more lost. My advice is to ask a woman."

The heat was stifling and O'Toole, who was wearing cargo shorts and a Mexico 70 T-shirt, began to sweat profusely the moment his sandalled feet touched the sidewalk. Hugo, to the contrary, looked as if he were strolling through Hyde Park on an autumnal day.

As they approached the first intersection, Hugo lowered his sunglasses and looked his friend in the eye. "Please don't think I'm intruding, but María seems to be enamoured of you, Vincent."

"And I of her," the Irishman admitted. "We've been getting on just grand. In many ways, she reminds me of my darling Kathleen, may she rest in peace."

"I'm genuinely delighted. You two would make a wonderful couple."

In his mind's eye, Vincent blew his Kathleen a kiss and she smiled right back at him. A tear formed in the corner of his eye prompting him to change the topic. "So, how are you and Sofia getting on? When I see the two of you together, it's as if you've known each other all your lives."

"I thought her rather majestic when I first set eyes on her, and I still do. I love her entirely, Vincent."

"The temper on the woman though," said Vincent whistling through his teeth. "Jesus, she's given me a fair old slap on a couple of occasions."

"Ha! I'm glad I'm not the only one."

"You grabbed a tiger by the tail when you met that one, Hugo. But just look at how she's turned your life around."

"She has indeed. And I'm enormously glad of it."

They passed La Iglesia del Ángel Herido – the Church of the Wounded Angel – its pink stone façade and baroque bell tower lit magnificently in the sunshine. The harmonious clang of its three bells could be heard from the house every Sunday morning and also at seemingly random times for no identifiable reason. They rang out as joyously to call worshippers to Mass as they did to celebrate marriages, and the neighbourhood was all the more glorious for their unstinting service.

At that point Vincent quickened his step; he knew that the church's resident priest had the uncanny knack of appearing each time he walked by, as if alerted by an invisible alarm. "Come along, Hugo," he urged, suddenly walking at an Olympic pace, his elbows moving like pistons.

True to form, the padre had spotted him and appeared in a manner not dissimilar to a cuckoo from a Swiss clock. "Señor O'Toole!" he called out in a godly voice.

"Feck it!" muttered the Irishman under his breath.

"Aren't you going to introduce us, Vincent?" grinned Hugo, seeing the priest in his black cassock moving bat-like down the stone steps.

Vincent flashed Hugo a murderous look before wiping the sweat from his brow with a handkerchief. "Hugo, meet Father Pedroza. Father, this is my friend, Hugo."

"Pleasure," said the Englishman, shaking the clergyman's hand.

"My full title, though it is rather a mouthful, is Father Rogelio Sánchez Pedroza. Do you live in the neighbourhood, Hugo?"

"I do," he replied guardedly, sensing what was

coming.

The priest had the look of a hawk which had just pinned its prey to the ground. "So, would you be interested in joining our congregation on Sunday?"

"Sadly, I'm agnostic but, as I'm sure you're aware, Vincent is a Roman Catholic born and bred. So I guess you'll be seeing a lot more of him in the coming weeks."

O'Toole pinched the back of Hugo's arm as hard as he could while continuing to smile genially at the priest.

Father Pedroza gazed mournfully at Vincent as if he were his only lost cause, as if he might forfeit his place in the Kingdom of God should he fail to bring the Irishman back into the fold. "I have tried so hard with señor O'Toole," he sighed. "As God is my witness, I have asked him many times to come into my church to confess any sins he might have so that I may offer him divine absolution. But he shows no interest."

"Vincent, why haven't you gone into Rogelio's church to confess your sins?" asked Hugo, receiving another fierce pinch to the back of his arm.

"Because, dear Hugo," said the Irishman through gritted teeth, "if I was after confessing all of my sins to the good Father it would take so long he would need to bring a mattress."

"We'll put you down as a maybe then," grinned Hugo.

Vincent, seeking to extract himself from the tight spot he was in, made a show of pointing to his watch.

"Hugo, just look at the time!" he said with high drama in his voice. "It seems we have taken our eye entirely off the ball."

"A previous engagement?" asked Father Pedroza narrowing his eyes.

"Exactly that, Father," said O'Toole, grabbing Wilde by the sleeve of his paisley shirt. "Come along, Hugo. Those books might be gone by the time we arrive. I'll see you around, Father."

Handshakes and goodbyes were briskly exchanged. Once he was out of earshot of the priest, Vincent admitted to Hugo that he had often considered going to the church, perhaps with María by his side, but was loath to commit himself. "Being born of the Catholic faith is a bit like belonging to Fight Club," he explained, allowing Hugo to help himself to one of María's fritters. "Except the first rule of Catholic Club is that you can never leave, even if you stopped paying the membership fee a long time ago."

"It seems to me that you need to give this some serious thought," said Hugo. "By what you are saying, faith still clings to you in the hope that you will one day give it a second chance."

Vincent once again saw his lovely Kathleen in his mind's eye, bright-eyed and valorous, in the days before the cancer had taken her away from him. The same days in which he had lost his faith in God. "You're a good friend, Hugo," he said, his voice quavering. "I don't always say it, but I want you to know that I consider you a dear, dear friend."

"I know you do," said Hugo. He fought to keep his own emotions in check. "I feel the same way about you, you big ape."

"None of this means that you don't look a prize eejit in those clothes, though. Come on, Austin Powers, let's find this fecking bookshop before I drown in a pool of my own sweat."

They turned left on Avenida Serenidad into the industrial smell of hot tarmac and exhaust fumes. The sun was relentless. Vendors trudged wearily through a shimmering heat haze between rows of slow-moving cars, trying to sell cartons of cigarettes and bottles of water. The afternoon heat was so intense that it sent birds back to their trees and made motorists ill-tempered. Amid the cacophony of car horns and shouted insults, a straw-hatted, turkey-necked owner of a donkey and cart remained indifferent to the uproar around him and met each taunt directed at him with an insouciant shrug.

"Is this not a fine city, Hugo?" declared Vincent, his face red in the heat. "And isn't it grand not having to see citizens preoccupied with their phones as they stumble about the place?"

"Yes, on both counts," agreed Hugo. "It's also liberating to not have to wear a face mask everywhere we go."

O'Toole allowed himself a little chuckle. "And to think that Stephen Hawking once said that if time travel really was possible, then how come we're not overrun by tourists from the future? Well, just look at us now. We are those tourists from the future!"

"Indeed we are," said Hugo, feeling tremendously privileged to be in such a position. "And it makes you wonder how many more of us there are."

As María had intimated, the bookshop was hard to miss, especially as its stucco façade was painted in a flamingo pink. Above the shop's sign four ornate balcony grills, resplendent with potted petunias, further emphasised its kerb appeal.

Hugo stood back to admire the pilastered shopfront and pocketed his sunglasses. "Utopía del Libro. This is the place, Vincent."

The door opened with a cheery ding-a-ling and the friends were met by the heady aroma of furniture wax and incense smoke. The wooden floor was conker brown and polished to a gentle sheen. Vincent was inexorably drawn towards a pedestal fan that swept the room and afforded him some much-needed relief from the heat.

They were still adjusting to the duskiness of their surroundings when, out of the gloom, came a silvery voice enunciated in perfect English. "Good afternoon, señores! Feel free to browse at your leisure and please let me know if I can be of any assistance."

Señor Volante, a convivial man in his mid-fifties with dancing eyes, rimless spectacles and a Father Christmas beard, was sitting behind a large reception desk from which there appeared to be no visible means of escape. In front of the desk, belly down on the floor, lounged a plump bulldog with the ill-tempered face of Benito Mussolini which regarded the visitors with lukewarm interest before drifting back to sleep.

Leaving Vincent to jig in front of the fan, flapping the hem of his T-shirt up and down in an inferior version of the can-can, Hugo approached the shop owner. "Good day to you, señor," he said, doffing his baggy cap and offering his hand across the desk. "You must be Eduardo. I've heard good things."

Volante viewed the Englishman over the top of his spectacles and stood briefly to meet his handshake before sitting down again. "At your service, señor…?"

"Wilde. Hugo Wilde. And the giant's name is Vincent. Your shop was recommended to me by María Bravo."

"Ah, María," sighed the proprietor, suddenly lost in teenage remembrances and shared secrets. "We grew up in the same neighbourhood. A truly wonderful lady. You really should sample her cooking if you ever get the chance."

Hugo's smile broadened. "She actually cooks for me at my house."

"Oh, how splendid. Then you are indeed a fortunate man, señor."

Wilde complimented the Mexican on his excellent command of the English language. "Your English is better than mine," he declared.

Volante blushed, disarmed by Wilde's princely charm. "You are too kind, sir. Before becoming a bookseller, I was a professor of English literature at the

National Autonomous University, here in Mexico City. Perhaps misguidedly, I consider myself something of an authority on all things English and could probably make a decent shepherd's pie if I put my mind to it."

Hugo turned to gaze upon the seemingly endless rows of books. Like humans, they came in all shapes and sizes: some were tall and slender, others squat and well upholstered, many were wrinkled with age.

Eduardo took pleasure in the Englishman's interest and beamed from ear to ear, the pride he had in his extensive collection clearly evident. "Look at them, Hugo. Each one seemingly as dead as a pharaoh," he said, waving an arm as if casting seed. "But dead they are not. A book, you see, comes alive when it is being read and some of these have lived a thousand lives."

Hugo took a moment to allow the proprietor's words to sink in, then explained to him his reason for being there. "My house accommodates a decent-sized library which I have hitherto neglected. You see, I left England some three months ago anticipating a short break and packed only three paperbacks."

The light of a reading lamp reflected in señor Volante's spectacles as he steepled his fingers. Hugo noticed that he wore a signet ring on each pinkie.

"So very sad, señor," said the Mexican. "For me, a library without books is like a night sky without stars."

"Oh, we have a great many books, Eduardo. It's just that only three of them are mine. María did mention that your collection includes novels printed in English."

"Indeed it does," Volante affirmed, before jiggling himself out of his chair and stretching belly down across the counter as if swimming towards the bookshelves. "You should find what you're looking for over there," he pointed, doing the front crawl yet going nowhere.

As Vincent joined him, Hugo was pleased to see that, besides a countless miscellany of novels written in Spanish, there was a section that showcased an assortment of English language publications. It further delighted him that a significant number were adorned with the orange cummerbunds indicative of the Penguin classics.

As the visitors continued to peruse, the shopkeeper scrambled across his countertop and slid onto the shop floor, a habit that had become second nature over a period of time.

O'Toole, with a whoop of delight, withdrew a book that had immediately caught his eye. "*The Ginger Man* by J P Donleavy. Now, there's a book!" he exclaimed. "Jesus, I haven't read this one in years. It's indecorous and spitefully hilarious, Hugo, you should give it a try."

"I very likely will," replied the Englishman, before turning to señor Volante. "Eduardo, if you are able to deliver, I'll take the lot."

Volante, as if he was suddenly the recipient of terrible news, slumped back against the counter in dramatic fashion. "All of them?" he gasped, putting a hand to his chest.

In the same way that an artist resents having to sell

their most treasured paintings, deep down Eduardo begrudged anyone actually buying his wares, despite this being the prime objective of shop owners the world over. To lose a whole section, lovingly built up over a period of time, was proving to be a very bitter pill indeed.

The impact that this contradictory dilemma was having on the proprietor wasn't lost on Hugo, who sought to lessen the fellow's dismay. "Would you prefer that I only took half of the books, Eduardo? You can even decide which ones."

The Mexican's mood brightened. "Really, señor Wilde? You would allow me that?"

"Of course. They are still yours, after all."

To give his guests something to do while he tallied up the cost of the books that he selected, señor Volante directed them to a pair of old leather armchairs and left them with a jug of iced lemon tea and two glasses. Once the publications were packed into boxes, Hugo wrote a cheque for the amount and handed the shopkeeper a card that bore his telephone number and address.

"Thank you, señor, I shall deliver them this evening," the Mexican promised. "May I offer you a lift to your next destination, gentlemen?"

O'Toole's eyes lit up. "Good man yourself, Eduardo. I couldn't face walking in that hellish heat again. Have you heard of Benito's? It's a bar on Avenida Pícaro."

"I know it. If you don't mind squeezing into a Volkswagen Beetle, I can take you straight there."

"You're a grand fella," said Vincent. "Will you join us so I can buy you a drink or two?"

Eduardo shuddered at the thought. "You are very kind, señor, but the type of guys who go there are puffed up with machismo. It would only bring back bad memories of my schooldays."

Hugo placed a comforting arm across the bookseller's shoulders. "Perfectly understandable, Eduardo. I'm not even sure if I should be setting foot in the place."

*

Afterwards, Wilde and O'Toole, who had been roped into an ill-advised taco-eating challenge at Benito's, stood on the neon-lit sidewalk outside the bar and flagged down a green taxi that had a band of sharp cartoon teeth painted across its doors and bonnet.

"Buenas tardes, señor!" said Hugo to the driver, sliding onto the back seat while Vincent crammed himself into the front. Flashing fairy lights, strung around the perimeter of the windscreen, supplemented the kitschy vibe. The Englishman had seen many of these eye-catching taxis around the city but, unlike Vincent, had never sat in one. "What is the meaning of all the teeth around the car, my friend?"

"It is a crocodile taxi, señor," replied the cabbie, who had something similar to a crocodile grin on his own cheerful face. "Do you like it?"

"I love it," said Hugo. "What is your name, señor?"

"Óliver, sir," said the driver pulling away. "Like

Óliver Twist. And you?"

"I'm Hugo. And the big lump sitting next to you is Vincent."

The three were soon chatting uproariously in their contrasting accents until, with the bonhomie in full flow, Óliver, abruptly pulled over to the kerb without warning. Much to Hugo's surprise, a thickset Mexican gentleman clambered into the taxi next to him as if it were the most natural thing in the world to do.

"Stand down, soldier," chuckled Vincent over his shoulder as Wilde shifted in his seat and adopted a trained state of vigilance. "He's not a carjacker. They like to share their taxis here." As the car pulled away, the Irishman gave the driver a friendly dig in the ribs. "It's a good job Hugo didn't have his gun with him, eh, Óliver?"

"He has a gun?" wailed the cabby, almost losing control of his vehicle while the passenger in the back cowered in his seat and held up his hands in surrender.

"God no," said Vincent trying to backpedal as fast as he could. "I was just joshing with you. Nobody has a gun. I wish I'd never mentioned a gun. There is no gun. Let's all just calm down."

With an international incident narrowly averted, the duo returned home in good spirits with stomachs tight as drums and clothes reeking of cigarette smoke. Their gaiety was boosted by the sight of Luna moodily flitting about the house with one half of her face painted in the style of a Day of the Dead skeleton, even though the celebrations were still several months away.

It wasn't long before señor Volante, wearing a silk cravat to rival any in Hugo's collection, arrived in a Volkswagen Beetle that was stuffed to the gills with a jumble of books. Between them, the three men ferried the boxes into the library where María served them a pot of tea and a banana sponge cake.

"I have known this man all my life, from when I was just a little girl," said the cook, tickling Eduardo's snowy beard before heading back to the kitchen. "He has always been such a sweet guy. So intelligent, too."

Señor Volante, who was perched awkwardly on a chaise longue, watched María leave the room. "I can see that she is very happy here, Hugo. This warms my heart."

The bookkeeper's seal of approval meant a lot to the Englishman. Though privilege was the inescapable ghost that hovered over him, it was in his nature to be humanistic. "Take care of the staff and they will take care of you," he said with conviction. "They are every bit as noble as you or I, and therefore deserving of our respect."

After seeing off his first cup of tea, Hugo shoved boxes aside to clear a path so that Volante could take a closer look at the bookshelves. "As you can see, Eduardo, my section is rather bare. Until today, these three were the only books to my name."

The bookseller looked at him approvingly. "I see that you are a fan of John Le Carré," he beamed. "I too follow George Smiley's clandestine adventures with great eagerness."

"As I'm sure you're aware, Le Carré was a British spy in real life," said Hugo, knowing more on the subject than he was letting on. "Which is why his books have that aura of authenticity about them."

"Imagine being George Smiley, living a seemingly normal life," the Mexican marvelled, "but at the same time having to live a secret one."

Hugo's grin widened. "I can't even begin to imagine."

The bookseller plucked one of Le Carré's paperbacks from the shelf. "*Tinker, Tailor, Soldier, Spy.* I've not heard of this one … May I?"

"Of course."

With the paperback nestled in his hand, Volante flipped open the first pages with a zeal that only a true book lover could ever understand. "How very peculiar," he frowned. "It says here that the book was published in 1974… You would think that whoever was responsible for typesetting that page would have noticed such a glaring error—"

"Ah! More importantly, it's time for another cup of tea," Hugo interjected, abruptly seizing the book from the shopkeeper's grasp and shepherding him towards an armchair.

CHAPTER SEVENTEEN

With guests set to arrive in five hours' time for a formal dinner party, Sofía awaited the arrival of Severiano Salazar, whose event-planning skills and attention to detail were likely to prove invaluable. Both Verónica and María had been prewarned that the butler, though officious, knew what he was doing, so they had been asked to make allowances. They were also told that if he overstepped the mark with his high-handedness they should report back to her.

"I will not allow anyone to be rude to my darlings," she promised them. "He is to be your guide, not your master."

The physicist had invited a mix of guests from various walks of life and differing nationalities, and she had worked with María to present a menu that offered comfort food presented elegantly. As well as the cook's signature Mexican appetisers and desserts, Sofía had gone with the times and asked María to cook *duck à l'orange* for the main course.

Hugo had earlier taken delivery of a black Cadillac, complete with extravagant tailfins, that Vincent had encouraged him to buy. They had named it 'The Batmobile' and taken it for a drive around the city before parking it near to the courtyard gate.

The jangle of the doorbell cavorted through the house, heralding the butler's arrival. Sofia, in high spirits, hurried to open the front door and there he stood, grim as a gravedigger. "Good afternoon, Doctor Ustinova," he said mournfully.

"Mr Salazar. So lovely to see you. Please follow me and I'll introduce you to everyone."

The butler made a show of wiping his shoes on the doormat then walked behind Sofia as she sashayed the length of the hallway. She turned right into the kitchen, where María, Verónica and Vincent were sitting at the table swapping anecdotes over cups of tea and coffee. Salazar sucked the life from the room just by entering it.

Sofia, brimming with enthusiasm, made the introductions. "Everyone, please give a warm welcome to Severiano. With his wealth of experience in hospitality, I think that tonight's dinner will prove to be a great success."

She went on to introduce him to Vincent and the two ladies, who rose from the table to shake the butler's clammy hand. They took stock of the new arrival from the soles of his glossy shoes to the crown of his brilliantined hair, and each took an instant dislike to him.

Vincent thought there was something damp and putrescent about the man; he imagined Salazar to be the sort of fellow who could mildew an armchair just by sitting in it.

"I would prefer it if we addressed each other by our surnames," said the butler in a wretched voice. "Otherwise we risk becoming too familiar with each other. You may all refer to me as Mr Salazar."

Sofia was taken aback and searched his face for a sign that he might be joking, but she could tell that he wasn't. "Oh. I see. Yes, of course. María's surname is Bravo. Verónica's is Valdez—"

"He can call me Lady Macbeth, for all I care," said Vincent.

"—and Vincent's surname is O'Toole."

The butler regarded the Irishman with disdain. "And what is *his* role in this household?"

"He doesn't have a role, Mr Salazar. Mr O'Toole is a permanent guest in this house. An honoured guest, for that matter."

"I see," said Salazar with the look of someone who had just trodden in something nasty. "Could you lead me to the room in which dinner will be served, Doctor Ustinova?"

"That would be the dining room," quipped Vincent as the butler followed Sofia from the kitchen.

Once they were alone again, the three companions looked at each other with utter disbelief.

"*Madre mía!*" exclaimed Verónica. "That man, when I touch his hand, I swear it is like touching the octopus."

María shook with laughter. "You are so right. I

164

never want to touch it again."

"And who does he think he is? I would rather take orders from the Devil," said Verónica firmly.

"I think he has more oil on his head than I have in my frying pan," María chuckled.

"And a face that would make an onion cry," said Vincent.

As the three continued to compare notes, a high-pitched shriek drifted in unexpectedly from the hallway. As one, they rushed to the doorway in time to witness Salazar cowering at the foot of the staircase while a perplexed Luna stood several steps above him, ethereal in a floaty white dress. Sofia was equally baffled as to why the butler had taken a funny turn.

"*Ay, caramba!*" he wailed, his expression one of pure terror. "Nobody warned me that the house was haunted!"

Affronted by the stranger's words, Luna ran down the remaining steps and kicked him hard in the shins, much to the amusement of everyone in attendance.

"Merciful God, please protect me!" squawked Salazar.

Sofia dashed to quell the disturbance and motioned for those who were laughing to shush. "Sir, sir! Really, it's OK," she soothed. "This young lady is also one of our houseguests… Luna, this is Mr Salazar, the new butler I was telling you about."

The teenager, slowly becoming accustomed to social niceties, offered her hand. "Hello, Mr Salazar," she said in her celestial voice. "I really should apologise for kicking you."

With much reluctance, the butler shook her hand, but secretly he would have liked to throttle her little white neck until she was dead.

There was a darkness to Mr Salazar, and Luna saw it immediately.

*

When it came to overseeing dinner arrangements, the butler was in his element, gliding about the formal dining room with practised panache. Having ironed a long tablecloth, he cast it across the table in a billowing flourish and proceeded to adorn it with a succession of plates and bowls, transforming it with every flick of his wrist and prod of a finger.

He demonstrated to Verónica how a succession of knives and spoons should be set to the right and forks to the left. The guests, he said, would be expected to work from the outside in. "I insist on perfection, Miss Valdez," he said, holding a soup spoon up to the light in his white-gloved fingers. "And will accept nothing less."

Salazar went on to clarify the function of different-shaped wine glasses, from the balloon type designed to hold the aroma of a robust Cabernet, through to the narrow-hipped Champagne flute that prolonged the wine's effervescence and helped to keep its chill.

His instructions, delivered in a funereal voice, came thick and fast. "When you pour red wine, the glass should be only one-third full to allow the drinker to swirl it around the glass. It is better to underfill than to overfill. Am I making myself clear, Miss Valdez?"

Verónica nodded, making minimal eye contact and almost too browbeaten to respond. Though she had already determined that she detested the man, the young housekeeper was nevertheless pleased to be learning some new skills.

"Napkins next," the butler continued. "They should be folded neatly and must not, on any account, be shaped into anything so tacky as a swan or a sailing boat."

When evening came the guests arrived in dribs and drabs, some dropped off by their chauffeurs, others by taxi drivers. Each was cheerlessly received at the front door by Mr Salazar who led them through to a chandeliered dining room that smelled of lit candles and decanted wine.

Most of the guests, though not all, were known to Sofia and Hugo and were warmly greeted by them as they entered the room. Sofia, glittering with jewellery and hair in a chignon, was resplendent in a silk-organza evening dress. Hugo, who enjoyed any excuse to dress up in the fashion of the era, had paired a ruffle shirt with a dark velvet suit and matching bow tie. Sofia smelled subtly of Chanel Nº5, Hugo more strongly of Old Spice.

By and large, the invitees were a companionable bunch who milled around getting to know each other and it didn't take long for an air of cordiality to prevail.

After *hors d'oeuvres* had been served and the guests seated at the twelve-foot-long dining table, Hugo clinked a butter knife against his glass and proposed a toast. "May you all live your dreams! Cheers, everyone!"

As a volley of salutes rang out, Sofia also rose from her chair and lifted her glass. "May our beds be broken by love!" she declared, eliciting a much greater eruption of cheers. Hugo was especially fond of Sofia when she was in a playful mood; he smiled at her and thanked his lucky stars.

A flotilla of food sailed to the table and soon the air was thick with the thrum of conversation, the chime of glasses and the clink of silverware.

O'Toole, who was sitting between Wilde and a Venezuelan poet of some renown, observed Salazar as he moved unctuously about the room. "So what d'you make of this butler, Hugo?" he asked, dabbing soup from his moustache with a napkin.

"I trust the fellow about as far as I can throw him, Vincent, but Sofia seems to tolerate him. She's even provided him with a spare house key, despite me warning against it."

"She gave him a house key? Jesus, I wouldn't give him the sweat from my armpit." O'Toole swirled red wine around his glass before continuing. "There's something dank and drippy about the man. I'm only surprised that he doesn't have a fecking mist rising from his head."

"So you don't like him then, Vincent?"

"I do not."

When asked about his occupation, Hugo's ongoing cover story was that he used to work for Her Majesty's government as a special envoy overseas. For her part, Sofia was the widow of a Soviet architect and a non-practising doctor of psychiatry.

Travis McAlpine, a convivial American diplomat, and his upbeat wife, Ruby, engaged Sofia in topics of conversation ranging from the break-up of The Beatles to the Cold War between their two nations. "Y'know, our President Nixon is a very forward-thinking guy," said the diplomat. "He's keen on strengthening relations with your Soviet Union, which can only be a good thing, right?"

"A very good thing," agreed Sofia.

Mrs McAlpine chimed in. "Now there's a man of integrity," she said with strong conviction. "I can see him going on to become the greatest president we have ever had."

Sofia kept a straight face. "Oh, I'm sure you are right, Ruby."

"And maybe we can cut you guys in on our space projects," smiled Travis. "Now that our astronauts have set foot on the moon, we'll be going there all the time."

"I'm picturing vast domed cities powered by nuclear reactors in which crops will be farmed and communities will prosper," ventured Sofia.

"You've got it," said the diplomat. "I have it on

good authority that perhaps as early as 1980 the first clusters of citizens will be raising their families on the moon."

The physicist clinked her glass against each of theirs. "Here's to humans living on the moon!"

Hugo, who had caught the tail end of the conversation, joined in. "We should all drink to that. Cheers!"

Ruby leant in, almost as if about to divulge a dark secret. "I should say at this point that Travis is known for his fanciful ideas. His latest notion is that we will all soon be able to carry telephones about our person without the need for cables. Can you even imagine?"

"I would like to see it," said Sofia.

"I can see y'all look doubtful, but it will happen sooner than you think," declared Travis with great confidence.

Relishing their company, the diplomat asked to switch seats with Sofia so that she and Ruby could get to know each other better and he could cosy up to Wilde. "So, Hugo, how are you finding life here in Mexico?"

"Well, it's a devil to obtain a pint of ale, the cricket scores or a decent cup of tea, but we absolutely love the place and its people."

"Hugo also misses his favourite china teacup and saucer," interjected Vincent with a roguish smile. "But Travis, while we're on the subject of tea, let us remember that glorious day when a band of stout-hearted Americans threw English tea chests into Boston

Harbour because of their imperialistic arrogance."

"Yes, let's," grinned the diplomat.

"A shameful waste of tea," said Hugo.

Travis warmed to the conversation. "I find the English something of a paradox, Hugo. Y'all seem to have an inborn arrogance yet at the same time don't take yourselves seriously. How is that even possible?"

"I guess that the arrogance stems from the time we ruled the waves," reasoned Hugo. "Nowadays, we would struggle to run a whelk stall. It is an indisputable truth that in England, a man can fail at everything he puts his mind to and be all the more loved for doing so."

"Very good," chuckled the diplomat. "Let us drink to the English."

"And to our American friends," said Hugo.

"And to the Irish," added Vincent.

The award for best guests of the night went to the irrepressible General Ricardo Contento and his voluptuous wife, Josefina, who had been a famous screen actress in her time. Because Hugo had recently earned the general a princely sum of money through his stock-market tips, the great man had earlier gifted him a ceremonial sword sheathed in a filigreed scabbard.

"Hugo, this is for you, my good friend," Contento had announced in an orotund voice. "It is a sword that once belonged to President Antonio López de Santa Anna. He was a great hero to the Mexican people, but also a great villain. He died poor and blind, with only one leg and possibly only one sword. And now it is yours."

The general was a vision of Mexican masculinity. His hair, though white-winged at the temples, was otherwise as dark as it had been in his youth. Continuing with a habit that had become second nature to him, he wore an army dress jacket emblazoned with a colourful array of ribbon bars. Josefina, who had successfully managed to squeeze herself into a scarlet evening dress, flirted with everyone, male or female, and found herself unable to utter a sentence that wasn't completely scandalous. To a captivated audience, she recounted the starry night that she and her husband had made love atop a cannon barrel at the Fort San Juan de Ulúa in Veracruz, and also the time they had drunk whisky with Frank Sinatra in Acapulco.

Mr Salazar, who hoped to ingratiate himself with anyone of importance, sidled up to Contento in a grovelling manner and refilled his red wine glass only one-third of the way up.

"What the hell?" snorted the General, his brass buttons glinting in the candlelight. "I am not a child on his first holy communion. Fill it up, man!"

The award for worst guest of the night went to none other than Owen Dudley, an English author whose Mexican fiancée must have done something terrible in a previous life to have ended up with him.

Dudley, a self-righteous know-all whose forehead was more pronounced than his intellect and who talked like a hippy despite looking like a square, had become increasingly intoxicated as the evening progressed. After the meal was finished, and with eyes glazed, he tapped Hugo on the shoulder and interrupted a conversation he was having with Carlos the stockbroker. "Hey, Wilde. I suppose it feeds your ego to have Mexicans working for you?"

A self-styled visionary in a turtleneck sweater, the author had already nettled Hugo with his wine-soaked pontifications and this was one sting too many. "Were you addressing me?" he bristled.

As Dudley's voice grew louder, ears pricked up all around the table. "I said that I suppose it makes you feel superior to have Mexicans as your subordinates?"

"Well, there's a job for you washing the pots if you'd like to redress the balance, Owen."

"You're making light of it, man, but you are demeaning these people by condemning them to a life of low wages and servitude."

An icy gust of silence blew across the table. Dudley's fiancée, an artist whose abstract paintings graced the walls of the house, buried her face in her hands.

Sofia pushed back her chair and threw her napkin onto the table. "What a sanctimonious creep you are!" she raged. "I am going to slap that smirk right off your face!"

"And I will slap him after you!" shouted Josefina.

"Count me in also!" yelled Madame Díaz-Zorita.

Hugo touched Sofia's wrist. "As much as it would please me to see it, no one is going to be slapped tonight." He turned to his accuser. "Sir, you talk brilliantly on a subject about which you know nothing. I treat my staff as I would like to be treated myself. And no one has dragged them kicking and screaming from their houses. They have each come of their own volition."

With all eyes on him, Dudley took another slurp of wine and wagged a scrawny forefinger. "I am opposed to social injustice in all of its forms," he said with a pomposity that was completely at odds with the doctrine he was preaching.

"And I am opposed to brainless idiots in all of their forms," Sofia blazed.

Dudley, despite his girlfriend urging him to be quiet, continued his rant. "The only way to ensure social progress is to wrest control from the bourgeoisie and give it to the workers."

"Says a man who doesn't even tip taxi drivers," huffed his fiancée.

"You are talking to someone who has experienced communism first-hand," said Sofia bitterly. "Yes, it all sounds so utopian in theory, but I can assure you that it's no fun in reality."

Hugo, seeking to end this tedious discussion so he could get the party back on track, held Dudley in his steely gaze. "For your information, our staff are protected by written contracts and remunerated handsomely. They receive sick pay, holiday pay and overtime pay. On top of that, they can eat as much as they damn well like. You, sir, are no longer welcome in this house."

The windbag pulled a face. "I shall stay here for as long as I want."

Hugo looked to O'Toole, who had been simmering quietly in his seat. "Vincent, will you show Mr Dudley the door?"

"With the greatest of pleasure," said the Irishman hauling Dudley out of his chair by the scruff of his jacket and the seat of his pants. The man's legs pedalled furiously as if on an invisible bicycle. Vincent carried him through the dining room to an enthusiastic round of applause and whistles.

"You'll be hearing from my lawyer!" the author shouted.

"Yeah, yeah, sure we will," said O'Toole.

Sofia apologised to Dudley's fiancée. "I will totally understand if you need to go with him, Carmen, but I would dearly like us to remain friends."

"I am not going anywhere," said Carmen. "This is the best fun I have had in a long time. And he is such a hypocrite, living off the money his parents send him and giving none of it to charity. I am done with him."

General Contento lit his Cuban cigar from a candelabra flame. "I do not understand this guy," he shrugged. "Does he think that everyone who has servants treats them like slaves?"

"Our staff are part of our family," Josefina added. "I would die for each one of them."

Sofia fished a Champagne bottle from its ice bucket and walked around the table, refilling glasses.

"I predict that there will be many more like him in the future," she sighed. "People of privilege speaking heroically on behalf of those with whom they have no intention of mixing."

Despite its one uncivil guest, the dinner party proved to be a roaring success. Everyone sang the praises of María's cooking, swamping her in hugs and boozy kisses when she was called to join them in the dining room. The guests ended the night in the library where Madame Díaz-Zorita, accompanied by Sofia on the Steinway, entertained them with arias from *Tosca* and *La Traviata*.

After taking their bows, Sofia raised a glass and issued a final salutation. "Thank you all for coming. In Russia, we say that it is better to have a hundred friends than a hundred roubles. I love you all!"

During the course of the evening, Mr Salazar had developed a burning curiosity as to why Sofia had twice denied him access to the wine cellar. Much to his chagrin she had, on both occasions, sent Hugo to fetch the bottles instead. As someone who looked for any opportunity to procure an advantage, be it financial or exploitative, he resolved to find out what the big secret was. In order to do that, he had to first figure out where they kept the key.

CHAPTER EIGHTEEN

Beneath his wolfish smile, Rubén Cuevas congratulated himself on timing his stratagem to perfection. With night drawing in, he had surveyed the tenement block in which Gerardo the trumpeter lived. No sooner had the local community settled into their evening routines than the musician's son set out on an errand of some kind.

Delighted that the father would be alone, Cuevas jogged up two flights of concrete stairs and strode along a dimly-lit walkway to their apartment. He rapped on the door and stood to one side in case the older man had the good sense to peek through the spyhole.

Gerardo opened the door with an amused look on his face. "Pablo, did you forget someth—?" Before he had time to react, the musician was bundled inside with the thief's hand around his throat.

Cuevas kicked the door shut with his heel. "I know you have money, *cabrón*," he hissed, slapping the blade of his knife against Gerardo's forehead. "If you show me where it is, I won't hurt you."

"I would rather die than hand over money to a dog like you," the musician croaked, bracing himself for what was sure to come.

Rubén cracked Gerardo across the face with the back of his hand. A runnel of blood trickled from the older man's nose and seeped into his little white beard. "Don't be an asshole," snarled the robber. "I swear to God that this will only get worse for you."

"God is not with you, Cuevas." Gerardo raised his chin in an act of defiance. "On the day of reckoning, you will be sent straight to Hell."

Cuevas led him into the living room by his hair and immediately caught sight of the colour television set and a shiny new telephone. "Who gives you the money for such luxuries, *cabrón*? Is it that fucking gringo you hang around with?"

Gerardo straightened himself, resisted the hand that gripped his hair and conjured a carefree smile. "Ha! He kicked your ass, didn't he? Now there's a real man, not a sad excuse for one."

Cuevas flew into a rage and slammed the butt of his knife into the musician's face, breaking two of his teeth. "Tell me where the money is, *cabrón*. Tell me, or I will kill you where you stand!"

Still the older man smiled, his teeth red with blood. "These walls are very thin, Cuevas," he lisped. "You had better hope that someone bigger and better than you doesn't come to my rescue."

The thief spat his chewing gum into Gerardo's face. "Give me the money, motherfucker. Or you will not see another day."

"Then I am stuck between a rock and a hard place. The money is for my son's future and he is the person I love most in this world. So, if those are the only options open to me, I choose death."

Rubén the Bull, with the Devil on his back, pinned Gerardo to the floor and throttled him until the light was gone from his eyes.

An actress in a soap opera seemed to scream at Cuevas from the TV, jolting him from his frenzy. Panicked by what he had done, he stumbled to his feet and hastily fled the scene.

*

Pablo's visits to the tented community in Citadel Park were always received with a great deal of expectation and excitement, and tonight's was no exception. All who crowded around him had a look of unbridled joy on their malnourished faces.

"You are our only saviour, Pablo," said Blanca Ríos, a moon-eyed girl whose parents were lost to drug addiction.

"What little I do comes from the heart," he replied, doling out tortillas, cheese and ham to a circle of outstretched hands. "I wish I could do more."

Félix Osorio, the most timid of the orphans, inched forward and greeted Pablo with a shy smile. "Where is your father tonight, Pablo? He knows I like bananas."

"I still have your bananas, my friend. He was just feeling tired and needed to put his feet up."

"If anybody deserves a rest, it is him. Please send him my best wishes."

As ever, the night was haunted by noisy insects and moving shadows. Pablo sat by torchlight among the homeless under a raven-black sky, keenly listening to their stories and offering advice where he could. His disposition, like that of his father, was always one of ungrudging kindness. When it was time to leave, he picked up his empty knapsack and said his goodbyes.

Upon his return, Pablo's precinct was ethereally quiet save for the echo of his footsteps and the barking of neighbourhood dogs. He was surprised to find the front door ajar and a clutch of keys on the hallway floor. An outburst of audience laughter could be heard emanating from the TV.

Pablo tiptoed quietly into the living room in case his papa had fallen asleep in his armchair. The first thing he noticed were the soles of Gerardo's feet, one bereft of its slipper. Then he saw that his father was on his back and staring resolutely at the ceiling.

"Papá?" he yelped, not yet cognisant of the fact that his father was dead. Frantic with fear, the boy dropped to his knees and shook him gently. "Papá! Wake up! Wake up! Oh, dear God, please wake up!"

CHAPTER NINETEEN

When Sofia had first taken it upon herself to home-school Luna, nothing could have prepared her for the aptitude that the girl showed from the outset. The teenager was blessed with a voracious curiosity and a genius beyond anything the physicist had ever witnessed. Luna had no appetite, however, for nonsensical small talk, simpering flattery or fatuous gaiety. She valued instead the derring-do of great adventures, the hidden gifts of nature, and the authority of learning.

Within a matter of weeks she had gained an advanced understanding of core scientific disciplines, and after two months could negotiate probability theory as ably as a Bedouin navigates the Saharan desert.

Though it was clear to Sofia that her prodigy had the potential to set the science world alight, she dwelled on the fact that she also was limiting Luna's progress by not allowing her access to laboratories. She was worried about the attention that this would bring upon someone who, despite outward appearances, was a non-human.

The Russian sought to inspire Luna in the same way that she was once motivated by Dr Yelena Nazarova, her university professor at the Moscow Institute of Physics and Technology.

"Science should be audacious," Dr Nazarova had once proclaimed in her strident voice. "It shouldn't be all about drab men in lab coats getting all the credit for something their female assistants have done. You will be leaving them for dust one day, Sofia."

Because of Sofia's passion for teaching and Luna's thirst for knowledge, their lessons in the library often continued well into the night, prompting María to bring them a tray of food and refreshments while Hugo and Vincent dined in the kitchen. It was on one such night, deep into the Russian's explanation of stochastic analysis, that their concentration was interrupted by the sound of the telephone ringing shortly after 11pm.

"Really, who could that be at this time?" huffed Sofia, setting off to answer it. "What a nuisance. It had better be important."

*

Vincent cursed the nonexistence of in-car satellite navigation as he and Hugo struggled to find Pablo's part of town. With only an unwieldy street map at their disposal, they took several wrong turns in the Cadillac before reaching his apartment block sometime after midnight.

The police contingent had consisted of two uniformed officers who made no effort to preserve the crime scene and who promised, with scant enthusiasm, to file a report. A coroner appeared in the midst of this slipshod investigation and yawned through a series of routine questions before sending Gerardo's body to the morgue. Photographs were taken and statements scribbled on notepads, but seemingly little else was done to probe the murder of a gentleman musician.

The officials had dissolved into the night by the time Hugo and Vincent appeared at the front door. Pablo, who was being consoled by neighbours, rushed into the Englishman's arms the moment he caught sight of him. "I am so sorry that I make a nuisance to you by the telephone, señor," he sobbed, struggling to form words. "You say to me that if I have any trouble to call to you. Now, I have the worst trouble."

Hugo ushered him into the living room. The neighbours, sitting at a Formica dining table, smiled beatifically at the two foreigners despite not having the faintest idea who they were.

Hugo sat the youngster on a sofa and got down on his haunches. "You did the right thing by calling me. Do you know who did this to your father?"

Despite his tears, Pablo's eyes blazed with hatred. He looked left and right then lowered his voice. "It was Rubén Cuevas. And I swear to God, señor, that I will kill him."

"How do you know it was Cuevas?"

The boy produced a piece of spent gum from his

trouser pocket. "Because I find *this* next to my father. And one of my neighbours, she see Cuevas running from here."

"And are the police going to arrest him?"

"We are poor, señor," Pablo shrugged. "When a person is killed here, maybe nothing happens."

As he broke down in a convulsion of sobs, Hugo glanced at Vincent who knew that his friend had already made the decision to mete out his own brand of justice.

"What am I to do without my papá?" wailed Pablo. "He was everything to me."

Hugo wrapped the boy in his arms. "You're coming to live with me, Pablo. I will look after you."

*

Sofia had waited up and wasn't in the least surprised when Hugo and Vincent returned from their mercy dash across town in the early hours with Pablo in tow. She sought to reassure the forlorn teenager by welcoming him with a comforting hug. "Oh Pablo, darling. I am so sorry that we finally meet under such sad circumstances."

The youngster was too traumatised to return Sofia's embrace and merely stood limp in her arms.

Hugo stepped forward, carrying some of the boy's belongings in a battered suitcase. "Pablo will be staying with us for the foreseeable future, Sofia. He's all alone in this world."

"Of course," she replied without hesitation. "He

can stay with us for as long as he wants."

Hugo mouthed the words *thank you* to her and placed a fatherly hand on the boy's shoulder. "Let's take you to your new bedroom, shall we, Pablo?"

The pitiful look on the boy's face and the tremble of his lips almost broke Sofia's heart. As he trudged upstairs, howling from the pain of his loss, even Vincent was reduced to tears.

CHAPTER TWENTY

After a fitful night's sleep, Pablo woke to the crushing realisation that his father had passed from this life and that his own could never be the same. He buried his face in a pillow and sobbed as quietly as he could, tormented by a nightmare that wouldn't release him from its grip.

An incantation of subterranean noises bubbled up from the depths of the house: the creak of floorboards, the murmur of conversation and the rattling of pans. In stark contrast to his previous bedroom, this one was spacious and came equipped with its own bathroom. After a stand-up wash with a soapy flannel, Pablo slipped into jeans and a short-sleeved shirt. He walked to the entrance door and gripped its handle while summoning the courage to face his benefactors and whoever else might be present.

He had scarcely stepped out onto the landing, bewildered by its many doors, when his attention was arrested by a white-haired girl who moved like a whisper. Luna stood before him and cocked her head to one side, as would a curious dove. They were both momentarily lost for words, as if they had once met each other in a distant dream.

Luna immediately recognised the boy. She had seen him and his glossy black hair often in her mind's eye, a fact that she would keep to herself for now. "Hello. Do you speak English?" she asked.

"Yes," he replied, unsettled by her unfathomable eyes.

"Who are you?"

"My name is Pablo, señorita. And yours?"

"I'm not telling you."

"That is not friendly."

"I'm not a friendly person."

"Oh."

"Why are you here?"

Pablo hung his head. "My father, he is killed, señorita. Mr Hugo take me here last night."

"I see," said Luna, thrown from her high horse. "Please forgive me, Pablo. My name is Luna."

"It is okay. You did not know."

In an uncharacteristic display of congeniality, the forest girl took Pablo by the hand. "Come downstairs with me. I will show you where we eat breakfast."

When the two walked into the kitchen hand in hand, Sofia, Hugo and Vincent were left open-mouthed with astonishment. María compensated for their shared stupefaction by welcoming the new boy in Spanish. "Good morning, Pablo. I am so sorry for your tragedy. Whatever you want, just ask. These people are kind and welcoming. I know you are hurting right now, but you are safe here."

It was all Pablo could do to remain composed. "I know this is true, señora. But I hurt so much. How will I ever find happiness again?"

The cook, who was also alone in the world, held his cheeks with floury hands and kissed him on his forehead, leaving behind a perfect lipstick smudge. "You will find happiness, beautiful boy. You will. I will see to it that you do."

*

It came as no surprise to Pablo that the coroner's report returned a verdict of 'natural causes' for his father's death. The case, such as it was, was closed without further investigation.

A vigil was held at Gerardo's apartment, where he made a very dapper corpse. He was displayed in an open casket, dressed in his favourite linen suit and sporting a flamboyant kipper tie. His hands were arranged as if in prayer and his trumpet tucked underneath them so he could continue to play it in the afterlife. The casket was the finest the funeral home had to offer, made from polished mahogany and lined with clouds of white satin. Its exorbitant cost had been met by Sofia and Hugo, who had stepped in to cover all the funeral expenses to save Pablo from any additional stress.

As well as a dependable contingent of good friends and neighbours, a gaggle of distant relatives had travelled up from Puebla on the off-chance that there might be some money kicking around. The wake was an altogether noisy affair, with food and refreshments and a spirited game of dominoes in its midst.

As well as a continual outpouring of grief, there was much drinking of tequila, lighting of candles and muttering of prayers, with everyone agreeing that Gerardo had touched their lives in one way or another. Mourners crowded round the casket and adorned the trumpeter's body with prayer cards and rosaries of the Virgin Mary, together with black-and-white photographs of Gerardo as a young man. He seemed peaceful in death, leading many of the attendees to remark that he was lost in the loveliest of dreams. One after another, they touched his body and wished him a safe passage into the afterlife.

The vigil continued through the night. Pablo was still leaning over his father's body and crying wretchedly when the undertakers arrived to collect the casket in the morning.

"A day will never pass where I don't feel bad for not being there to save you, Papá," he wept as the funeral director solemnly closed each of the casket's two lids.

By Mexican standards, the funeral was not a lengthy affair. Gerardo had always made it clear that, when his time came, he wished to pass into the next life with the minimum of fuss. The Mass was held at a local church where the padre, a thin man with unruly teeth, praised the musician for his service to God and for raising his son in the Catholic tradition. There wasn't a dry eye to be seen as the priest recited beautiful passages from the Bible, and Gerardo's casket received a standing ovation when it left the church.

Accompanied by the mournful dirge of a brass band, the congregation made the short walk to the cemetery to gather like crows at the graveside. Gerardo was to be buried near to his beloved Rosa, and marigolds had been placed around his grave so that their scent would lead him to her. While the women mourners wailed and the men tried to remain stoical, the priest inscribed the sign of the cross on the casket lid and sprinkled it with holy water, prompting a lone trumpeter to strike up with a soaring rendition of 'La Golondrina' as a heartfelt farewell.

When the time came for the casket to be lowered into the ground, Pablo threw himself across it, desperately calling out for his father. He had to be restrained by Jesús the organ grinder. "Please do not upset yourself, Pablo," said Jesús. "If I know your father, he will play his trumpet all the way to Heaven."

Inconsolable in his grief, the boy sobbed in the organ grinder's strong arms as the casket was buried under shovelfuls of dirt.

CHAPTER TWENTY-ONE

By his fourth day at the big house, and with all of his artwork and worldly possessions transported from the apartment, Pablo had emptied his well of tears and could conduct a conversation without breaking down. Touchingly, while sitting with Hugo and Vincent at a wrought-iron patio table in the fountain courtyard, he even showed concern that if he didn't return to work soon his customers might start to look elsewhere.

Hugo placed a hand on the boy's shoulder. "Now that you are under my roof, Pablo, you will never need to shine another shoe."

"But I like to shine shoes," said the youngster brightly, showing the first shoots of recovery.

"Well, you can polish mine if you want. Even Vincent's, if you can bear the smell."

"You'll get my shoe up your arse," said the Irishman.

A shy smile broke on Pablo's face. "It would be an honour to shine your shoes, señores."

As butterflies flitted about the courtyard, Hugo moved onto weightier matters, specifically the real reason he had asked Pablo to join them outside. The

Englishman leaned forward in his chair, elbows resting on the table, and looked the boy squarely in the eye. "Pablo, do you know where Rubén Cuevas goes to in the evening?"

The mention of the brute's name sparked a ferocity in the youngster's eyes that seemed unsuited to a face so innocent. "My friend Miguel, he tell me that Cuevas drink every night at a bar near to his house."

"Do you know the name of the bar?" asked Hugo.

"The name is Barra de Sirena."

Vincent produced a notepad and pen. "Could you draw us a map?"

A sudden look of alarm appeared on Pablo's face. "Señores, you must not go there. This place have many bad men and is very dangerous. Especially for gringos, I think."

"We'll be fine," smiled Hugo. "Let us worry about the bad men."

"But, señores, already I have a plan for Cuevas—"

"Trust me, kid, you cannot do what we can do," said Vincent, pushing the pad forward. "So your only job is to show us where the bar is."

Pablo put pen to paper and began to draft a map. "Oh, señores, you make me very scared for you."

*

Hugo and Vincent's daytime reconnaissance mission involved the Irishman driving the Batmobile into a shabby part of town populated by rats and ne'er-do-wells. Guided by Pablo's well-crafted map, O'Toole cruised the narrow potholed road where the bar was situated.

"There it is. Barra de Sirena," said Hugo.

Vincent pulled over to a weed-strewn kerb. "And you had the nerve to say that my bar was disreputable? Benito's is like a gentlemen's club compared to this booze shack."

"I'm inclined to agree with you, Vincent."

They stepped from the car into a sudden gust of wind, and a flock of plastic bags took to the air as if startled. The surrounding buildings, which were served by a cat's cradle of overhead cables, were grey and soulless. A putrefying stench of open sewers hung heavily on the breeze and scabby dogs roamed the streets.

Hugo removed his sunglasses and surveyed the bar. In the harsh glare of daylight, and without the night-time embellishment of its neon signs, it looked like a large cowshed rather than a drinking establishment. "If you could guard the car, Vincent, I'll get to know the lay of the land."

He surveyed the barbed wire on top of the concrete walls and peered through the bar's grimy windows, then he walked the perimeter and noted the entrances and exits. A man, who Hugo presumed to be the owner, suddenly burst out from a side door with a beard of shaving foam on his plump face and a towel around his neck.

"*Oye! Qué deseas?*" the Mexican barked, jabbing his razor in Wilde's direction.

Hugo adopted the pretence of an unworldly tourist who had simply lost his bearings.

"So sorry, señor. *No hablo español,*" he shrugged.

"Go to Hell!" shouted the man before retreating inside and slamming the door.

Vincent leant back against the Cadillac as his pal returned with a satisfied grin on his face. "You seem to have this knack of making friends wherever you go, Hugo."

Hugo chuckled. "Well, if that's the sort of welcome one can expect at this hostelry, I shall be taking my custom elsewhere."

"So, what are your thoughts?" asked Vincent as they slid into the car.

"Rather handily, there's an outside urinal around the back for the customers. If I can catch Cuevas on his own tonight, then all the better."

Vincent woke the car's throaty engine. "Sounds like a decent plan. We need to do away with this bastard."

That night, under the all-seeing gaze of a pearly moon, O'Toole parked the Batmobile a safe distance from the bar so as not to bring attention to it. Wilde sat in the passenger seat wearing his special-ops combat gear and shoulder holster. "Of course, another great thing about living in 1970 is the absence of CCTV cameras," he grinned, completing a function check of his Glock handgun.

Vincent wasn't keen on the idea of his friend going in on his own. "Are you sure you don't want me to mingle with the locals in the bar, Hugo? With my handlebar moustache, I'd fit right in."

"Having a moustache makes you no more a Mexican than your wig makes you a judge, Vincent."

"Excuse your cheek. I'm quite entitled to offer my help, Hugo."

"And it is warmly welcomed, my friend, but you're already doing enough by being my getaway driver. Now listen, the first thing I'm going to do is look through the windows to see if he's there. If so, I'll hide in the shadows, hoping that he'll answer the call of nature at some point."

"Grand. And if you're not back in ten minutes, I'll know it's on."

Hugo stepped from the car and zipped up a bomber jacket that concealed his firearm. The bar's fluorescent sign hovered in the darkness and a cacophony of rock music blared out from unseen speakers. With his head down and his hands in his pockets, Hugo slunk along the uneven pavement and stole past a raucous bonhomie of drunken lowlifes, one of whom was Cuevas himself. He coasted into the backyard where the ceramic latrine lurked under a green neon light, bathed in a witch's glow.

High above, a ghost ship moon was moored in an inky sky, presenting the perfect backdrop for a righteous execution. The Englishman found a vantage point in the darkest recesses of the mosquito-infested yard and sat there cross-legged in calm anticipation.

*

In the hour that followed, several men stumbled from the bar to the latrine where they belched, whistled and farted while discharging great streams of urine. One respectfully sang the chorus of the Mexican national anthem with his hand across his heart before unzipping himself and playing the time-honoured game of 'hose the cigarette butt'.

It was another thirty minutes before Rubén the Bull clumped into view. He had unbuttoned his fly and was in full flow when the Englishman appeared in his peripheral vision. Eerily green under the neon light, the Mexican's expression was one of nonchalance, rather than surprise. "You like to watch me take a piss, huh, gringo?" he grunted, continuing to empty his bladder. "Perhaps you can wipe my ass when I have a shit?"

Hugo made a show of winding a silencer into the barrel of his Glock. "I want to teach you that bad things happen to bad people, Rubén," he said coolly.

Cuevas buttoned himself up and faced the Englishman. The moon reflected in his tarry eyes as he let rip with a throaty laugh.

"You have brought a toy to scare me, huh, *Inglés?*" he grinned, producing a large knife from under his beer-stained shirt. "You made a big mistake coming here, *cabrón.*"

"I see you've bought yourself a new knife," smiled Hugo.

Cuevas licked his lips and carved a figure of eight in the air. "Go home, gringo, or you will lose your eyes. You don't have the *cojones* to use that gun."

"We'll see, shall we?"

With practiced speed and precision, Hugo snatched the knife from the Mexican's grip and at the same time fired a bullet through his hand at point-blank range.

Cuevas promptly jumped about the yard like a scalded cat. "Waaaaaah! Waaaaaah!"

"I do hope that wasn't your writing hand," said Hugo.

"Son of a bitch! Waaaaaah! Waaaaaah!"

Wilde watched with mild interest as the Mexican whirled around in a state of panic, splashing blood in a neat circle. A stroboscope of lightning suddenly convulsed the sky, silhouetting rooftops and power lines. Without further ado, and to the distant rumble of thunder, Hugo stepped forward and shot Cuevas twice in the head.

CHAPTER TWENTY-TWO

On the morning after the execution, Hugo's consciousness was seized by an unsettling sense of *déjà vu*. Vincent and Pablo were sitting at the wrought-iron patio table, just as they had been the previous day, wearing the same clothes and having the exact same conversation. The scene in the courtyard was tranquil, albeit bafflingly familiar. Butterflies flitted from one flower to the next and sunlight danced on the fountain's cascade of water.

Vincent produced a notepad and pen and slid it to Pablo across the table. "Could you draw us a map?"

A sudden look of alarm haunted the boy's face. "Señores, you must not go there. This place has many bad men and is very dangerous. Especially for gringos, I think."

O'Toole turned to Wilde, expecting him to cut in, and instead saw an expression of complete bewilderment on his face.

"God Almighty, Hugo, you look as if you've seen a ghost. Are you okay?"

Wilde furrowed his brow and continued to gaze at

his friend with incredulity. To him, the entire scene was like a hallucination. "Please excuse us for a moment, Pablo," he said, rising from his chair. "Vincent, could I speak to you in private?"

"Ooh, I've said something I shouldn't," grinned the Irishman, scraping his chair back and casting the teenager a convivial wink.

Hugo led him to a far corner of the courtyard. "Why on earth are we discussing the same things we discussed yesterday?" he enquired, his voice an intense whisper.

"What in God's name are you on about? I'm only doing what we agreed upon earlier."

The Englishman folded his arms. "And what was that, exactly?"

"That we would ask Pablo where this Cuevas fella hangs out in the evenings."

"But we've already done that."

"Done what?"

"Found his watering hole. You drove me there, Vincent. I shot him in the head last night, remember? And then you drove me home—"

"Go on with your nonsense, Hugo. Perhaps you should get out of the sun."

Hugo massaged his temples. "What day is it today, Vincent?"

"It's Friday."

"Friday, not Saturday?"

"That's what I said."

Hugo clicked his fingers, struck by the sudden

realisation of what had occurred. "Of course! It's the time-travel paradox, Vincent. We weren't able to avenge Gerardo's death because Cuevas wasn't destined to die last night."

O'Toole gave Hugo a sidelong glance and took a moment to marshal his thoughts. "Hey, wait. You're telling me that we've already executed the plan, only to be caught up in some kind of *Groundhog Day* time loop?"

"That is exactly what has happened."

"And that bastard is free to walk the streets of Mexico City without a care in the world?"

"Apparently so."

*

Unable to resist the call of nature any longer, Rubén Cuevas drained his beer glass and threaded through a sweaty throng of fellow inebriates. Under the glimmer of an alabaster moon, he cleared his nasal passages and headed for the urinal's emerald glow. He had unbuttoned his fly and was in full flow when he became aware of someone in his peripheral vision. The man stood half in shadow and looked on in silence.

"You like to watch me take a piss, huh, *cabrón*?" Cuevas grunted, continuing to empty his bladder. "Perhaps you can wipe my ass when I have a shit?"

The man laid his cowboy hat on the ground and stepped forward. Cuevas shook himself dry. "Hey, don't I know you?" he snorted. "You're the dopey organ-grinder guy."

Jesús the organ grinder pulled a fabric *lucha libre* mask from his waistband and stretched it over his head. The red disguise was embellished with yellow flames and had cut-outs for the eyes, nose and mouth. "You might know me better as Johnny Diablo," he said in a grave voice. "In my entire career, I was never unmasked in the ring. Only my family and closest friends are aware of my true identity."

Cuevas buttoned his fly. "Yeah, I saw you on the TV a long time ago. So what? Get to the point, asshole."

Johnny Diablo rolled his neck and cracked his knuckles. His dark eyes glared through their oval cut-outs. "My point is this, Cuevas. You murdered my dearest friend, one of the kindest men ever to have lived. I had to attend his funeral knowing that you were still alive."

Cuevas drew his knife. "Then I will send you to him, *cabrón*."

Diablo, drawing on years of training, grabbed the killer's knife hand in his vicelike grip and flipped him in one fluid movement, snapping Rubén's wrist bones in the process. As Cuevas screamed on the ground in agony the wrestler put him in a headlock, lay underneath him and executed a rear naked choke from which there was no escape.

"This is for Gerardo," growled Johnny Diablo, wrapping his legs around Cuevas and pulling back with all his might.

With his eyes bulging from their sockets and lungs heaving on empty, the villain tried to cling on to life but it was slipping away from him forever. High above, a sheet of lightning illuminated the night sky and, at that moment, Rubén Cuevas wondered why he had never witnessed such beauty before.

CHAPTER TWENTY-THREE

Wishing to emulate the French poets she had seen in monochromatic photographs, Luna wore a black beret paired with a Breton top, baggy jeans and a scarlet neckerchief.

Wherever the teenager went, a book went with her, and she headed for the park carrying a hardback copy of Elena Garro's *Los Recuerdos del Porvenir* in her knapsack. In the space of just eight weeks she had taught herself to read Spanish proficiently and the book's title, which translated to *The Memories of the Future*, put her in mind of her own extraordinary set of circumstances. There was a poetic expressiveness to the writing of Spanish-speaking authors such as Gabriel García Márquez, Jorge Luis Borges and the aforementioned Elena Garro that had lit a fire in Luna's imagination, inspiring her to read their stories in their original language.

As she hastened to the park, Luna held a parasol aloft to protect her pale skin from the sun. She was followed eagerly by the same clique of finches that pecked at her bedroom window each morning, asking to be let in.

The day was clear, with an endless blue sky and the faintest wisps of white cirrus. As she walked through its wrought-iron gates, the park welcomed Luna with a verdant embrace, reconnecting her with nature's extravagance. She turned in a circle with arms outstretched, energised by a kaleidoscope of green colours: shades of pistachio, jade, sage, shamrock, juniper and fern.

Much to the bafflement of their owners, dogs strained at their leashes to make Luna's acquaintance. A Jack Russell with a piratical splodge of black fur around one eye broke free altogether, its chain trailing behind, and yapped excitedly in her presence.

"My apologies, señorita," said the flustered owner. "I do not understand. My Lola has never done this before."

"It's fine," replied Luna, scratching the dog under its collar. "She just wanted to say hello."

A little later, spooked by a roller skater, a muddle of pigeons took to the air. As they rose they shat liberally on the statue of a former Spanish king who was captured in perpetuity astride a sturdy horse. With mere finger holes for pupils, the king gazed out blindly, unable to see the world around him or even the stallion beneath him.

Luna hurried along, disregarding the legion of iron benches that sat heavily upon sun-scorched grass. Her preferred seats were to be found in the highest branches of the oldest trees. As is true of humans, each tree has its own personality, and she had a knack for knowing which ones were welcoming and which were temperamental. She gave two sullen oaks a wide berth and instead opted for an obliging ash tree that shook its leaves eagerly to grab her attention.

Hiding behind its wide trunk, Luna checked that the coast was clear and, with the parasol hooked to her knapsack, briskly skittered to a height of thirty feet. She lay upon a sturdy bough, feet dangling either side, and made herself comfortable using the main trunk as a headboard.

From this vantage point, Luna could see much of the park's geometry and the city beyond. She gazed upon a landscape of lawns and flower beds that were neatly bisected by pathways. She saw refreshment kiosks and gazebos alongside shaded seating areas where people could escape the heat. Her favourite features, two giant chessboards, had been painted onto square paving slabs and attracted a daily gathering of players and spectators.

Sunlight shimmered through the leaves of the tree as she fed sunflower seeds to her retinue of finches. The start of a new novel carried with it a sense of occasion, and the alphabets in Luna's mind started to shuffle their letters in anticipation. She opened the book and began to read.

*

Some time later, Pablo entered the same park via its northern gate. He was on his way to see Magic Miguel, who had telephoned to say that he had some exciting news to share. They had arranged to meet near the chessboards. As he approached, Pablo saw his friend accosting a stiff-looking gentleman who, despite the ruinous heat, was dressed in full butler's uniform.

"Isn't it a lovely day, señor?" said Miguel, stepping into Salazar's path.

"It is also a busy day. Get out of my way, you brat."

Pablo, who had arrived in the midst of their exchange, sought to reason with the butler. "Sir, please don't speak to him in such a way. He is just trying to make a living—"

Salazar shouldered them both out of the way without breaking his stride. "You parasites disgust me. Go bother someone who actually gives a shit."

"It is your loss, señor!" Miguel called out after him. "You have missed out on the most amazing magic trick!"

Pablo put his arm around his friend. "Forget about that sourpuss, Miguel. You said on the telephone that you had some exciting news?"

*

Luna had whiled away the best part of four hours absorbed in her book when she was alerted to a familiar voice drifting up from the pathway below. She shifted her position on the bough and gazed down at the top of Pablo's head. He was chatting in Spanish with a raggedy, snub-nosed teenager who was relaying the news that a man called Rubén Cuevas had been found dead outside a bar near to his home.

Luna observed that Pablo, rather than being upset, seemed pleased. He then gave the other boy some money and suggested he buy himself an ice cream. She leant forward as they ended their conversation with a hug and the dishevelled one scampered off in the direction of an ice-cream trailer, the hems of his overly long trousers dragging along the pathway.

Pablo, as if suddenly gifted with a sixth sense, looked directly up at her. "Luna! How did you get up there so high?"

"Mind your own business!"

"But I would like to know!"

"It's easy! You should try it!"

"I will!"

The teen struggled to get to grips with the wide trunk but his shoes skidded on the bark each time he tried to gain a foothold. "It is impossible!" he hollered. "You used a ladder, I think."

"Of course not! I am just a better climber than you!"

Pablo blew on his sore fingertips and walked around the tree, expecting to find some metal stakes driven into its trunk. In the meantime, Luna pelted the youngster with twigs and loose scraps of bark. She even threw her parasol at him.

"Hey! Stop that!" he laughed, brushing the detritus from his mop of black hair.

It pleased Luna to have distracted Pablo from his heartache in such a knockabout fashion. "I will come down to you," she yelled, adjusting her beret. "But you must not look!"

"Why not?"

"Because how I move about the tree is a secret, you fool!"

While Pablo turned his back, she coasted down the tree trunk and landed weightlessly on the grass before tapping him on the shoulder. Secretly infatuated with her, Pablo saw Luna as someone he could love for an eternity, but he knew it was best to keep such thoughts to himself.

"You may escort me back to the house," she instructed.

*

Hugo walked into señor Volante's bookstore to make a proposition that he hoped the proprietor would find attractive. En route, and acting on impulse, he had purchased an antique cricket bat from a curio shop that had lured him into its cluttered depths.

"*Buenos días*, Hugo!" greeted a bow-tied Volante from the custody of his reception desk. "Are you so English that you have to walk about the city with a cricket bat tucked under your arm?"

"I bought it merely to remind me of home, Eduardo. How the devil are you, my good friend?"

"I'm fine, sir. How are Sofia and Vincent? And María, of course?"

"All tickety-boo. Oh, and María has sent you a little something—" Wilde set his cricket bat down and handed Volante a paper bag containing bread buns filled with fried pineapple.

"She knows I love these!" Eduardo enthused. "I have such a sweet tooth." He clambered nimbly across his desk and sat on the edge of it with the bag in his lap and feet dangling. "So what brings you here, Hugo?" he asked, prodding his spectacles onto the bridge of his nose.

Hugo joined him on the edge of the desk. "I have a proposition, Eduardo. One that is offered with the very best of intentions."

"You have me intrigued," said Volante stroking his Santa beard.

"I have taken a recently orphaned Mexican boy under my wing. He's as bright as a button and has bags of potential. The only thing he lacks in life, aside from a mother and a father, is a good education."

"How old is the boy?"

"Sixteen. His name is Pablo. I was wondering, Eduardo, if I could commission you to school the lad at my home and give him the education he deserves. I will, of course, reward you amply for your services. Just name your price."

Señor Volante steepled his fingers and contemplated the offer. A thin line of smoke from an incense stick curled around him. "How many days a week are we talking about, Hugo?"

"Only as many as you would feel comfortable with."

A broad smile appeared through Volante's beard.

He swivelled on the seat of his pants and offered his hand. "It's an exciting proposition, Hugo. Yes, I would love to do it."

Hugo slid from the desk and shook Eduardo's hand warmly. "That's fantastic! He's an admirable young man. You won't regret it."

"And, please, you do not have to worry about the money. Just to be fed by María in your beautiful house would be payment enough."

"Think of María's food as a wonderful perk in addition to your remuneration," said Hugo." What about the running of your bookshop when you are with us?"

Eduardo looked upwards and pointed to the ceiling. "My best friend lives with me in the apartment above the shop, and he is always happy to step in."

"Perfect."

"I would just like to add that it *is* a two-bedroomed apartment—"

"I don't need to know your sleeping arrangements," said Hugo patting Eduardo's knee and casting him a wink. "I'm just delighted that you can help me out at such short notice."

"It will be my pleasure, señor."

"And your best friend – perhaps you could bring him over to our house for a meal sometime? We would love to meet him."

Eduardo nodded at the Englishman, his impression of the man validated. "He would like that, Hugo. His name is Rafael, but you can call him Rafa."

*

Luna spun her parasol, fluttering shadows across her face, as she waited for Pablo to unlock the back gate to the fountain courtyard. Once opened, Copernicus raced out to greet her, winding in and out of her legs and purring rapturously.

Luna got down on her haunches. "*Nå, hva' så?*" she cooed, tickling the underside of the cat's chin.

"Wow. What was that you said?" asked Pablo.

"Just a greeting in Danish," she said airily. "If you speak to him in any language, he understands what you are saying by the tone of your voice. All animals do, if you know how to gain their trust."

The forest girl walked to the fountain, removed her beret and splashed cool water onto her face. Then, with a composed air, she sat down at a patio table in the shade of a crab-apple tree. A gauzy-winged dragonfly darted about her head and settled on her shoulder. "You must be thirsty, Pablo." She furled her parasol and laid it on the cobbled ground.

"Of course," he replied.

"Then why don't you ask María for a jug of her lemonade and two glasses? We could talk for a little longer, if you would like."

"I would like that very much!" he beamed, before scampering to unlatch the stable door that led into the kitchen. The cook was nowhere to be seen, though a pan of *mole* sauce was blipping away on a very low heat.

Pablo returned to the doorway and called out to Luna. "María is not here! What should I do?"

"Use your initiative!" shouted Luna.

"What is initiative?"

"Just take the lemonade from the refrigerator! Or must I do it myself?"

"Okay"

Pablo opened the refrigerator door and pushed aside a Tupperware container of salsa to get the jug of lemonade. Just as he had it in his grasp, a ghoulish voice boomed out, causing him to jump out of his skin and spill lemonade onto his shirt.

"You filthy little thief!" barked Severiano Salazar. "So you thought you would follow me from the park, heh?"

Pablo, who had almost dropped the jug in his panic, timorously placed it on a work surface and held his hands out in a placatory manner. "Please, sir. I am not a thief. I live here in this house—"

"Do not take me for a fool, boy," snarled the butler, grabbing him by his ear. "I will have you thrown in prison."

"Ow! Sir! Please! You are hurting me!"

Luna, alerted by the clamour, rushed into the kitchen and promptly booted Salazar hard in each shin. "What are you doing, you imbecile? Leave him alone!"

Pablo retreated in a state of shock, cupping his reddened ear. Luna shielded him, prepared to fight on his behalf if necessary.

Severiano's eyes blazed like hot coals. "You would side with a common thief, little girl?" he hissed, directing a bony finger at her. "Just you wait until I tell Mr Wilde!"

María, roused from a light siesta by the ruckus, wandered into the kitchen from her private quarters and tried to make sense of the standoff that greeted her. She saw the upset on Pablo's face and immediately went to comfort him. "I heard you shouting, Mr Salazar," she scolded. "Surely not the behaviour of a gentleman?"

"The boy is a dirty little beggar, Mrs Bravo. He followed me from the park and tried to steal lemonade from the refrigerator."

Luna stepped forward, causing the butler to retreat. "He is not a beggar, you idiot. And he returned from the park with me."

"Are you even allowed out in daylight?" sneered Salazar.

María sought to bring the butler up to speed. "Since you were last here, Mr Salazar, Pablo has become the latest honoured guest in this house. And you should treat him as such."

"You are like a clucking hen, woman," replied the butler, rubbing his bruised shins. "Who knows what diseases the wretch might have? We should at least check him for head lice."

María held Pablo close. "How dare you talk this way! You are a man with rust in his heart!"

"That may be so," said Salazar, "but it is a big

mistake to invite such a boy into a civilised house. A lemon tree will never grow mangoes, no matter how well you treat it."

Sofia rushed into the kitchen and noted that the air was thick with hostility. "I heard raised voices," she said sturdily. "Can someone please tell me what the hell is going on?"

"Mr Salazar and I, we fight like the cat and the dog," said María contritely. "But we have made our peace."

"Just a simple misunderstanding," the butler added.

"Good, because I don't want discord in the house. Especially in front of the youngsters."

"May I just add," said Salazar, "that women are perhaps too emotional when it comes to matters of importance and that they should stick to what they do best."

"Which is?" bristled Sofia.

"Cooking and cleaning, Madam."

Sofia somehow resisted the urge to slap his nasty little face. " Mr Salazar, either you must think me very stupid or yourself highly intelligent, but I can assure you that neither assumption is true."

"Of course, Madam," he said with a slimy smile.

Sofia ignored him; his impertinence and disingenuity was beginning to wear thin. "Luna and Pablo," she said switching her tone. "Would you care to join me in the library?"

Just as Sofia and the two teenagers were trooping

towards the library, Hugo breezed through the front door and grabbed their attention by shaking a brown-paper carrier bag. "I come bearing gifts," he said, propping his cricket bat against a side table. "A book for you, Luna. A book for you, Pablo. And one for you, my love."

"Thank you, my happiness," said Sofia with a kiss. "But what is the cricket bat for?"

A ceiling fan skittered a flickering shadow across Hugo's face. "It's not just any old cricket bat," he beamed. "It's a Gunn & Moore vintage model hewn from English willow."

Luna inspected the bat with scant interest and gave it an inquisitive sniff before passing it to Pablo. She noted that it smelled faintly of crushed grass and linseed oil.

Sofia was less than enthused. "From how you describe it, anyone would imagine it to be a thing of rare beauty, but it is really just a battered old lump of wood, no?"

"A battered old lump of wood?" gasped Hugo with faux indignation, taking possession of the bat. "Look at its elegant design, its cane handle, its lovely patina." He gave himself some space and went through his repertoire of batting strokes, starting with a solid forward defence followed by a stylish cover drive, then a valorous hook shot and a reverse sweep to finish.

"I really like it," Pablo bubbled.

"You like everything," huffed Luna.

Sofia folded her arms. "Now that you have this

curio, what do you plan to do with it?"

"A cricket bat could incapacitate a burglar just as easily as it could send a leather ball racing to the boundary. With that in mind, I'm going to hang it here in the hallway."

Sofia gifted Hugo a charitable smile. "Boys and their toys. Now, let us return to more important matters. Come along, darlings!"

The scientist peeled away abruptly, inviting Hugo to follow them to the library. She informed him that she had asked María to prepare a tray of light refreshments.

"I've been casting my eye over your artwork, Pablo," she said over her shoulder, her heels clacking rhythmically on the tiled floor. "And really, it is exceptional. I must introduce you to some of my artist friends."

Pablo, unaware that he possessed anything more than a passable talent, assumed that Sofia was simply trying to lift his spirits. "Thank you," he said, his short legs struggling to keeping pace. "But I think that you are too kind."

"Not at all," she continued, leading her entourage into the library. "I was blown away. What do you think of these, Hugo?"

The Englishman stopped in his tracks, wide-eyed with astonishment. Sofia had spread the paintings on the parquet floor. Some were framed, others were unfurled and weighted down. Each was rendered in the Mexican folk-art tradition, and most of them depicted surreal, dreamlike scenes.

Hugo shook his head in wonderment. "I saw these on your apartment wall, Pablo, but I had no idea that they were actually yours. You have a rare gift, young man."

Pablo was touched by Hugo's kind words and gazed at the paintings with renewed confidence.

Of the four of them, Luna was the most awestruck. She circled the assembled pieces in a daze of disbelief and gaped at Pablo as if he were the eighth wonder of the world. "Your surname is Quiroz?" she asked, suddenly kneeling before a picture and pointing to his signature.

"It is," said the young artist proudly.

"You are Pablo Quiroz?"

"Yes, of course."

Luna's expression was suddenly one of complete bewilderment as she sat back on her heels trying to gather her thoughts. When Mr Salazar paraded into the library with a tray of drinks and dainty sandwiches, she used the interruption to discreetly ask Sofia to accompany her to the attic room, citing a matter of some urgency.

Intrigued, the Russian pursued her prodigy upstairs, along the first-floor landing and up the last rickety flight. Luna briskly unlocked her door and ran over to a colourful art poster that depicted a barefoot young lady floating above rooftops in a starry sky, wearing a black party dress. "Look at the signature," she exhorted.

Sofia scrutinised the bottom-right corner of the poster. There, in red paint strokes, was Pablo Quiroz's name. The date below it read 1972, two years into the future.

"Oh! How wonderfully crazy," said Sofia, once-more realising that the laws of physics should make some allowance for supernaturalism. "Really, I am as surprised as you, darling."

The teenager's voice was jittery with persistence. "But look! There's more—"

Sofia remained open-mouthed, for in the lower margin of the poster was the title of the painting: *Luna*.

"Seeing my name on a work of art was the reason I ordered the poster in the first place," Luna explained. "And the girl even looks like me."

"Darling, we must keep this to ourselves," Sofia urged, holding the teenager's hands. "Otherwise the spell might be broken, so to speak."

"I won't say anything to anyone," promised Luna. "Not even to Pablo."

CHAPTER TWENTY-FOUR

Mexico City was under the canopy of darkness as O'Toole coasted the Cadillac along its glittering boulevards. Ribbons of red-and-yellow light drizzled across the car's glossy roof and Afro-Cuban music trumpeted from its push-button radio. Hugo was sitting alongside him, while Sofia, Pablo and Luna occupied the back seat.

"Here it is! This is the park," said Pablo excitedly. "Parque de La Ciudadela."

As Vincent slowed the car, he was flagged down by a leathery-skinned man in a cowboy hat who stepped out in front of him waving a dirty red rag.

"This person, he is a *franelero,*" explained Pablo. "He will help you to park if you give him a little money."

"I know," grumbled the Irishman. "I've had to deal with these jokers before. They'll vandalise your car if you don't grease their palms."

O'Toole bartered with the hustler, employing obstinate shakes of the head and dismissive hand gestures before settling on an amount that suited them both. The *franelero* removed a trash can he had used to block a parking space and guided Vincent into it. As the group left the vehicle, the rogue favoured them with a courtly bow and patted the car's bonnet to signify that it would be in the safest of hands.

The night was heavy with humidity. Carrying large holdalls, they walked under the sulphurous glow of swan-necked streetlamps, their shadows bobbing on the paving slabs. Venturing into the dim recesses of the park, the makeshift family switched on their torches and approached the tented community, slashing the darkness with light sabre beams.

Their appearance had initially provoked alarm among the homeless until Pablo's beaming face suddenly slid into view. Only then did agitated murmurings give way to an outpouring of joy. Even the older kids, intoxicated through solvent abuse, raised a smile.

Pablo introduced his *de facto* family to the orphans before a miscellany of blankets, socks and other necessities were rationed fairly from holdalls. The youngster had earlier revealed to the others that the life expectancy of those sleeping rough was just twenty-five years of age, which further fired up their willingness to help.

Because of her disposition to secrecy none of the family had hitherto known that Luna could speak fluent Spanish, yet there she was, dispensing chicken soup from a thermos and chatting to the homeless with astonishing proficiency. Not only had she taught herself to read in Spanish, she'd also learned to enunciate it properly by talking to the park gardeners and spending a great deal of time with María in the kitchen.

Vincent allowed some of the younger kids to use him as a climbing frame while Sofia and Hugo released bottles of Coca-Cola into a tide of outstretched hands. Before setting out, the adults had listened with great sadness as Pablo relayed some of the orphans' tales of domestic abuse and social abandonment. Now that they were witnessing the hardship first-hand, Sofia and Hugo wanted to do more. Much more.

In a quiet moment, Sofia shared with Hugo her sudden aspiration to build an orphanage. "You must think me crazy," she sighed, waving away a mosquito that was bugling in her ear.

A grin spread across Hugo's face. "Not at all, darling. I was thinking the exact same thing. But you once told me that foreigners couldn't legally purchase a property in Mexico."

"You forget that I am a Mexican citizen," she smiled, pointing to the stars.

*

Sofia woke from a dream in which she had eagerly surfed the internet for local real estate, and immediately bemoaned the fact that the World Wide Web was yet to be invented. "How annoying! How annoying!" she huffed, digging a sleeping Hugo in the ribs so she could share her frustration.

"What's annoying?" he asked, rubbing the sleep from his eyes.

"That everything takes so long to do without the internet."

"You woke me up to tell me that?"

"I found this amazing plot of land in the city centre that would have been the perfect site for an orphanage, only to realise that it was just a stupid dream."

"Poor you."

Sofia shoved a pillow into Hugo's face and thumped it several times.

"Have you quite finished?" he asked from underneath the pillow.

She removed it and kissed his lips. "You are too annoying, darling, but you also have love from the top of your head to the tips of your toes."

"High praise indeed from a madwoman."

They made love to the sound of doves cooing on their balcony, then shared a hot shower before heading downstairs to enjoy a breakfast of eggs Benedict followed by churro waffles.

While she washed dishes, María trilled along to the chorus of a Sonny and Cher song that was playing on the radio. The windowsill in front of her was crowded with pots of fresh cilantro, oregano, thyme and marjoram, statuettes of the Virgin Mary, pictures of Mexican saints and a number of lit candles. Directly in the middle of this chaotic shrine sat a silver-plated bowl of holy water into which she dipped her fingers each time she felt the need to cross herself.

Pablo, buoyed by the previous night's mercy dash, was all smiles and seemingly restored to his former self. Luna, meanwhile, who had been reading Charles Darwin's *The Voyage of the Beagle*, thought the breakfast table the perfect place to sing the praises of Captain Robert Fitzroy, "a man who inspired loyalty and compelled obedience with little use of the cat." Pablo, unable to grasp all that she was saying, wondered how a ship's captain was able to control a tough crew of mariners with a household pet, but thought it best not to ask.

Just as Hugo was about to ask if anyone had seen Vincent, the Irishman wandered into the kitchen larger than life and as bald as a baby's bottom. Momentarily lost for words, Hugo set down his knife and fork and leant back in his chair to take it all in. "Vincent, you've—"

"I don't want to hear it," growled O'Toole.

"But you look—"

"Shush."

"Doesn't he look handsome?" beamed María, opening her arms in an operatic fashion.

"Very handsome," agreed Sofia. "I prefer him without the wig."

"It was María's suggestion," mumbled Vincent, his arms crossed and hands tucked into his armpits.

"And a great suggestion it was too," said Hugo, thinking that his friend resembled a circus strongman even more than he had before. "A vast improvement."

The Irishman edged closer to María, his dome

shining under the glow of a ceiling light, and lay a hefty arm across her shoulders. "While we're all together, I would like to officially announce that María and I are dating."

"Really, this is the most wonderful news," enthused Sofia, getting up from the table to congratulate them with hugs and kisses. Hugo followed suit, as did Pablo. Luna shook their hands.

"I hope this doesn't mean that you're both moving out?" asked Hugo, concerned that he might be saying farewell to a daily diet of good food and playful banter.

O'Toole's grin was as wide as the River Liffey. "Don't worry, Hugo, this place is far too good to walk away from."

"Thank God for that. I'd rather lose a kidney than I would María."

"We must have a celebratory dinner this evening," suggested Sofia. "Hugo and I will do the cooking."

"Couldn't we just eat out?" replied Vincent, pulling a face.

"Ignore him," said María, putting a hand over his mouth. "We accept your kind offer, Sofia."

*

For the purpose of finding a vacant plot upon which to build an orphanage, Sofia had arranged a morning appointment with Hector Cabrales, an estate agent acquaintance with an office in Bosques de las Lomas, a district eight miles to the west.

Hugo, meanwhile, had set himself the task of

transforming his ground-floor study into an art studio for Pablo. The room would provide ample space for the young artist to work in, and was served with a north-facing window that offered natural light throughout the day. Additionally, Pablo's horizons were to be further broadened under the tutelage of Eduardo Volante who was due to arrive at any minute.

No sooner had Vincent and the Batmobile joined the rush-hour traffic on Avenida Destino, chauffeuring Sofia to her morning appointment, than señor Volante arrived at the mansion in his Volkswagen Beetle.

Hugo greeted the bookseller at the front door before he had the chance to ring the bell. "*Buenos días,* Eduardo! Delighted to see you."

"Likewise, Hugo. I had to set off early as they are still digging up half the roads in this city to build these new subway lines. The old streetcars suited me just fine."

Señor Volante, with his luxuriant beard sparkling like snow, was a picture of elegance in a cream suit and matching Panama hat. A billowy cravat and black-and-white salsa shoes completed the ensemble. Cheerily swinging a brown-leather briefcase, he followed in Hugo's wake, walking through the house in the way that a sightseer hurries through a museum on a guided tour. Barely breaking stride, he paused fleetingly to admire a colourful abstract painting, a French console table, a Tiffany lamp and a Japanese ginger jar. At one point he spun in a small circle, head tilted upwards, to worship some chandeliers before continuing on his way.

"Your house doesn't become any less beautiful on a second viewing, Hugo," he remarked, gliding his fingers across the latticework of an Arabesque wall panel.

He closed his eyes and inhaled the smell of fresh coffee and cinnamon doughnuts. "Ahh, I can tell that María is not too far away." Hugo led him into the kitchen, where the bookseller's spectacles misted up in a cirrus of steam. "*Buenos días,* María!" he hailed, raising his hat.

María stopped what she was doing and trotted forward, wiping her hands on her apron. "My sweet friend, Eduardo!" she cooed, standing on tiptoe to kiss his cheeks. "Because I knew you were coming, I made you *buñuelos*. Sit, sit. I will bring you a fresh coffee."

Eduardo's eyebrows performed a little dance. "Perhaps a *café de olla*, María?"

María smiled broadly and primped her hair. "Of course! One *café de olla* coming up."

Pablo, who was sitting quietly at the kitchen table with Copernicus at his feet, went almost unnoticed in the prevailing enthusiasm until Hugo made the introductions. "Eduardo, this fine young fellow is Pablo. Pablo, meet señor Volante—"

The youngster, reassured by the fact that señor Volante was clearly a kind, affable gentleman, rose to shake his hand and greeted him in Spanish. "It is a pleasure to meet you, sir. I will study hard and you will not be disappointed."

Volante smiled warmly. "With such a positive attitude, I have no doubt that you will do well, Pablo." He paused to thank María for bringing him a cup of spiced coffee and a plate of cinnamon fritters. "Señor Wilde has asked me to help you with your English as well as your general education, so we will speak in English for much of the time. How does that sound?"

"It sounds wonderful, sir!"

"Señor Wilde has also mentioned that you are as bright as a button, Pablo, and that you have great potential. I see it, too. You will do very well."

Señor Volante strongly reminded Pablo of his own dear departed father, and he couldn't have been happier at the prospect of being under his tutelage. Hugo and María looked on like proud parents and shared smiles. Copernicus, who was not at all interested in who was educating whom, sat back with hind legs pointing to the ceiling and licked the part of him where his balls used to be.

Sofia and Hugo had determined that the dining room would double as a classroom for lessons. The table served as a prodigious desk, with Eduardo sitting at its head and Pablo at a right angle to him.

While Hugo could be heard noisily relieving the study of its all fixtures and fittings, master and pupil began to cultivate a climate of mutual respect. The boy took instruction extremely well, retaining all that he was taught, and for his part señor Volante was delighted to have landed such an eager student. The tutor's voice was gentle, like the lapping of waves, and he knew how to extract the best from Pablo in the shortest amount of time. He expounded philosophy as freely as most men discuss football, and proved not only to be a great linguist but also to have an encyclopaedic breadth of knowledge, knowing as much about Renaissance art and polar ice caps as he did about pronunciation and prepositions.

Volante was impressed by Pablo's homespun command of the English language and addressed any verbal missteps without a hint of condescension. María replenished them with refreshments throughout the day. At one point Luna tried to eavesdrop unseen from the hallway, but a plume of cigar smoke betrayed her presence. The boy blossomed under Eduardo's considerate supervision and by mid-afternoon had greatly expanded his English vocabulary.

Hugo's study, apart from receiving a lick of paint, had been left as it was before the rest of the house was redecorated and refurbished. The Englishman considered it therapeutic to drag all of the furniture and furnishings from the room and to remove shelves and brackets from its walls. He smoothed screw holes with filler, sanded down the plaster and, in an adherence to conformity, coated the room with white emulsion to create a pure space in which Pablo could work and hang his paintings.

The artist himself, keen to see how his studio was progressing, had brought señor Volante along with him. Verónica, who was meticulously folding the first sheet of a toilet roll into a triangle, offered them a cheery greeting from the downstairs restroom as they continued to the study.

They walked in on Hugo as he was tidying his paint pots and equipment into an orderly pile. He was dressed in a T-shirt and blue jeans; it didn't escape Eduardo's notice that the Englishman's bare arms were brawnier than his long-sleeved shirts had suggested.

The room was now devoid of clutter and bathed in a white radiance. Hefty dustsheets covered the floor entirely. Hugo ran a hand through his paint-flecked hair. "So what do you think, Pablo?"

The boy's eyes grew bright and he rushed to hug his champion. "I love it! I cannot believe what you do for me." He looked to señor Volante for validation, a prompt to reassure him that his English grammar was on track. A reassuring nod and a graceful gesture from his tutor was all that he needed to correct himself. "I cannot believe what you *did* for me."

"Bravo!" said Hugo, patting the boy on the back. "If you're not careful, you'll be talking like me soon."

"Jolly good!" shouted Pablo, causing both Hugo and Eduardo to crease up with laughter.

Once their mild hysterics had subsided, Wilde thanked Volante for his expertise. The Mexican responded by stating that Pablo had made his job so much easier. "The kid has a bright future," he said. "It's a rarity to witness such promise."

Hugo checked his hands to ensure they were free of wet paint and draped his arm across the tutor's shoulders. "Eduardo, do you have any plans for tonight?"

"Nothing special. Why do you ask?"

"Did you know that Vincent and María have announced that they are a couple?"

"I did not, but naturally I am delighted for them both."

"Well, we are hosting a celebratory meal in their honour this very evening and would love for you and Rafa to join us."

A broad smile lifted the contours of Eduardo's snowy beard and crinkled his eyes. "You remembered his name! Yes, of course, Hugo. We would be delighted to attend."

*

Sofia and Vincent arrived home not long after señor Volante had left. They headed straight for the kitchen where Hugo, María and Verónica, together with Luna and Pablo, were sitting around the table engaged in a companionable conversation.

The sight of Vincent's bald head made Hugo do a double take as he hadn't yet become accustomed to it. "So, how did you two get on?" he asked, setting down his cup of tea.

It was clear to them all that Sofia was fizzing with excitement because she was hopping from foot to foot and grinning from ear to ear. "We looked at a few sites and properties, but one clearly stood out from the rest," she enthused. "It's a former school, built in the 1920s, and not too far from here."

Hugo visualised how easily an old school could be converted into an orphanage and immediately warmed to the idea. "Sounds as if it could be a contender. When can I see it?"

Sofia's eyes lit up. "I told the realtor that I would phone him back the moment I knew you were interested."

"I'm definitely interested. Any time on Monday will be fine."

Sofia turned to the phone on the kitchen wall and leafed through her address book. "Really, you are just adorable, my darling. I shall call him now."

O'Toole nodded at his friend. "The school is perfect, Hugo. The plumbing and electrics need an overhaul, but the building is sound."

Hector Cabrales was closing the Venetian blinds in his office against the late-afternoon sun when the phone on his desk rang. "Please forgive me for one moment," he said to his client, plucking the handset from its cradle. "*Bueno.* Hector Cabrales—"

"Mr Cabrales, it's Sofia Ustinova. My partner has confirmed that he would like to view the property on Monday."

"But he is here with me now, Doctor Ustinova."

The physicist held the phone limply in the palm of her hand and fell silent. All eyes were upon her, everyone in the kitchen wondering what the person on the other end of the line had said to rattle her. Space-time contradictions were once again being turned on their head. She stared open-mouthed at Hugo, who in turn gave her a quizzical look and asked what was wrong.

"Hello? Doctor Ustinova? Are you still there?" enquired the realtor, his disembodied voice hanging in mid-air.

Entirely perplexed, the Russian restored the phone to her ear. "Yes, yes. I'm still here… You said that my partner is with you?"

"I did indeed. Mr Wilde arrived shortly after you left the office. Do you want to speak to him?"

Sofia kept her composure. "No, that won't be necessary… It's just that he didn't tell me that he was going to see you."

"I take it that this person *is* your boyfriend?" laughed Hector, giving Hugo a chummy wink.

"Of course he is," said Sofia, trying to think on her feet. "English, handsome, six feet tall, always smiling—"

The realtor nodded in Hugo's direction. "That's him."

Sofia glanced at the real Hugo as a tumult of thoughts erupted in her brilliant mind. Only one made any sense: the probability of extra-terrestrial involvement,.

"One more question, Mr Cabrales, and then I shall leave you in peace. Has Mr Wilde mentioned why he's there?"

Hector smiled at Hugo as the replicant continued

to sit patiently and quietly in a cantilevered office chair. "He wants me to draw up a purchase agreement for the school... Hey, do you two need to talk this over?"

"No, no, it's fine. I shall leave it all up to him ... and, um, please give him my love."

"Will do. Catch you later, Doctor Ustinova."

"*Hasta luego,* Mr Cabrales."

Sofia replaced the handset on its wall mount. Everyone had stopped what they were doing, including Copernicus, who'd taken a break from licking his nether regions.

"What was that all about?" asked Hugo.

"I'll tell you later," said Sofia putting a hand to her forehead. "Right now, I need a stiff drink."

CHAPTER TWENTY-FIVE

The next morning, Hugo was sitting reading in a leather wing-back chair as the streets outside resounded to church bells merrily calling worshippers to Sunday Mass. Because the words in books had become blurry of late, and because he'd begun to hold restaurant menus at arm's length, Hugo had finally surrendered to the realisation that he was of an age where reading glasses would have to be considered.

Vincent walked into the library with the tips of his handlebar moustache curled to perfection and wearing a suit and tie for the first time since his wife's funeral. He stopped for a long moment to regard Wilde's attire. His friend, absorbed in a leather-bound volume of *Les Misérables*, was resplendent in a velvet smoking jacket over an open-necked shirt and cravat. "Jesus, Hugo. I can't quite figure out if you're supposed to be Noël Coward or Sherlock Holmes. You're even wearing monogrammed slippers, for crying out loud."

Hugo lay the book's ribbon marker across the page he'd been reading. "And a very good morning to you too, Vincent. I do feel that a *robe de chambre* lends a certain sartorial elegance to one's wardrobe. Speaking of which, you look the bee's knees, my friend."

Vincent self-consciously fussed with his necktie. "Well, I've taken your advice, and am reconnecting with my faith, starting today. María and I will be attending Mass this morning and Pablo's coming with us."

Perhaps in receipt of this news, the bells of the Church of the Wounded Angel seemed to clang even more joyously. The Englishman congratulated his friend, knowing how much Vincent's faith had meant to him until his wife's death. Hugo also took a moment to acknowledge the fact that the man standing before him was a far cry from the unruly hellraiser of old. He recollected with great fondness the night that the Irishman had drunkenly walked naked through the war-ravaged streets of Pristina playing an awful tune on a trombone that he'd borrowed from a local bandsman.

"Y'know, Vincent, I was thinking about you just before you walked in," said Hugo patting his book as if it were a pet. "You caught me at the very moment where Jean Valjean is carrying valiant Marius to safety through the Paris sewers. It reminded me of that fateful day in Kosovo when you picked me up in a fireman's lift and ferried me to the medic's truck."

"Sweet mother of Jesus. If it had been a filthy sewer I needed to carry you through, Hugo, I'd have let you bleed out on the side of the road."

"Oh, stop it, you romantic fool. You'll have me all

misty-eyed."

His big moustachioed face suddenly diffident, Vincent stepped forward to offer a robust handshake. "On behalf of María and myself, I would like to thank you for the meal that you and Sofia cooked in our honour last night. That was a nice thing you did and it meant a lot to us both."

Hugo saw the earnestness in his friend's Irish eyes and it touched him deeply. "Come here, you big ape," he said, rising from his chair. "Let's hug it out."

They shared a brawny embrace which culminated in Vincent lifting Hugo high off his feet in a demonstrative bear hug.

"A-ha! While I'm up here, I'll give your bald head a shine," said Hugo, vigorously buffing Vincent's dome with his jacket sleeve.

María stepped into the room wearing a tweed skirt suit, white satin gloves and a pillbox hat with a net veil. Sofia and Luna, acting as her ladies-in-waiting, stood proudly behind her. "Ay, ay, ay!" yelled the cook upon witnessing the men's horseplay. "You two are like children in the school playground."

Vincent unhanded Hugo and stood utterly transfixed before his sweetheart. Hugo imagined love hearts popping from his friend's eyes.

"You look pretty as a picture, my darlin'," Vincent cooed, lifting María's veil and kissing her on both cheeks.

"I totally agree," said Hugo, adding to the kisses.

The cook had a tear in her eye as she produced a

crucifix and chain from her purse. "This is a gift I give to you, Vincent," she said placing it in his ginormous hand. "The crucifix reminds us that there is no true love without sacrifice."

Her words brought a lump to the Irishman's throat. He kissed the representation of Jesus and fastened the chain behind his head before tucking it into his shirt. "I shall wear it always, my little darlin'," he said, his eyes twinkling with Gaelic charm.

Pablo appeared in the library's doorway, slightly forlorn in the black suit that he had worn for his father's burial. The family recognised his sadness and swamped him with hugs and kisses. Verónica appeared from nowhere and joined in. Luna patted him on the back.

Vincent lay a heavy arm across the boy's shoulders and held María's hand. "Right, if you're all done smothering the lad, we three believers have a date with God."

As María, Vincent and Pablo ascended the stone steps of the Church of the Wounded Angel, an ethereal shaft of sunshine came down upon them from the heavens and the bells pealed ever louder. The trio crossed themselves with holy water and took their place in a pew, receiving companionable smiles from those around them. María, for the hundredth time, entreated Vincent to pray to Our Lady of Guadalupe, a Mexican version of the Virgin Mary, who had once appeared before a lowly peasant and spoken to him in his native tongue.

"Our Lady is the mother of all Mexicans," she explained, pointing to a likeness of the hallowed saint on a leaded window in which she was surrounded by an aureole of radiant light. "And the peasant was Juan Diego, who became the patron saint of indigenous Mexicans."

Throughout the service, Vincent felt a reawakening in his soul. Though he couldn't sing along to the Spanish hymns or understand any of the sermons, he savoured the familiarity of the ritual: the deference of the congregants; the sonorous sound of the church organ; the smell of lit candles, and the smoky perfume of an incense burner as it was swung down the aisle by an altar server.

Having absolved Vincent of all his sins in the confessional a few days earlier, and because he was as conspicuous as a walrus amid a colony of penguins, Father Pedroza's eyes were unavoidably drawn to the sight of the giant Irishman in the crowd. The priest wondered with great compassion what terrible affliction had caused the poor fellow to suddenly lose all his hair.

Vincent looked up to the rafters through dewy eyes, hoping to catch sight of his dear Kathleen floating in a golden light and surrounded by a choir of angels. Though he didn't see her, he felt her presence and trusted that she was safe in the hands of the Lord.

The congregation was united in spirit and prayer and at the end of mass, María, Vincent and Pablo shook hands with strangers who would one day become friends.

As the worshippers filed from the church, Father Pedroza stood at the top of the steps in his white Sunday finery and greeted as many of the congregants as was humanly possible. When Vincent stood before him, blocking out the sun, his heart swelled with pride. "Señor O'Toole! I cannot tell you how many times I have prayed for this day. You once told me that God was no longer in your heart and that tequila had become your new patron saint. No doubt María has played a big part in this."

María smiled bashfully and Vincent held her closer. "Absolutely, Father. This beautiful lady has brought the light back into my life and I love her to bits."

The priest, a conjurer of poetic metaphors, offered the couple some spiritual guidance. "Always remember that love, much like our faith in God, is the kite we must fly even on a windless day." He blessed them both with the sign of the cross.

Vincent and María bade Father Pedroza goodbye and rejoined Pablo at the base of the steps. As the three walked home arm in arm, Kathleen O'Toole looked down from afar and gave them her blessing.

CHAPTER TWENTY-SIX

Mexico City, 1942

Having recently turned sixteen, Severiano Salazar was set to begin his first day as a junior manservant to the family of Érik de Generar, a famous and extremely wealthy industrialist of murky repute. Born into a lower middle-class family, Severiano's parents had long since lost all faith in him and instead devoted most of their time, love and money to Próspero, his flawless younger brother. Severiano's father, a deceitful man with hidden gambling debts, worked in the purchasing department of the company that Señor de Generar owned. By spotting the vacant position on a staff notice board, he had happened upon a golden opportunity to get his rancid son out from under his feet.

"This will be the making of you, my boy," said his father, lying through his teeth. "I have it on good authority that the best households train their staff in all aspects of service, from appreciating the world's finest wines through to greeting the world's most illustrious dignitaries. While you are living under their roof, you will undoubtedly sleep on satin bedsheets and eat like a king!"

Less than one week later, on the same day that Mexico declared war on Germany for torpedoing five of its oil tankers, Severiano stood at the front door of the industrialist's house at the appointed time, trembling with apprehension and clutching a small leather suitcase.

His father, who had frogmarched him onto three separate buses and walked with him for the remainder, shook his hand stiffly and wished him luck. "Give it your best, Severiano, and remember to write to your mother when you can." Mr Salazar then fled the scene, his trench coat flapping about him like a cape, leaving his son to stare fearfully at the imposing oak door with its enormous iron hinges.

After taking a deep intake of breath, Severiano clutched the brass door knocker and gave it three sharp raps. While waiting for a response, he set down the suitcase and ensured that the top of his hair was neatly parted in the centre, greasing it down with his bony fingers.

The door opened and a vampirish butler with knife-edge creases in his trousers loomed over him. "Yes?" said the man curtly, his lips a cruel red.

Severiano proffered a slip of paper which was summarily ignored. "My name is Severiano Salazar. I am here for the position of trainee manservant, señor."

"Come to the back of the house, boy!" growled the butler.

"The back, señor?" said Severiano, furrowing his brow.

"The back, you simpleton! The back! Where do you suppose the back of the house is?" With that, the butler slammed the door in Severiano's miserable face.

Because of the sheer size of the house, it took the boy several minutes to reach its rear. Once there, he rapped on another knocker, set down his suitcase and slicked his centre parting again.

The door opened abruptly. "Yes?" snapped the vampirish butler, as if he'd never set eyes on Severiano before.

"You just sent me around to the back door, señor," said the boy hesitantly, trying not to seem as if he was stating the obvious.

"So I did. What took you so long? Come in, boy, and wipe your feet."

The house was Moorish in design with peacocks strutting around its large central courtyard. Countless photographs of Érik de Generar pictured alongside movie stars and prominent politicians dotted the wide corridors. On one of them, he was even snapped rubbing shoulders with President Ávila Camacho and his wife. Because Severiano had ignored much of his father's puffery, he hadn't hitherto realised that his employer was such an influential man.

"My name is Frederick Lobo," said the butler, walking at a pace that he expected Severiano to match. "But you will address me at all times as Mr Lobo.

Have you got that?"

"Yes, Mr Lobo," the boy mumbled, unnerved by the man's long fingernails and the icy air that surrounded him.

"I understand that you were taken on by Señor de Generar's executive secretary without the formality of an interview," the butler continued. "You are therefore here on a trial basis only. It is I who will decide whether you are to stay or leave. Is that understood?"

"Yes, sir … Mr Lobo, sir."

"They are called bifurcated stairs," said Lobo, noting the astonishment on Severiano's face when he was confronted by a monumental staircase that split off into two different directions. "You are not to use them. The staff accommodation, including my own, is accessible via a back staircase, to which we shall proceed."

Severiano was taken to his quarters, a bedchamber with scarcely enough room to swing a cat. It occurred to him that rather than sleeping on a bed with satin sheets as his father had envisaged, he would be lying on a thin mattress under a rough woollen blanket. As for his father's assertion that he would be eating like a king, it transpired that Irma Gómez, who ran the kitchen, had all the culinary skills of a jailhouse cook. She served up soups as thin as puddles and loaves that could have doubled as doorstops.

The butler cursorily introduced Severiano to the staff: the cook, her kitchen maid, and Ignacia, a wild-eyed Chilean housemaid who glared fiercely at the new boy as she ground corn on a stone *metate* to make dough for tortillas.

At every opportunity, Mr Lobo made it abundantly clear that he was the boss. Severiano was soon in awe of the man, regarding him as both charismatic and monstrous at the same time.

"Just as you are to be my understudy, I also oversee the housekeeper, the cook, the maids and the laundress," Lobo said, speaking in clipped sentences and staring into Severiano's soul. "You are an unpleasant creature, Salazar, but thankfully I know how to make a silk purse from a sow's ear. Here is your uniform. You must wear it at all times."

Severiano was put to work immediately carting consignments of food and wine from a succession of delivery vans to the storeroom in between ironing the master's shirts and undergarments. He was told that Señor de Generar owned a shirt for every day of the year and that his walk-in closet was the size of a doctor's waiting room. He was further told that only Mr Lobo and Señor de Generar himself were allowed access to it.

While he was in the process of pressing yet another item of clothing, wearing a uniform two sizes too big for him, Severiano wondered how his young life had come to this. He had dreamt of moving to America where he would learn to speak like Clark Gable and dance like Fred Astaire, where he would marry Joan Crawford, even though he didn't particularly like women, and own a mansion in Beverly Hills.

As it was, he was a friendless individual whose only highpoint in life had been the day in which he had hospitalised his brother by slipping rat poison into his coffee. Against his parents' expectations, he had been absolved of all suspicion. The attending doctor, who didn't know his arse from his elbow, had declared the brother's sickness to be nothing more than a severe bout of food poisoning.

Before lunch was due to be served the mistress of the house, señora Miriam de Generar, accompanied by her Tweedledum and Tweedledee kids, showed her expressionless face in the kitchen to enquire if all was running smoothly. She disappeared almost as soon as she had arrived, nodding like a cockatoo to everyone she passed.

Señor de Generar was an altogether different kettle of fish. Upon his return, the well-upholstered tycoon waddled into the kitchen full of bonhomie and asked to be introduced to the new boy. Severiano was immediately summoned from the laundry room and de Generar's eyes lit up upon seeing the lad's weaselly face.

"Well, what a fine boy!" he proclaimed, licking his lips and waving dainty fingers that seemed disproportionate to his size. "Not handsome by any means, but a fine addition to the household, eh, Mr Lobo?"

"Only time will tell," said the butler dryly.

The industrialist, as if to mark his turf, occupied the centre of the kitchen and started to orate a speech which made it clear to the newcomer that the mansion was under patriarchal rule. "Let it be known, Salazar, that I am the head of this house, not my wife. Her role, you see, is primarily one of child-rearing and the performance of conjugal duties."

Although the ladies in attendance looked daggers at the misogynistic buffoon, his chauvinistic precept seemed perfectly reasonable to Severiano.

"I am the one who pays your wages," de Generar continued, directing a manicured finger at his scullions. "I am the one who is out meeting heads of state while you lot are attending to menial tasks, so don't you forget it."

"Yes, sir!" said Ignacia, clicking her heels and giving him a military salute.

De Generar did a double take, unsure whether the Chilean was being sarcastic or not. She grinned back at him, her feral eyes defiant. "Well, go about your business, everyone," he blustered, wiping his fat neck with a handkerchief and heading for the door.

He paused to cast the new boy a sly wink. "No doubt, I will see you later, Chico."

"It's Severiano, sir."

"Must it be Severiano?" said the master irascibly. "Mother of God, you are a finicky fellow."

*

Something about Severiano had piqued Mr Lobo's interest and he observed the boy in the way that a lizard watches a fly. He saw that the lad was shifty, noticed the insincerity in his thin smile, and was thrilled by his spiteful nature and complete lack of empathy. In short, he saw the devil within.

Lobo slyly observed his understudy from an upstairs window as the teenager took delivery of a consignment of avocados at the back door. "You don't know it yet, Salazar," he muttered to himself, "but you, dear boy, are a sociopath." The butler was certain of this because it took one to know one.

*

Once night had fallen, Severiano crept about the house like a vengeful ghost, exploring areas that were off limits to the staff and skulking in the shadows each time he heard footsteps approaching. He'd happened upon de Generar's enormous walk-in closet and, acting on impulse and knowing they would not be missed, had stolen a pair of shoes from the master's vast collection.

After everyone else had taken their turn, Severiano availed himself of the staff bathroom. He hung his uniform on the back of a rattan chair before filling the claw-footed tub with cold water. As he scrubbed his clammy skin under the dim glow of a naked lightbulb, he heard the door rattle against its bolt. "It's engaged!" he yelled out to whoever was on the other side.

The rattling stopped.

"Severiano, it's me, Señor de Generar. I wondered if I might come in for a friendly chat?"

The youngster hung his scrawny arms over the rim

of the tub. Water dripped from his fingers. "I am in the bath, sir."

"Pleased to hear it. Then maybe I could give you a thorough clean while we have our chat?"

Severiano's face soured. "I would not like that, sir."

There was a pause on the other side of the door. "Not a good time perhaps?"

"No, sir."

Another pause. "So, you would like me to go then, Severiano?"

"I think it would be best, sir."

*

Mr Lobo, immaculate in his butler's uniform and seemingly appearing from nowhere, encountered Severiano on the staff corridor the following morning. The boy's face, he noticed, was even more miserable than it had been the previous day. "Salazar. I trust you slept well?" he asked.

"Sleep is the least of my worries, Mr Lobo."

The butler's satanic eyes smouldered. "Really? You must tell me more," he pressed, despite already knowing the answer.

Severiano hung his head. "If I may be so bold, sir, the master is the problem."

Lobo gnawed the air with his sharp teeth. "Go on—"

"The way in which he comes on to me makes me feel sick to my stomach," Severiano said, waving away the memory of last night as if it were cigarette smoke.

"The man disgusts me. I do not think I can stay in this house any longer."

Lobo took a moment to consider his answer. "Hmm, now you can see why my last understudy left, and also the one before him." He lifted Severiano's chin on the tip of his fingernail, forcing the boy to look at his terrifying smile. "What if I were to tell you that there is a way to hit the master where it hurts, yet without it costing you your job?" he suggested. "And it doesn't end there. You could earn yourself a great deal of money in the process. How does that grab you?"

"It sounds good," said Severiano, keen to avoid the ignominy of returning home to his parents in disgrace. "It also sounds too good to be true."

"Not so. Everyone has a weakness that can be exploited," said the butler lowering his voice. "You already know de Generar's weakness, as do I."

Although he was almost incapable of showing it, Severiano's mood brightened appreciably. "So, what are you saying?"

"I have been working on a plan to extort money from the boss by obtaining evidence of his debauchery and threatening to take it to the newspapers. It occurs to me that you might be able to add the finishing touch."

Mr Lobo went on to explain that señora de Generar, whose father was a high-ranking politician and a close friend of the president, was wholly unaware of her husband's extra-marital affairs and his sexual kinks.

Miriam was an influential figure on the city's social scene; were she to find out about his dalliances, she would do everything in her power to drag his name through the mud and make him a social pariah.

"He will pay a small fortune to save his reputation," said Lobo, raising a prophetic finger. "With that in mind, I am going to set a trap for him and would like to enlist your help."

A vindictive leer appeared on Severiano's face. "What do you need me to do?"

*

During the course of the day Severiano stuck grimly to his allotted tasks, lighting fires, cleaning bathrooms, polishing shoes and taking care of deliveries. For reasons known only to herself, Ignacia smiled salaciously at him each time he passed her in the courtyard, though she might just as well have smiled at her own foot for all the good it did.

Mr Lobo, for the purpose of implementing his cunning plan, had earlier provided Severiano with a spare door key to his plush bedroom and an unwieldy camera of the type that press photographers bring to murder scenes and movie premieres. The butler had talked his understudy through the plan of action several times until he was certain that it would run like clockwork.

"I have set the focus, so you don't need to," he had instructed while getting the boy used to the feel of the camera. "All you need do is stand three feet away from the bed and press this red button. Leave the rest to me."

Severiano prided himself on being a quick learner and felt perfectly capable of fulfilling his nefarious role with cool-headed precision.

"And one last thing, Salazar," said Lobo, skewering the youngster with a penetrating stare. "No matter what you see in that room, no matter how unpalatable, you must not let it throw you. You must hold your nerve. Do you understand?"

"I understand perfectly, Mr Lobo."

*

Throughout the evening, Severiano nervously observed the Bakelite clock in his bedroom for what seemed like an eternity. Validating the precept that a watched pot never boils, the clock's filigree hands seemed to resent being stared at and were reluctant to budge. Even so, the minute hand had crept inexorably towards the predetermined time of 11pm and moths begun to flutter in Severiano's stomach.

With senses heightened, he stepped out onto the dark landing and crept towards Mr Lobo's room, his inky shadow haunting the walls. Never had a camera been so ungainly nor a heartbeat so rapid and, before he was even ready, the door was upon him.

He heard laughter, unrestrained and earthy, emanating from within. Severiano held the camera by its flashgun and fumbled for the door key before slowly turning it in the lock. He froze, thinking that he must have been heard, but the laughter continued unabated. His mouth was dry and he could scarcely breathe, but there was no turning back.

He opened the door and, in one heart-stopping moment, burst into the room. Time stood still as he took in the astonishing scene before him. Señor de Generar was wide-eyed and naked in the middle of the bed with rabbit ears on his head and a feather boa around his neck. Also naked, and on either side of him, were Mr Lobo and Ignacia.

Severiano stood three feet away and took aim. The flash bulb popped in an explosion of light, illuminating the horrified tycoon and his two smiling companions.

"You little shit!" shouted de Generar, covering his button-mushroom penis with a pillow. "How dare you invade our privacy?"

"Thank you, Salazar, that will be all," said Mr Lobo calmly.

Severiano turned on his heels, the flash-bulb glass crunching underfoot, and desperately tried to unsee all that he had witnessed.

*

"To the victor comes the spoils," announced Mr Lobo three days later, presenting Severiano with his share of the blackmail money after the youngster had answered a knock at his bedroom door. "You are holding the equivalent of six months' wages, just for doing five minutes' work."

Though he remained appalled by his handler's

predilections and hadn't been able to look him in the eye since that night, a wide smile crept across the boy's face, an occurrence as rare as a meteor strike. "I appreciate this, Mr Lobo. I have never seen so much money."

The butler waved the boy's gratitude away. "Ignacia will receive the same amount and I have taken the lion's share. Once I'd shown that dupe the photograph, it was a *fait accompli*. He knew I had him by the balls."

Severiano, not wishing to be reminded of Señor de Generar's ghastly balls, stuffed the banknotes into his pockets and thanked his mentor once again.

"I don't want thank yous," the butler hissed, baring his spiteful teeth. "Thank yous are for losers. As you journey through this life, Salazar, remember that everyone has a secret that can be exploited."

CHAPTER TWENTY-SEVEN

Señor Volante arrived for his latest teaching stint and was met warmly at the front door by Hugo, who had abandoned his smoking jacket in favour of a more subdued trouser and shirt combination.

"How is Rafa?" asked the Englishman.

"He is very good, thank you," the Mexican beamed. "And of course he sends his best regards."

María was out of the blocks the moment she heard the doorbell jangle. She came rushing from the kitchen to greet her childhood friend with cilantro hugs and chipotle kisses.

"Mmmm, you smell so wonderful, María," said the bookseller, tipping his hat to her. "A feast for the nose as well as the eyes."

The cook fluffed her friend's white beard with her fingers. "Would you like some pancakes with your coffee, Eduardo?"

Volante's eyes lit up. "Is the Pope a Catholic? Of course I would like pancakes!"

"Then I will bring them to you," beamed María. "And how about you, Hugo?"

"Count me in," he smiled. "Thank you, María. We'll be in the library, if you would be so kind."

Vincent poked his big head round the kitchen door. "Hey! You'd better not be chatting up my girlfriend, Eduardo."

Volante put up his dainty fists. "I will fight you for her, señor."

"Jesus. In that case, she's yours," grinned the Irishman.

Hugo escorted Eduardo to the library, where an atmosphere of studious calm prevailed. Sofia was reading on the chaise longue with her legs tucked underneath her, while Luna was belly down on a Persian rug engrossed in *The Structure of Scientific Revolutions*, by Thomas S Kuhn.

Once the usual pleasantries had been exchanged, Volante surveyed the bookshelves and was pleased to see that they were now replete with an extravaganza of well-chosen publications. Luna, seizing any opportunity to test the fluency of her Spanish, sat up cross-legged on the rug and immediately engaged the tutor in a quickfire conversation. Eduardo, astonished that he didn't have to modify his speech to allow her to keep pace, talked with her as he would a local. The Dane had reached the stage where she could read a Mexican broadsheet as easily as she could peruse a food menu, and took great satisfaction in being able to eavesdrop on conversations in cafeterias and on buses.

Sofia sat forward on the chaise longue and made a point of showing Volante a ragged fringe of paper that existed inside the book she was reading. "Really, there is nothing quite so annoying as a page torn from a book," she grumbled. "What would prompt a person to engage in such vandalism?"

Eduardo took a moment to ponder the question before speaking. "Perhaps there might have been a line on that page so relatable to the person who read it that they could no more resist ripping it from the book than you or I could resist the urge to smell a lily," he speculated. "It may have reminded them of a personal triumph, or perchance a family member who had passed to the other side. It might even have evoked memories of a lover who had once set their pulse racing."

"But it's still annoying," Sofia reiterated.

"Oh, yes. It is still annoying," said Eduardo with an insouciant shrug.

María bustled in carrying a stacked plate of banana pancakes on a silver platter. "I shall return with a pot of coffee and a jug of water-melon juice," she announced, caught in two minds as the loud cries of the water-delivery man suddenly drifted in from the street.

"*Aguaaa! Aguaaa!*" the vendor called out at the top of his lungs, trilling his tricycle bell.

"I'll take care of the drinks while you're dealing with the water guy," said Luna springing to her feet.

"Thank you so much, my princess," replied the cook, trotting off to find her purse.

Eduardo and Hugo, meanwhile, had helped

themselves to pancakes.

"Before I set off to fetch him, how is Pablo faring with his lessons?" asked the Englishman.

"Incredibly well, considering that it is not yet two months since the death of his father," said the tutor, knitting his hands and twiddling his thumbs. "Pablo is an intelligent boy. Had he been able to attend a better school, he would have excelled in most subjects. But, casting personal tragedies and lack of opportunities aside, his future is now very bright – thanks, of course, to you and Sofia."

"Well, that's very kind of you," said Hugo. "We're both extremely proud of him."

"It bodes well that yours is a family that doesn't entirely rely on a television set for its edification," Volante continued. "It is my firm belief that future generations will lose both the capacity to think for themselves and the ability to lift their backsides from an armchair."

Sofia entered the conversation and stressed to the tutor that she and Hugo wanted to give Luna and Pablo every chance in life. She went on to say that they hoped each youngster would go on to realise their potential.

Eduardo fished a cloth from a jacket pocket to clean his spectacles. "Clearly, they are both exceptional in their own way. And I think it was Jean-Paul Sartre who suggested that life begins on the other side of despair, an assertion that is certainly true in their case."

While Hugo was heading upstairs to fetch him, Pablo stood before a bedroom shrine that he'd adorned with photographs of his parents and garlanded with marigolds. Also jostling for prominence were food offerings, tin-framed images of various saints, an assortment of tealights and incense sticks and a statuette of the Virgin of Guadalupe. As was his custom every morning, Pablo lit candles for his mother and father and murmured a prayer asking that they remain safe in God's presence and happy in each other's arms.

He stood before a mirror and ran a comb through his hair in readiness for the day's tuition. Since coming to the house, his face had become fuller and he'd put meat on his bones, testament to the steady stream of nutritious food from María's kitchen. And, as was evident in the mirror, he was on the first rungs to becoming a man; a caterpillar of downy fuzz had recently crawled across his upper lip, and his voice had dived a few octaves deeper.

He had also subscribed to the Charles Atlas 'Dynamic Tension' program, having seen a comic-strip advertisement for it in a magazine. The strip depicted the story of Mac, a seven-stone weakling who had suffered the ignominy of having sand kicked in his face by a bully on the beach. Mac's girlfriend, irritated that he didn't stand up to the brute, called him a 'little boy' and promptly broke off their relationship. Thanks to Mr Atlas's unique bodybuilding method, where no lifting of weights were necessary, the skinny teenager was able to return to the beach with muscles aplenty and exacted sweet revenge on his former tormentor by punching him on the jaw.

The defining moment for Pablo came when the boy's ex-girlfriend, captivated by his new-found virility, said, "Oh! Mac! You ARE a real man after all!" And, as if that were not enough, a beautiful female who was presumably unknown to Mac and who happened to look great in a bikini, made no secret of her admiration by exclaiming, "Gosh! What a build!" This astonishing reversal of fortune, and the fact that it was obviously a true story, sold the program to Pablo and so he sent off for the book. Despite faithfully following Mr Atlas's isometric exercises every day for a month, his physique remained lean rather than muscled, but he lived in the hope that one day he would be able to emulate Mac's magnificent transformation.

Hugo knocked on Pablo's door and called through it, informing him of Mr Volante's arrival. Grabbing his exercise books and pens on the way, the boy opened the door and brightened the morning with his sunshine smile.

Hugo draped a fatherly hand his shoulder as they descended the stairs. "Señor Volante tells me that you are doing very well, Pablo. It goes without saying that Sofia and I could not be prouder."

"This makes me so happy, señor Hugo. I want to learn everything in this world, and señor Volante, he teach to me many, many things."

"Good to hear, Pablo. And how is the art coming along?"

At this, the boy beamed with unalloyed delight. "My art is my *pasión,* señor Hugo. It is my love, my heart," he rhapsodised, patting his chest. "Here, I am free to paint all of my dreams with only a brush in my hand."

They joined señor Volante in the dining room where the teacher had spread a time-worn atlas and several reference books across the table. Copernicus was curled in on himself and sound asleep on a sunny windowsill. Hugo bade tutor and pupil a fruitful day and returned to Sofia and Luna in the library.

In the intervening hours, as well as familiarising him with the past participles of English verbs, señor Volante regaled his eager student with tales hewn from momentous events in history including the Chinese Age of Invention, the rise and fall of the Aztec civilisation, Hannibal crossing the Alps on the back of an elephant, the storming of the Bastille and the story of how the bowler-hatted Wright brothers had built the world's first aeroplane. His avuncular charm and mellifluous retelling of history had Pablo completely in his thrall. Never before had a student been so committed or so thankful, and at the end of each lesson he made a point of expressing his deep gratitude.

"The pleasure is all mine, dear boy," replied señor Volante. "There is no greater honour on earth than to share one's wisdom with those who seek it."

*

At the cessation of the day's lessons, and after helping señor Volante to carry his books to his car, Pablo took advantage of the late-afternoon daylight to put paint to canvas. Inspired by the work of Mexican surrealists, the white walls of his studio were adorned with a growing collection of his paintings.

He was possessed of a speculative imagination that allowed intuition and unorthodoxy to take the place of observation, and his compositions somehow managed to be both nightmarish and romantic at the same time. As he was on a transformative journey and hadn't yet mastered his craft, he regarded his work either with a sense of fulfilment or a feeling of dissatisfaction. Among many other things, he depicted a fisherman in a rowing boat that was, upon closer inspection, a giant human ear. He characterised a chimpanzee in a monocle and deerstalker hat, and a sisterhood of nuns huddled together on a platform of floating ice. He painted giraffes with rocking-horse legs, put flamingos on roller skates and portrayed a mother who, having given birth to a fish, seemed to love her abominable newborn no matter what it looked like.

Influenced by señor Volante's story of Hannibal and his marauding army crossing the Alps to do battle with the Romans, Pablo started work on a stylised painting that he hoped would represent the audaciousness of such an attack. Just then he heard an unanticipated noise swishing in from the hallway and felt the draught of something by his ear. To his surprise, in a flash of feathers, a finch had darted past him and flown headlong into a window pane. A pitiful sight, it lay motionless on the windowsill, flat on its back with its little claws in the air. Pablo, assuming that it was merely stunned, conveyed it gently through the house and out into the fountain courtyard, where he hoped it would once again take to the air. But it didn't; it remained lifeless in his hands.

He rushed back into the house, called out for Luna and found her clattering on a typewriter in the library. "Please help me," he asked, desperation in his voice. "This bird, it fly into the window, but now it does not move."

Luna carefully took the finch from his hand. It was one she recognised. "Why did you bring him to me?" she asked with keen interest as she carried it out to the courtyard.

"Because I know that they like you … the birds and the animals, I mean."

Once outside, Luna parted the bird's tiny beak and blew softly into its lungs, then she massaged its chest gently with one finger. Soon the creature was up on unsteady feet, wondering what on earth had happened. Once recovered, it thanked her with an exultant chirp and flew off to join its friends and family.

"You did the right thing by coming to me," said Luna, switching to Spanish.

Pablo was lost in the crystalline brightness of her eyes. "Please, Luna, keep talking to me in English. It will help me to improve."

"I could speak to you in Danish, if you would like," she teased.

"Oh, I am not so ready for that," he said shyly, looking down at his feet. "Um, Luna, I want to tell you that I had a dream about you last night—"

"You can keep your filthy dreams to yourself."

"No, it was not like that," he squirmed, blushing vividly. "I dream that you were in much danger and I, um ... *rescató*—?"

"Rescued."

"Yes, I rescued you."

Though her countenance gave little away, Luna was touched that Pablo had dreamt about her. She, of course, had dreamt about him long before they'd even met and had secretly continued to do so with increasing regularity. She noted the pride that Pablo had in his imaginary heroics and appreciated the pluck it had taken for him to speak of it.

"Then I must thank you for your bravery," she said graciously.

"Oh, it was my pleasure," he replied unable to hold her piercing gaze. "But it was only a dream."

Luna, enjoying his discomfort, jabbed him in the arm. "So when are you going to show me your artwork?"

Pablo was taken aback but delighted that she had expressed an interest. "Really?" he gasped. "You would like to look at my paintings?"

"No, I would like to listen to them," she said

sarcastically.

Beyond excited, Pablo ushered her into the house. "Please, please. I would love to share with you."

Luna marched ahead of him for almost the entire length of the hallway then turned into his studio. The space was light, airy and covered in paint-spattered dust sheets. In its centre was an artist's easel, adjacent to which was a trestle table covered in reused fruit tins filled with paint brushes of differing sizes. In front of the easel was a wooden stool, which was every bit as paint spattered as the dust sheet beneath it.

She patrolled the room, stopping every now and then to study Pablo's finished paintings. She felt that the space had a curatorial feel and offered a fascinating insight into the artistic workings of his mind. Pablo, meanwhile, waited on tenterhooks, desperately hoping that she would approve of his art. She saw by the look on his face how much her opinion meant to him and realised that this studio was both his sanctuary and the epicentre of his creativity.

"I really like them," she said, staring directly at him. "Your paintings are like your dreams, yes?"

The relief on Pablo's face was palpable. "Oh, thank you!" he exclaimed. "Yes, some are like my dreams, some are like my nightmares."

Luna had looked to see if she could spot herself in any of the paintings and was disappointed not to have done so. Nevertheless, she sought to offer her encouragement in a way that didn't make her seem too eager. "You should definitely pursue this dream," she prompted, fiddling with an aluminium tube of acrylic paint and choosing her words carefully. "I can see you being famous one day."

Pablo was flabbergasted; this was the first time that Luna had paid him anything akin to a compliment. "Famous?" he sputtered. "Thank you, but I am not good enough to be famous."

Luna moved forward and stared deep into his Bambi eyes. "Listen to me, Pablo, and listen carefully. You are going be famous." The artist opened his mouth to protest, but she cut him dead. "You are going to be famous, and I know it to be true. So shut up."

"Okay."

Luna caught sight of what appeared to be a page that had been ripped from a magazine and pinned to one of the walls. It depicted a grainy black-and-white photograph of a Herculean man who was dressed in nothing but a baggy pair of leopardskin swim trunks. "Who is this?" she frowned, reading an honorific that stated 'The World's Most Perfectly-Developed Man.'

"Oh, he is señor Charles Atlas," Pablo beamed. "One day I hope to be just like him."

Luna was less than impressed and moved on from Mr Atlas without feeling the need to ask further questions. An idea had occurred to her, though, and she strode towards the window to survey the sky. "Pablo, would you like to walk with me to the park?" She spoke with her back to him, turning her head east and west. "It's still glorious outside and you know how I love to be among the trees." Had she turned around at that moment, Luna would have seen the unbridled delight on Pablo's face.

"I would love to walk with you," he enthused.

"Good. Then let's go."

They passed Hugo in the hallway. He had surfaced from the cellar with three bottles of wine tucked precariously under one arm and had carefully set them down so he could lock the door behind him. "Where are you two off to?" he asked, slipping the key into his pocket.

"To the park," said Luna casually.

Hugo had somehow gone from being an elite assassin to a concerned parent in a matter of months. He resisted the urge to tell them to be back for their supper and instead gave them money and wished them a good time.

As Luna and Pablo walked through the fountain courtyard, the late-afternoon sun broke through the clouds and an orchestra of crickets played their violins in celebration. The teenagers locked the wrought-iron gate behind them and stepped out onto a street that was alive with the noise of traffic and the trundling of carts.

Pablo, just as his father had taught him, ensured that he walked on the outer side of the sidewalk, keeping Luna to the inside. "Why do you love the trees so much?" he asked her.

"Because trees are the highest life forms on the planet," she said, opening her parasol. "Without them, nothing would exist. But try telling that to the idiots who chop down our forests."

While she was on the subject of environmental destruction, Luna shared her contention that humankind's lack of respect for nature would one day cause irreversible damage to the planet. Despite not being able to understand the gist of what she was saying fully, Pablo nodded politely and made all of the right noises as she warned of rising sea levels and punishing extremes of weather.

"You make me very afraid for the future," said Pablo, passing a man who sold fruit from the trunk of his car.

"Don't be. Even though the governments of the world are incredibly selfish and stupid, they are surely not so stupid that they won't wake up to this."

As they continued on their journey, Pablo recalled seeing Hugo appear through the cellar door earlier with key in hand. This prompted him to air an issue that had plagued him for some time. "Luna, could you please tell me something?" he asked hesitantly. "Did you ever go down to the basement?"

She stopped walking and looked at him for a long moment. "Only once. Why do you ask?"

"Oh, because nobody is allow," he said with a shrug. "Only señores Hugo and Vincent, and señora Sofia are allow. Is there a big secret?"

Luna smiled to herself. "Some things are best kept a mystery, Pablo," she replied, thinking about her own secrets. "They will tell you when the time is right. I am sure of it."

"But I am worry that it is a very bad secret," he winced.

"Oh, no, it's not bad at all. You have no need to worry."

Pablo's subsequent enquiries about her past life in Denmark pushed Luna into being economical with the truth, so she deftly brought the topic of conversation back to his childhood. He talked freely about family holidays to Puerto Vallarta when it was little more than a sleepy fishing village, and how daunting Mexico City had seemed to him when they had first arrived in the dead of night with all of their worldly possessions crammed into the back of a tarpaulined fruit truck.

They picked up the pace and reached the northern entrance to the park, where Pablo stopped at a trailer to buy ice creams, a pineapple one for himself and a coconut one for Luna. Birds could be heard calling to her from the trees as the two sat upon low plastic chairs provided by the vendor.

"I am seventeen tomorrow," announced Pablo in the midst of their conversation, as if heralding a momentous event.

"Then we might share the same birthday," said Luna, not sounding very interested. "It was at this time of year that my adoptive father found me abandoned in the forest."

"Oh. It is sad that you do not even know your birthday."

"I couldn't care less, *amigo*. There are far worse

things in life."

As they seemed to be getting on so well, Pablo gingerly seized the opportunity to air a sentiment that had remained uppermost in his mind from the moment he had first set eyes on her. "Luna—" he began, looking down at his feet. "Even before the day we meet, I think we know each other, yes?"

Luna knew the truth of what he was struggling to say but preferred to deny its existence. "How could we already know each other if we hadn't even met?" she snapped. "What a ridiculous thing to come out with."

Though wounded, Pablo saw no sense in stopping that which he had started. "I saw you in my dreams for many years. And here you are."

Luna dropped her half-eaten cone in the trash and wiped her sticky fingers on a serviette. "Aren't you the lucky one! Come on, let's get moving."

*

After entering the park, and having only achieved a distance of one-hundred yards, they encountered three uncouth teenage boys. The trio were greasy-haired and walked with a synchronised swagger, hogging the pedestrian pathway and talking loudly. Because of her white hair and conspicuous appearance, the ruffians stared openly at Luna as they strutted past. It was an everyday nuisance that she had become accustomed to since moving to the city, but one she found impossible to ignore. "Hey! Do you want a photograph?" she shouted, stopping them in their tracks.

Their leader, a troll with tendrils of oily hair hanging over a spotty forehead, was the first to speak. "So, the ghost girl speaks Spanish," he grinned, continuing to swagger on the spot. "Listen, why don't you go back to the coffin you climbed from, you little freak."

As he and his cohorts cackled like hens, the trees shook their branches in anger, causing a wild flurry of leaves to pepper the air. Luna threw the reprobate a venomous glare and calmly composed her riposte. "Perhaps we could strike a deal?" she countered, furling her parasol. "I will go back to my coffin on the understanding that the three of you return to your swamp."

One of them, who could have been Billy the Kid in a previous incarnation on account of his squirrel teeth and neckerchief, stepped forward and prodded Pablo in the chest. "You need to keep your little girlfriend in check, *cabrón*," he snarled, "because it won't be her who gets the beating."

Luna, stormily protective of Pablo, dropped her parasol and clenched her fists, prepared to take on anyone who would do him harm. She recalled that Scout Finch had split her knuckle on her cousin's front teeth in *To Kill a Mockingbird* and was about to do the same to Billy the Kid when, to her complete surprise, Pablo stepped in between her and the louts.

"She can say whatever she wants," he announced proudly, remembering the true story of how Mac had the last laugh after having sand kicked in his face. "I do not give in to bullies and will fight anyone who disrespects her."

The delinquents looked at each other with grins on their rotten faces and promptly burst out laughing again.

Luna tried to pull Pablo back by his shirt, worried that he might get hurt, but he stood firm, his voice decidedly heroic. "Please stay out of this, Luna. Do you not remember how I came to your rescue in my dream last night? Everyone knows that you cannot argue with fate." With that, he jutted his chin like a flamenco dancer and put up his fists. "Come on! Who wants it first?"

Scarcely had his words been uttered than Billy the Kid rushed forward and, with one wild punch, sent Pablo crashing to the ground where he lay out for the count. Luna, shrieking with rage, reacted by leaping through the air and smashing her elbow into the aggressor's face.

The boy staggered back with blood dripping through his fingers. "Arghhh! You broke my nose, you little bitch!"

Luna hissed like a cat and inched forward, wild-eyed and ferocious, ready to fight. The boys backed off, almost tripping over themselves in their haste to get away. Meanwhile, Pablo was regaining consciousness, helped along by an old lady who had shoved a small brown jar of smelling salts under his nose.

"What *are* you?" sputtered the leader of the gang, pointing a judgemental finger at Luna as two park maintenance workers arrived at the scene to send them on their way.

"Go back to your swamp, cabrones!" she shouted, waving them off with a dainty hand.

The maintenance staff, together with a small crush of concerned citizens, milled around asking questions until they were satisfied that the youngsters' injuries amounted to nothing more than a swollen eye and a bruised elbow.

Once the crowd had dispersed, Pablo sheepishly thanked her for stepping in to defend him. "The old lady, she tell me that you jump in the air and hit him."

"I did."

"How did you learn to do this?"

"My adoptive father taught me a few things."

"I am sure that he was a great man."

"Well, you would be wrong."

Pablo winced as he touched the swelling around his eye. "Maybe I should not listen to my dreams," he said dolefully.

"Nonsense. You must always listen to them," Luna insisted. "Sometimes they do come true."

A shy smile broke across the boy's face. "If I had to do it again, I would still fight to protect you, Luna."

"What nonsense! I don't need anyone to fight my fights," she huffed, giving him a shove. "Come on, let's forget about the park and go back to the house."

CHAPTER TWENTY-EIGHT

September, otherwise known in Mexico as 'the Patriotic Month', proved to be a busy one. Sofia and Hugo, as well as contributing to a succession of glitzy charity events, had set aside enough money to provide a local hospital with a new dialysis machine. In the meantime, María and Vincent, wishing to avoid any fuss, had flown to Las Vegas to get married in a kitschy chapel on the Strip. They honeymooned at the Hilton, where they dined within earshot of Zsa Zsa Gabor (and one of her husbands), and watched Elvis Presley, resplendent in a white gull-wing-collared jumpsuit, sing his heart out in front of a twenty-five piece orchestra.

Mr Salazar continued to snail about the house whenever he was called upon to oversee a dinner or drinks party, and Verónica found herself secretly and hopelessly in love with a courteous young delivery driver tasked with bringing floral arrangements to the property. Pablo remained at home having his horizons broadened under señor Volante's private tutelage, while Sofia and Hugo took Luna on day trips to visit

Mayan ruins and various other tourist attractions that had long been of interest to her.

The thing that had recently usurped almost all of Luna's many passions was the time-honoured pastime of chess. Captivated by the spirited contests she had seen played in the park, she had set her heart on learning the game. Having memorised a multiplicity of strategic moves, she asked Hugo, who had played the game competitively at Eton, to teach her its finer points. To his complete astonishment, and despite her never having played before, Luna beat him after just three matches. Not only that, she went on to force Sofia, a high-level player, to concede on their fifth contest.

Bolstered by her prodigious success, the teenager entered the park's annual chess tournament. In front of a rapt audience, she upset the odds by overthrowing the reigning champion, Ismael del Toro, in the final. Luna had keenly studied the maestro's game from her perch in the treetops over several weeks and noted his strengths, of which there were many, and his weaknesses, of which there were few. As she had hoped, the seasoned player responded to her 'Ruy Lopez' opening by counterattacking with the 'Sicilian Defence'. Taking advantage of his eagerness to play a combative game, she eventually provoked her wily opponent into an uncharacteristic mistake that allowed her to execute a clinical checkmate.

The defeated champion, recognising the emergence of a rare and special talent, shook Luna's hand and congratulated her on her victory. "You are a strong player, señorita. It was an honour to do battle with you."

"And I with you, señor. You were my inspiration, sir."

Del Toro looked his young vanquisher in the eye. "What is your name, señorita, that I may one day boast that I competed against you."

"My name is Luna, sir. Luna Wilde."

*

The sixteenth day of the month heralded Día de la Independencia, the national holiday celebrating Mexico's declaration of independence from their Spanish oppressors. Late into the previous night, Mexico's dictatorial president Gustavo Díaz Ordaz – whose government had ordered the horrific slaughter of student protestors at Tlatelolco only two years earlier – had delighted the nation by clanging the same bell that Father Miguel Hidalgo y Costilla had rung before delivering his rousing call to arms speech back in 1810.

Sofia and Hugo's unique family, who numbered Vincent, María, Luna, Pablo and Verónica, eeled through the crowded streets to join the celebrations at the Zócalo. Luna had stated from the outset that she had a strong aversion to crowds and noise and would likely decamp if it all became too much, but the smiles on everyone's faces somehow made it seem worthwhile.

The hearts of the people were filled with national pride. Mexican flags flew from every balcony, bunting was strung above every avenue and cries of *¡Viva México!* rang out from every mouth. When the national anthem blared out from a cluster of loudspeakers, Pablo sang along as heartily as a Welshman opens his lungs to 'Land of my Fathers', or as lustily as a Frenchman sings along to 'La Marseillaise'.

The prevailing enthusiasm was infectious: ticker-tape rained down on military parades; mariachi music could be heard everywhere, and children waved foil windmills on little sticks. The bars, cafés and restaurants were bursting at the seams and music billowed out from every door. Despite Sofia and Hugo's proclivity for gourmet food and fine dining, the family lunched together at a casual *taqueria* restaurant, which was recommended by María and whose plastic plates during the celebration were in the red, white and green of the Mexican tricolour.

"The green represents hope," said the cook, explaining the symbolism behind the colours of the flag. "The white is the purity of our faith, and red is for the blood of those who fought for Mexican independence."

Though the restaurant was thick with cigarette smoke, something that Sofia and Hugo had struggled to grow accustomed to since travelling back in time, it served up tasty tacos stuffed with braised meats and fresh cilantro, topped with dashes of fiery sauce. Luna opted for a black bean version.

"*Buen provecho,*" said the head waiter with practised ceremony after he had set the steaming plates on the table.

María presided over the food, her eyes shining like wet pebbles. "The cuisine here is simple, but tasty," she said, squeezing a wedge of lime over Vincent's food without being asked. "A little bit of Heaven on your tongues."

She persuaded Sofia and Hugo to forgo their knives and forks in favour of eating with their hands. Everyone got stuck into the tacos, some with more finesse than others.

"Would you look at yourself, Hugo? Such a typical gringo," mocked Vincent as the Englishman bit into the taco as if it were a sandwich, causing its entire contents to spill out onto the plate. "You have to eat like a Mexican, my friend. Come in from the side, like so—" In common with María, Verónica and Pablo, the Irishman craned his neck slightly and demonstrated the correct way to tackle a folded tortilla, earning a thumbs-up gesture from a gentleman on an adjacent table.

"And yet half of it is on your moustache, Vincent," quipped Hugo, winking at Luna and cheerfully scraping the misplaced taco ingredients back onto his tortilla.

Though the day had been bright for the most part, the heavens had begun to turn grey. The sun caught the first droplets of rain that fell upon the restaurant's windows and projected lava-lamp patterns on the faces of the diners who sat closest to them. While Sofia and Hugo's inclusive family were halfway through their meal, the sky sagged under the weight of its cargo and collapsed in a cataclysmic downpour.

"It looks as if we might be staying here a while longer," remarked Sofia as the rain came down heavily, the sound of it percussive against the restaurant awnings.

"Suits me," said Vincent. "Let's order wine."

Luna's eyes lit up. "I'll have some!" she said.

"Absolutely not. You are under the legal age," tutted María.

"But who would know?" Luna protested.

"Ah, a little won't hurt her," said Vincent. "My auld fella was letting me drink the froth off his Guinness before I was fully potty-trained."

"Could I have some wine too?" asked Pablo.

Vincent threw his hands in the air. "Oh, Jesus. I'm keeping out of this."

The adults went on to share two carafes of house wine while the youngsters had to make do with glasses of limeade. By the time the family had seen off an immoderate amount of the restaurant's *tres leches* cake, the downpour had run its course. As one, they stepped out onto a wet sidewalk that had released its smell of city grime into the air. They paused to allow Luna to light a cigar then headed home under the drip of wet flags.

Reflected in a car window, Sofia caught a fleeting

glance of her future self gazing straight back at her through a transtemporal prism. She took Hugo by the elbow and allowed the others to walk on ahead, chatting exultantly as they did so. "Darling, look at them. They are the family that I have always wanted," she said, her voice brittle with emotion.

Hugo caressed her face with the back of his hand. "And they're also the family that I've always wanted. This is where fate has taken us, Sofia, and I wouldn't change a thing."

*

That evening, as night drew in, the group gathered in the kitchen to prepare an informal meal to mark the historic day. María had earlier cooked a quantity of tomato rice which she'd transferred to the refrigerator together with a large bowl of spicy chicken thighs. She marshalled the troops, enlisting the help of those present to stir pots, prepare fresh salads, reheat enchiladas and set the table.

Sofia, who had elected to fetch the wine while Hugo was busily chopping onions, dashed upstairs to collect the cellar key from their bedroom. She had just retrieved two bottles of Malbec from the basement and was halfway through the cellar door when the front doorbell jangled noisily on its coil, heralding an unanticipated caller.

"I'll get that!" she hollered, carefully setting down the bottles on a side table.

On the other side of the front door, wretched as

ever, stood Mr Salazar in his butler's uniform. "Good evening, Doctor Ustinova," he said sullenly, moonlight shining on his brilliantined hair.

Sofia was taken aback. "Mr Salazar. I wasn't expecting you. Have we got our wires crossed?"

"Not at all, Madam. I am here to recover my waistcoat," he replied, gazing longingly at the key in her hand. "I left it in the laundry room. It was uncomfortably hot for me while I was doing the ironing, you see."

The physicist, imagining that Salazar must live and sleep in his starched uniform, wondered why such a minor issue couldn't wait. Nevertheless, she invited him in. "Go on ahead," she instructed. "I just have to lock up."

The butler produced his oily smile and directed a bony finger at the two bottles on the table. "With respect, Doctor Ustinova, may I humbly remind you that I have capably managed many wine cellars in my twenty-eight years of service."

"I am sure you have, Mr Salazar," she said sharply. "But we can manage it perfectly fine on our own."

He retreated, bowing obsequiously as he did so. "As you wish, Madam."

The butler slunk off to the staircase, where he paused to watch Sofia as she secured the cellar door. Just the mere sight of the key turning in the lock intensified his compulsion to unearth the secrets that his employers seemed determined to hide. Lying in his dismal bedroom at night, he often allowed his mind to run away with him as he fantasised about the illicit treasures that might be in the basement: perhaps a stockpile of Nazi gold, a collection of Fabergé eggs, a masterpiece stolen from the Louvre, or maybe a cache of looted antiquities. In one of his more extravagant fantasies, Salazar had even hoped that Wilde and Ustinova had kidnapped an heiress and were keeping her chained to an iron pipe until the ransom was paid.

He coveted that key as keenly as Gollum had coveted the Ring. He sensed that once he had exposed their shameful secret his silence would need to be bought and a great deal of money could be made.

The laundry room was a short distance from the top of the stairs. While Salazar was retrieving his waistcoat, Sofia walked by towards her chambers with key in hand. Once she had disappeared from view, he tiptoed towards the master bedroom and furtively observed her through its open door, hoping to find out exactly where she kept the key.

Before opening a lacquerware musical box, an heirloom passed down from her maternal grandmother to her mother and then to her, Sofia cranked its winding key several revolutions; it was something she liked to do for sentimental reasons. She lifted its lid, prompting a tiny ballerina to pirouette to the tune of the 'Dance of the Sugar Plum Fairy'. The butler, once he had observed her placing the cellar key in the box, tiptoed away and hastened down the staircase.

Sofia caught sight of the top of his head as he scurried off. Leaning over a balustrade, she called out to him. "Mr Salazar. Did you find what you were looking for?"

He gazed up at her, holding the waistcoat aloft in his twiggy fingers. "I did, Madam. Thank you, Madam. I will see myself out."

Oh, yes. I definitely found what I was looking for, Salazar thought as he left the house.

CHAPTER TWENTY-NINE

By the grace of alien intervention, and having signed an abundance of legal documents, Sofia and Hugo had become the new owners of the grounds upon which a disused school was still standing proud. Consistent with the couple's vision for the orphanage, a local architect named Ray Flores had drafted detailed plans to conserve much of the existing school building and extend its footprint. These plans were reviewed by a civil engineer, whose principal role was to survey the site and oversee each stage of the building work. Furthermore, they had enlisted the services of a site manager and a team of skilled contractors who had experience in working on similar projects.

Apart from it sheltering an infestation of cockroaches, which were soon eradicated by a pest-control team, the old school was solidly built and in a decent state of repair. The other residents of the block were pleased to hear that something was finally being done with the site as it had become rather an eyesore. For some time, they had seen the plot reduced to a playground for vandals and a local dumping ground.

To reverse the trend, flyblown heaps of trash and a tatty forest of tall weeds were cleared away to reveal a workable area of concrete and asphalt over which a scattering of jacaranda trees stood guard.

Sofia and Hugo, with Pablo in attendance, arrived on site to observe the start of the building process from the street side of a chain-link fence. The air was alive with the machine-gun rattle of jackhammers cutting into hard surfaces and the clang of mechanical diggers.

Once the ground was broken up along the marked lines of the proposed building's foundations, the footings were excavated first by machine and then by hand by mahogany-skinned men who were used to hard toil in muddy trenches. In addition, separate channels were harrowed to lay sewage and other underground pipes.

As a steady procession of loaded wheelbarrows were trundled along dusty planks and clattered into large skips, Pablo felt the eyes of his father gazing down on him from Heaven and imagined how happy he would be to see his dreams being realised.

"This fine school is the acorn from which a mighty oak is destined to grow," said Hugo without preamble, leaving Pablo struggling to translate and decipher the metaphorical thrust of his statement.

The project architect, looking the part with a hard hat atop his head and a shirt and tie peeking out from his overalls, opened the school's old iron gate and bade them all good morning. While furling his site drawings into a tight scroll, señor Flores assured them that the team hadn't yet encountered any snags and that everything was proceeding as planned.

He nodded towards a huddle of middle-aged citizens who were viewing the building work with keen interest from the sidewalk and chatting animatedly. "Former pupils of the school," he said with a big smile. "The renovation is bringing back wonderful childhood memories and they have come here to share their stories."

"So are they happy with what we are doing?" asked Sofia hopefully.

"Of course," replied Flores. "Some of them will have made lifelong friends at this school. And it is likely that some would have had their first kiss here. They all want to see it reborn."

While he was speaking, an elderly lady with soulful eyes and taffeta orchids in her silver hair hobbled over to express her gratitude. "Greetings, señora and señores," she said, slightly out of breath and smelling of talcum powder. "With news of this orphanage, you have made an old woman very happy. You see, at the age of thirty I was one of the very first teachers at this school on the day it opened in 1922. And when it closed its gates for the last time, a little of my heart closed with it."

Sofia hugged and kissed her warmly. "Then you will be pleased to hear that the orphanage will also have its own classrooms."

The lady clasped her veiny hands to her chest.

"By saying this you have opened up my heart again, Madam."

"May I ask your name, señora?"

"Magdalena Velázquez," said the retired teacher proudly. "And you?"

"I'm Sofia," replied the physicist, engendering a rush of handshakes as she made the introductions. "This is my partner, Hugo… This is señor Flores, the architect for the project. And the handsome young man next to me is Pablo."

"You are Russian," observed señora Velázquez, her eyes as wise as Galileo's.

A look of delight bloomed on Sofia's face. "Is it so obvious?"

"I'm good with accents," said Magdalena with a mischievous smile. "I taught English here for many years."

Sofia asked Hugo for his notepad and fountain pen. "Magdalena, if it is not an imposition, could you please write down your address? We would love to invite you to the grand opening, whenever that should be."

The teacher's eyes lit up. "Oh, Sofia, that would be wonderful. I am already excited."

Displaying beautiful penmanship, Magdalena wrote her name and address in ornate handwriting that belonged to a bygone age.

She returned the notepad to Sofia. "My dear, what you are doing here is admirable, truly admirable," she said, fighting back tears. "We can point the finger at adults for the stupid decisions they make in life, but an orphaned child can never be blamed for the situation in which they find themselves."

CHAPTER THIRTY

Not wishing to hide Luna's light under a bushel any longer, Sofia thought it high time that the girl's genius was recognised further afield by those who could take her to where she needed to be. Though books had given wings to Luna's mind, it was the physicist's face-to-face tuition that had provided her with a scientific knowledge so highly developed that it would likely draw acclaim from the foremost academics on the planet.

Sofia and Hugo had initially wanted to keep their charge out of the spotlight, afraid that somewhere along the line Luna's otherworldliness would be exposed, leading to intense medical scrutiny from the scientific community and thereafter catching the rabid attention of the world's media. They had sat down with her to gauge her feelings on the subject and to discuss at length the pros and cons of her stepping into the limelight, especially given her tendency towards introversion. To their utmost surprise Luna was open to the idea and remained so even when they reiterated the many pitfalls that could jeopardise her freedom.

Before asking Luna's opinion as to whether she was prepared to take the next step, Sofia had made a generous donation to the Institute of Theoretical Physics in the south of the city. She had also decided that hosting a cocktail party in their honour would be a great way for Luna to announce herself to some of the institute's luminaries. The facility employed eighteen technicians and forty-six full-time professors, the most prominent of whom was the world-renowned Hungarian physicist, József Boros.

Once she had received confirmation that a contingent of scientists and their team would be attending her *soirée*, Sofia wandered through the house searching for Luna so she could tell her the news. She encountered Verónica in the library where she was polishing the leaves of a rubber plant with a damp cloth. "Verónica, have you seen Luna?"

The housekeeper gestured towards the fountain courtyard. "I think she is outside, Madam."

When Sofia reached the sunlit patio, María was standing there with arms akimbo looking up at the crown of a tree as if something of special interest was about to occur. Once her eyes had grown accustomed to the sun, Sofia followed the direction of the cook's rigid gaze and saw Luna sitting high in the tree's branches with a grey squirrel in her lap.

"Luna! Get down from there!" shouted María. "Either you will break your neck or the *ardilla* will bite you!" She turned to Sofia for help. "Sofia, what is this thing called in English?" she asked before performing a mime that mimicked buck teeth and a bushy tail.

"It's called a squirrel."

"Luna! Get down from there! The squirrel will bite you!"

"He's my friend!" yelled Luna, stroking the rodent's fur.

"How can you be the friend of a squirrel?" María hollered.

Sofia sought to reassure her. "Don't worry, María, I'll get her down."

"She thinks she can be a friend with the squirrel," said the cook with a demented look on her face.

"I know, I know. Leave it with me."

"*Madre Santísima.*" María shook her head several times as she trudged back to the kitchen.

Sofia, joined by Copernicus, kept her gaze upon Luna as she advanced along the leafy borders of the courtyard, snagging her sleeve on a spiteful cactus in the process. "What is his name?" she enquired once she was underneath the tree. Copernicus hissed up at the creature but thought better about engaging with it.

"Animals don't give themselves names," said Luna airily.

"Of course. How uninformed I am."

Undeterred by her adopted daughter's fractiousness, Sofia conveyed the good news. "József Boros has confirmed that he and some of his team will be attending my little get-together this Saturday. What do you say to that, darling?"

Suddenly motivated, Luna relinquished the squirrel, leapt to her feet and traversed the branches like a tightrope walker. After checking that María wasn't watching from the kitchen window, she shimmied down the trunk in the blink of an eye and stood before Sofia with a rare smile on her face. "I say that it is very exciting," she beamed, relishing the prospect of conversing with like-minded individuals.

"Good. But there must be no kicking of shins though—"

"I promise."

*

Saturday evening arrived, together with a symposium of scientists and their researchers. The guests were greeted solemnly at the door by Mr Salazar and escorted to the grand dining room where Verónica was on hand to serve chilled Champagne and a spectacular array of María's Mexican hors d'oeuvres.

A cordial mood prevailed among the associates, who were delighted to socialise with each other in a relaxed atmosphere without having to discuss mathematical calculations and the behaviour of electrons. Sofia, dressed in a floral hippy dress and white knee boots, worked the room while Luna, who was unaccustomed to hobnobbing with strangers, stood lonely as a scarecrow in her favourite beret and a pair of denim dungarees.

"I'll have one of those," she said, snatching a flute of Champagne from Salazar's silver tray as he toadied through the crowd.

"Are you even allowed to drink alcohol at your age, child?" sneered the butler, elevating the tray to prevent her helping herself to another one.

"Are you even allowed to ask stupid questions, Mr Salazar?"

He leaned in, close enough that she could feel the wintry mist of his breath. "Do not try to lock horns with me, you little bitch."

"And there it is!" said Luna, her vivid eyes peering into his soul. "Once again the monster bares his teeth. I know what you are, Mr Salazar, and I have you in my sights."

Sofia, who had threaded though the throng with a large gentleman in tow, interrupted their *contretemps*. "Luna, may I introduce Professor Boros?"

While Salazar slithered off into the crowd, Luna shook the professor's hand firmly and presented herself. The Hungarian was a great bear of a man with an Oscar Wilde mane of hair and a cigarette between his lips. Luna noticed an ink stain on the chest pocket of his corduroy jacket and also that he wore socks with his sandals.

"Sofia tells me that you have a rare precocity for all things science," he said to the teenager, folding his arms and fixing her with a penetrating stare.

"I like to think so," she replied.

Boros blew cigarette smoke from the side of his mouth. "But then she also informs me that everything you know has been gleaned from books."

Luna, knowing that Sofia had withheld from Professor Boros the part that she, as an eminent physicist, had played, went along with his offhanded appraisal. "Yes, only from books. But you can learn so much from them, wouldn't you agree, Professor?"

The Hungarian stuffed his hands into his trouser pockets and loomed over her. "With all due respect, one cannot become a scientist from reading books any more than a shepherd can consider himself an astronomer just by gazing up at the night sky."

"And with all due respect, József," interjected Sofia, "I think that you are greatly underestimating Luna."

Boros turned to Sofia and regarded her with an air of superiority. "Remind me again what your doctorate was in, Sofia—"

"It was in psychiatry," she lied through gritted teeth.

With the cigarette still stuck to his lips, the professor sighed deeply. "Forgive me for speaking candidly, Sofia, but I view psychiatry in the same way I do faith healing or phrenology. Yes, the management of mental health has its place, but the entire economic and ecological wellbeing of the planet is reliant on what we physicists do."

Sofia was already aware of Professor Boros's pig-headed arrogance and would have loved to take him on, given that her scientific knowledge was far more advanced than his, but she managed to keep her composure. Had she really been a psychiatrist, she'd have happily slapped every atom of conceit from his nicotine-stained face. It felt bizarre to see him standing larger than life before her, because she clearly remembered reading about his death from lung disease in 1996, when she was a twenty-one-year-old science student in Moscow. More importantly, she also recalled that he was a world-class chess player and an esteemed member of the Hungarian national team.

"József, if I remember correctly, you are something of a keen chess player, no?" she said almost coquettishly.

"Something of a keen chess player!" he snorted. "I'll have you know that I am a chess player of great renown. As a matter of fact, I beat the Nicaraguan champion only last week."

Pleased that the professor's ego had led him into her trap, Sofia made a submission. "Then how about this proposition, József? Though she only started playing three months ago, Luna has shown an extraordinary aptitude for the game. If she were to beat you, right here, right now, would you consider offering her an internship at the institute?"

"Ha!" the professor squawked. "What a comical idea! If by some miracle this little lady were to beat me in a game of chess, I'd place her in charge of the whole damn facility."

Sofia fixed him with her feline smile. "Then let us put my comical idea to the test, shall we?"

"You're not serious?"

"Deadly serious."

*

In due course, the guests decamped to the library where a chess board had been set up on a square table. Sofia, with Luna's assistance, had earlier removed any scientific text books that post-dated 1970 because the scientists and their researchers were sure to browse the shelves. The participants stood side by side before the match, their significant height difference accentuating the David and Goliath essence of the contest.

Professor Boros, never one to miss an opportunity to grandstand, addressed the spectators. "Now I know that each and every one of you dreamers would dearly love to see the great József Boros getting his comeuppance tonight, but I fear you will all be going home disappointed. Nevertheless, it should prove an interesting end to what has been a thoroughly enjoyable evening." Here he paused to introduce his adversary. "My opponent tonight is one Luna Wilde who, I'm told, is a genius in the making."

The gathering broke into an exuberant round of applause.

Professor Boros took two pawns, one black, one white, from the board and put his arms behind his back. He then presented his closed fists to Luna and invited her to choose.

"That one!" she exclaimed, slapping his left hand a little harder than he would have liked.

"White," he said upon opening his palm. "You go first, Luna. Statistically, you have an advantage over me already."

As they sat down, the Hungarian returned the

pawns to the board and didn't do himself any favours by slyly winking at the spectators. The crowd, without exception, were in the underdog's corner and hoped against hope that she could spring an unlikely upset.

The combatants faced each other and shook hands. While Boros was still tweaking his chess pieces in readiness to play, Luna promptly advanced her queen's pawn two squares.

"I was hoping that you might have opted for a bolder opening," he said condescendingly. "Something experimental perhaps, just to throw me off guard—"

Luna lasered him with a cold glare. "Are you going to talk all the way through the game, Professor?"

The Hungarian played his moves automatically and at great speed, hoping to fluster his young opponent, but she matched his briskness move for move with calm efficiency until it was he who became flustered.

As the pace of Boros's play slowed, and as he puffed out his cheeks, Luna resorted to gamesmanship by exaggerating the occasional yawn or drumming her fingers on the table.

"Would you stop that?" he huffed, lighting up another cigarette. "It's not at all sportsmanlike."

"Oh, I do apologise. I was becoming quite bored, you see."

Frustrated by his inability to put Luna's pieces under pressure, the professor eventually made a rash move which he instantly regretted. "I didn't mean to do that," he protested. "You broke my concentration."

Luna steepled her fingers and smiled at him. "Then

I will allow you to take it again, if you like."

"Of course not! We play on."

Boros was walking a tightrope, and both he and his young adversary knew it. The astonished spectators were captivated and a breathless silence prevailed. It wasn't long before the Hungarian accepted the helplessness of his position and conceded defeat by shaking his opponent's hand, eliciting a raucous round of applause from their audience.

"I don't really expect to be put in charge of your institute," said Luna, fishing two cigars from a dungaree pocket. "An internship would suit me fine."

A broad smile broke across the professor's face as he accepted one of the cigars. "It would give me the greatest pleasure to find a place for you on my team, Luna. And I promise that I will never underestimate you again."

The room erupted in a chorus of cheers and whistles while Sofia looked on with barely restrained pride.

Able to see the funny side of his humiliation and enjoying the beaming smiles of his associates, Professor Boros hitched up his trousers, drew back his shoulders, and addressed the group. "Nobody shall ever speak of this," he chuckled, jabbing a finger at their ranks. "Is that understood?"

Later in the evening, after the guests had departed, Mr Salazar approached Sofia to ask if his services would be required the next day.

"My apologies, Mr Salazar, I really should have

mentioned it sooner. We will be out celebrating the Day of the Dead festival tomorrow, so the house will be empty."

Empty. The word rang a bell in Salazar's mind and a frisson of excitement coursed through his swampy body. He almost wanted to do a little dance.

"Then I hope that you enjoy the experience, Madam. I shall see myself out."

"I am extremely grateful for your help tonight, Mr Salazar. You and I have had our ups and downs, but the evening was an incredible success with you at the helm. Rest up, and we'll see you next week."

"Of course, Madam."

CHAPTER THIRTY-ONE

On the morning after her triumphant chess match, Luna resisted appeals for her to join the rest of the household as they prepared to immerse themselves in the *Día de Muertos* festivities. She reminded them that she had remained sullen for much of the Independence Day celebrations, that noisy crowds weren't her thing and that they would likely have much more fun without her. A day spent reading George Orwell's *Nineteen Eighty-Four* – a future year in which she hadn't found herself living under the control of a totalitarian state – seemed a far better proposition.

*

The previous day Hugo and Vincent had driven Pablo to the cemetery in which his mother and father were buried so he could pay his respects. The graveyard was already bustling with lively groups of mourners sitting on picnic blankets among the tombs, singing songs and drinking *mezcal*, determined to foster a party atmosphere. It was commonly believed that the gates of heaven were opened between the last day of October and the first two days of November to allow the spirits of the deceased to reunite with their families.

"I know you are here with me, Mamá and Papá," Pablo murmured into the breeze, doing his best to remain upbeat as this was not a time of mourning. "I promise that I will live my life in the best way I can and that we will all meet up again one day."

While his guardians kept a respectful distance, the teenager laid a pathway of marigold petals and placed candles around his parents' graves to guide their way back to the world of the living. Before saying his goodbyes, he left his mother and father two opened bottles of water and some *Pan de Muerto*, a sweet-tasting bread that María had baked specially for the occasion.

*

Happy to leave Luna to do her own thing, Sofia and Hugo, Maria, Vincent and Pablo set out on foot to enjoy the unique occasion. Unbeknown to them Mr Salazar, predictably dressed in his butler's uniform, was monitoring the house from a safe distance on the other side of the road.

The sidewalks were already teeming with revellers heading for the historic centre, many with their faces painted to resemble skeleton skulls. The females, young and old, wore flowing Edwardian-style gowns and sported flower garlands in their hair, while the males paired black dinner suits with white gloves and top hats. Some of the celebrants, assuming that

Salazar was in character, complimented him on his ghoulishness and shouted "Happy Day of the Dead!" at him. Distracted by the merrymakers, and having fought off a persistent jostle of flower sellers, the butler, much to his annoyance, wasn't able to keep a tally as to exactly who had left the house.

After waiting a good while to confirm to himself that the coast was clear, Salazar adjusted the strap of the camera case he was carrying and crossed the road. Upon reaching the front door, he yanked the bell to determine if the house was really empty.

Just when Luna had reached the part in Orwell's book where Julia yells "Swine! Swine! Swine!" at Goldstein's telescreen image, the doorbell disturbed her serenity with its disagreeable jangle. Ensconced in a nest of pillows, she was wonderfully comfortable reading in bed and, in an instance of life imitating art, had wanted to shout "Swine! Swine! Swine!" at whoever was at the front door. So, to preserve her repose, she ignored the mystery caller, knowing that if their purpose was truly of any importance they would keep on trying.

A long pause ensued, a return to blissful quietude, and the longer it lasted the more Luna felt satisfied that the person had given up. But then, to her complete surprise, she heard the rattle of a key in the lock.

Salazar! she thought instantly. *Who else could it be?* Luna slipped quietly from the bed and pulled a knitted sweater over her nightdress. *What is he up to?* She slowed her breathing and stood motionless in the attic room, waiting for him to show his hand. Her keen hearing captured every sound below: the agonising creak of Salazar's shoes on the staircase, the waxy squeak of his palm on the banister rail, the wolfish rasp of his breath.

The butler reached the first-floor landing and Luna peeked down on him through a slight gap in her bedroom door. He disappeared into Sofia and Hugo's master bedroom for a short while, reappearing with key in hand and a grin on his face.

Luna's senses were on high alert. *The cellar. He's going down to the cellar.*

Once the butler was back at ground level, she floated barefoot down her rickety staircase in the manner of a heavenly messenger and continued along the landing. Ethereal and self-composed, she sailed down the main staircase and hovered above its lower steps.

Salazar was at the cellar door with his back to her, oblivious to her presence. Copernicus, sensing that the human was up to no good, appeared from nowhere to bite his ankle, but the butler sent the cat sailing through the air with a vicious kick to its midriff.

As Luna swallowed her anger, Salazar unlocked the door and disappeared inside. She glided above the hallway's terracotta tiles, silent as a cloud, and looked for anything that she might use as a weapon. To her delight, she saw Hugo's antique cricket bat resting on two large hooks attached to the wall. Luna recalled him saying that such a bat could incapacitate a burglar, so she grasped it in both hands and continued towards the basement.

She coasted through the open doorway and gazed down at Salazar, who was now bathed in the craft's glow and squealing with excitement. Unaware that Luna was hovering above the stairs behind him, he removed his camera from its leather case and prepared to take some shots.

"I wouldn't do that if I were you," Luna said in an unearthly voice.

Salazar spun round and completely missed the fact that Luna's feet were levitating a few inches above the steps. As he gazed up at her, flames of anger ignited in his eyes. "You little bitch!" he hissed baring his mildewed teeth. "I always knew that there was something strange about you, and now I have proof."

He directed a bony finger towards the craft as it began to hum. "What the hell is this thing? Who are you people?"

Luna's heels brushed the steps as she made her descent. "Give me the camera, Mr Salazar," she said coolly. "If not, I will be forced to hit you with this bat."

"You must be crazy to think that I would do that. I am going to take as many photographs as I want." A sly smirk danced across his thin lips. "And if you assholes do not pay me a very large sum of money for my silence, I will go to every newspaper in the city."

Luna gripped the bat's handle tightly as the butler turned to face the time machine. "This is my final warning, Mr Salazar—"

"Go to Hell!" he shouted over his shoulder, taking snaps in quick succession. "Someone should tie you up and put you in a zoo."

Luna planted her feet and whacked the Mexican hard across the back of his neck, causing him to drop the camera and crumple to the ground. She knelt beside him and was relieved to find that he still had a pulse.

The craft's Saturnian ring began to spin and its hatch glowed pink, inviting her to come aboard. She recalled the moonlit night in which she had dragged her adoptive father's corpse into a hole and did much the same with Salazar, hauling his insensate body into the machine's cabin.

In recognition of her effort, a burr of alien conversations filled the air and the machine began to pulse as if it were a living thing. Luna had alighted from the craft and was stooping to retrieve Salazar's camera when Copernicus streamed down the cellar steps, seemingly unharmed, to congratulate her on her heroism.

"You were the brave one," said Luna. "And as a thank you, I will read to you in bed."

*

The rest of the household returned home that afternoon with garlands around their necks and joy in their hearts. In the midst of their collective gaiety, Luna took Sofia and Hugo to one side and led them into the library to apprise them of what had happened.

"Well done, Luna. You did the right thing," said Hugo reverting to cloak-and-dagger mode. "Has anything happened since?"

"Shortly after I locked the cellar door, the time machine made a terrific noise," she replied. "But I thought it best to leave things as they are until you had returned home."

Sofia stuck her head into the hallway to check that María and Pablo weren't anywhere near the cellar door. "The coast is clear, so let's investigate, shall we?"

She unlocked the door and they descended into the basement where the time machine sat in total silence. Sofia placed a hand on its outer shell, causing the neon-pink outline of the hatch to come to life.

Hugo ventured inside first, in the event that Salazar had planned an ambush, but the brightly-lit interior stood empty. "It would seem that our friends in high places have spirited him away," he observed.

"But where to?" wondered Sofia.

*

Twenty-eight years earlier.
Mexico City, 1942

Severiano Salazar was about to slip rat poison into his brother's coffee. Then he stopped himself, wondering what had possessed him to even consider doing such a wicked thing.

"Próspero, have I been a good brother to you?" he enquired after surreptitiously tipping the poison into the trash.

"Of course you haven't been a good brother! You have always been an incredibly horrible brother," replied his younger sibling as he sat at the kitchen table. "Which is why I was so surprised when you offered to make me a cup of coffee just now."

Severiano was shocked by how shamefully he had conducted himself thus far in his young life and resolved to be a better person. "If it is not too late, Próspero, I would like to apologise for my inconsiderate behaviour and beg for your forgiveness."

Much to Próspero's astonishment, Severiano dropped to his knees before him in supplication.

"Severiano, what has brought this on? You know that I will always respect you, no matter how poorly you treat me." He held his older brother's hands and noticed with some relief that, for a change, they weren't unpleasantly clammy.

"I have had an epiphany, my dear Próspero," enthused Severiano, directing a scraggy finger heavenward and raising the volume of his voice. "From this day forward, I shall dedicate my life to the service of God."

"I am very happy to hear it," said Próspero leaning back in his chair. "But what about that coffee?"

CHAPTER THIRTY-TWO

By mid-December, the north winds had brought an appreciable chill to Mexico City. Hugo had cleared the guttering of autumn leaves, chimneys in the house had been swept and coal fires were lit on cooler evenings.

Señor Volante, like all Mexicans, was a master at networking. He had taken advantage of his long-standing friendships with administrators at the National Autonomous University to arrange for Pablo to have his artwork exhibited on the campus. This brought about an interview with one of the local newspapers whose cheesy article was unimaginatively titled *From Shining Shoes to Painting Pictures*.

Under the watchful eye of Professor József Boros, Luna was six weeks into her internship at the Institute of Theoretical Physics and wowing everyone with her intellectual capacity.

For their part, Sofia and Hugo had taken up salsa lessons, while María continued to work on Vincent's rudimentary grasp of the Spanish language. In the meantime, after a tentative courtship blighted by a litany of mixed signals, Verónica had delighted everyone by finally landing the courteous flower delivery guy with whom she had fallen hopelessly in love several weeks earlier.

Work on the orphanage had moved on a pace, with the compound being extended in different directions. The building would accommodate male and female dormitories at opposite ends and also comprise classrooms, along with segregated shower blocks and toilets. Additionally, there would be a staff room, a games room, a library and a refectory. Newly-built parapets enclosed flat roofs that would double as terraces, and the rough-hewn outer walls were rendered with clay to give the building a traditional feel. Doors and windows lent the structure the semblance of habitability, although the interior was still a shell and yet to benefit from the attention of plumbers and electricians.

The labourers were mostly a happy bunch whose sunny disposition was buoyed each day by the arrival of María and Vincent, who rocked up in the Batmobile with a bountiful supply of home-cooked food. Before a line of ravenous workers, they would set out a buffet fit for royalty along a table that the site carpenters had cobbled together from planks and wooden offcuts. As a further inducement to get the men to work like Trojans, O'Toole made a habit of providing them with a metal wash tub filled with ice cubes and bottles of Corona beer.

Señora Velázquez, often with her silver hair in rollers

and wearing a headscarf, dropped by periodically to bear witness to her old school's spiritual rebirth through the site's chain-link fence.

*

Three months later:

March 1971 saw the orphanage receive its finishing touches. In addition to the existing electrical wiring being upgraded to a modern standard, an alarm system had been installed and safety provisions made in the event of a fire. Antiquated water and gas pipes were removed and replumbed throughout and a commercial range cooker, of the kind used by professional chefs, was fitted in the refectory kitchen.

With an efficiency only bettered by God creating the entire planet in seven days, the workers plastered walls, painted ceilings, tiled floors, hung crucifixes in every room and installed appliances and water tanks. Delivery trucks rolled up at all hours of the day bringing consignments of furniture, schoolbooks and other requisite items. Metal-framed beds were organised into rows in the dormitories, desks were set out in the two classrooms and library shelves were stocked.

The grounds of the orphanage were landscaped and asphalt was laid to create a basketball court and a five-a-side football pitch. Once a security-grade chain-link fence and floodlights were erected on its perimeter, the only missing pieces of the orphanage's puzzle were the orphans themselves and the staff needed to take care of them.

Sofia and Hugo envisaged that the children's health and well-being would be supervised by a matron who would reside in a separate self-contained apartment on the campus. They interviewed the prospective candidates in the orphanage's library. Within two days, they had filled both teaching posts, taken on two cooks, hired a kitchen assistant, appointed an administrator (who doubled as an accountant) and found a janitor.

The position of live-in matron was targeted by a formidable widow of around fifty, whose hair was tied in a bun and who confirmed her name as being señora Mercedes Márquez. "Mercedes like the German automobile manufacturer, and Márquez like the Colombian writer," she said with clipped enunciation. "I was head nurse at the famous Hospital de Jésus Nazareno, which first opened its doors in 1524."

"You were there a long time then," quipped Hugo receiving a swift kick under the table from Sofia.

"Please ignore my partner, señora Márquez. He is often an idiot. May I ask what prompted you to apply for the position?"

The nurse, dressed in a black jacket and matching ankle-length skirt, sat ramrod straight and took a moment to answer. Sofia thought of her as being a cross between Florence Nightingale and Mary Poppins.

"As well as raising three children of my own, I have worked as a volunteer at various orphanages in my free time. You see, helping those less fortunate than myself has been a passion of mine for as long as I can remember."

Here señora Márquez's earnest face darkened as she shifted in her seat. "I have seen the good that these institutions can do, but I have also seen the bad. The children need stability and continuity. My aim would be to help you to turn this orphanage into one of the good ones."

The nurse's values went straight to the heart of what Sofia and Hugo were hoping to achieve. Moreover, they were each struck by the determination in her eyes. Sofia was the first to respond.

"Please be reassured, señora Márquez, that our intentions are honourable. We are acutely aware that there is no substitute for a family and that some orphanages cause more problems than they solve, but we passionately share your hope that this facility will be one of the good ones. Ideally, we would like to find the right kind of adoptive parents for these children so they can be loved and cared for in a stable household."

Márquez, not wishing to offend her kind hosts, trod carefully. "You have good intentions, I can see that. But know that this job is not a glamorous one. There will be fights, there will be tantrums. You will have children dumped at your gate by parents who are simply too poor to feed them. And there will be outbreaks of sickness. It is exhausting. I have seen for myself how the bitter pill of reality has dulled the appetite of those who meant well when they first started."

Sofia reached out across the tabletop and took the nurse's hand. "Our objective is to give these kids a brighter future. We will feed them, clothe them and educate them. More importantly, we will protect them. You have my word on that."

"Please judge us by what we do, not by what we say, señora Márquez," added Hugo. "Our intention is to cultivate a family atmosphere within the orphanage, and we only want to employ those who will put the children first."

"Then I have probably talked myself out of a most wonderful job with my directness," sniffed the interviewee, dabbing at her eyes with a lace handkerchief.

"On the contrary," said Sofia, walking around the table to wrap the nurse in an affectionate hug. "You are exactly the person we need."

"Oh, absolutely," agreed Hugo. "We are extremely fortunate to have found you, señora Márquez."

"Señor and señora, I am so happy!" exclaimed Mercedes, descending into tears. "This building means so much to me. Can you believe that right where we are sitting used to be my classroom in the 1930s?"

"Then you must surely remember our friend, Magdalena Velázquez?" Sofia ventured.

"Señora Velázquez!" trilled the nurse. "She was my teacher and my inspiration. I loved her so much. All of the children loved her. And she is still alive?"

"Very much so," replied Sofia. "In fact, you will be

able to see her at the grand opening."

*

Even with staff background checks completed, legal permissions granted and the institution registered, finding orphans to fill the orphanage wasn't as straightforward a task as Sofia and Hugo had anticipated. Under Pablo's guidance, those who were the most vulnerable and not yet lost to a life of solvent abuse and petty crime were brought to the orphanage. Some came willingly, overjoyed at the chance to finally have a roof over their head, others were initially too frightened to leave a tented community that had provided them with companionship and a degree of stability. At first they stepped timidly into the facility, wild-haired and apprehensive, having to be reassured by Pablo that they hadn't fallen victim to some cruel hoax.

From the janitor to the administrator, the team played their part in making the children feel safe and welcome. Señora Márquez wasted no time in establishing herself as the mother figure on whom the kids would all rely.

Not all of the children were orphans because of the death of their parents. Two had been born in a prison hospital; others were the progeny of drug addicts who were unable to look after themselves, much less anyone else. Wherever possible, relatives were tracked down and familial ties re-established. In the case of the children whose birth parents had abandoned them solely for financial reasons, every effort was made to reunite them, even if it meant only seeing each other at weekends.

Other homeless hangouts were visited in the succeeding weeks and, before long, the orphanage was operating at full capacity with a flourishing contingent of children.

*

The second Saturday in May 1971 heralded the official opening of the orphanage. Sofia and Hugo had intended to name it The Pablo Quiroz Orphanage, but Pablo, with his customary humility, asked that it be named after his father instead. There were two brass plaques bearing Gerardo Quiroz's name; one attached to the wrought-iron entrance gate, the other screwed to a wall beside the front doorway.

News of the occasion had spread far and wide. No one, least of all Sofia and Hugo, had anticipated such a large turnout. In attendance were local residents, ex-teachers and former pupils of the school. There were also police and government officials, representatives from the local welfare department, news reporters and an overbearing TV film crew. Fuelled by finger food and liquid refreshments, the event was brightened by a wealth of smiles as adults became classmates again and retired teachers were belatedly told how much their tutelage had shaped the lives of their students.

Knowing how much this day would mean to Pablo, his loyal friends Magic Miguel and Jesús the organ grinder were also there to celebrate the realisation of his father's impossible dream. With all eyes upon him, Pablo nervously orated a speech that he had practised several times over. Having fluffed most of his lines, he wrapped it up with a rousing finale.

"I hereby announce The Gerardo Quiroz Orphanage open!" he shouted to resounding cheers, cutting a ceremonial ribbon with a gigantic pair of scissors that necessitated the use of both hands. "This is for you, Papá," he muttered, gazing up at the sky, hoping to see his father floating on a cloud with a trumpet to his lips.

After inspecting the orphanage's pristine rooms and its sparkling facilities, the attendees bunched together in one of the classrooms as Magdalena Velázquez rolled back the years by standing before a blackboard to deliver a speech of her own. And how good it felt to be there; once more she was a carefree thirty year old in her second teaching position and with wedding plans on the horizon.

"As most of you are aware, I was one of the first teachers at this school when it opened in 1922, and it warms my heart to see so many of my former pupils back here with me again."

Magdalena took a deep breath and fought back tears. It was while she was at the school that she had met Alfonso, her teacher husband, who had sadly died from tuberculosis just one year into their marriage. Because their love was imperishable, she had decided to settle for a life of chastity and solitude. The school became her significant other, and its pupils her children.

"Please don't imagine, though, that my teaching journey was always strewn with roses," señora Velázquez continued with a hawkish gaze. "Some of you were very naughty. Very naughty indeed... I am especially looking at you, Hector Ramos."

The fifty-year-old grandfather buried his face in his hands and accepted the ensuing cheers and good-natured catcalls with a wave and a hearty chuckle.

"You all flew away, my beautiful doves. And God does not give wings to just anybody, so he must have seen something good in you. Now you have all flown back, having made something of yourselves. I am so proud of each and every one of you for what you have achieved in this life, and I love you all from the depths of my ancient heart."

There wasn't a dry eye in the room as the tearful former schoolteacher blew kisses to her audience and received a standing ovation. Once the applause had subsided, she beckoned señora Márquez to join her. "A final word, as I am certain you must be terribly bored by the sound of my frail old voice. Some of you will already know Mercedes Márquez, who was one of my star pupils—"

"She was in my class!" Hector Ramos interjected, prompting an eruption of exuberant cheers. "But I knew her as Mercedes Muñoz in those days!"

"Yes, and I remember you putting a mouse in my

hair!" Mercedes yelled back, eliciting more laughter in the ranks.

A starry twinkle had returned to señora Velázquez's failing eyes. She had imagined that all of her best moments were buried in the past but this transcendent day had helped her to forget about her rusty knees, her gnawing loneliness and even the cancer that was doing its best to kill her.

"Mercedes is the matron here," she announced, her voice croaky. "And I know from talking to her how committed she is to the welfare of these children. So I am certain that you will all join me in wishing her, and the orphanage, the very best!"

CHAPTER THIRTY-THREE

One year later.
March, 1972

While showering, Sofia noticed a lump in her left breast. It seemed to have appeared almost overnight, a small knurl of hardened tissue invisible to the naked eye. Though unsettled by the discovery, she wasn't unduly worried at first; she knew that most lumps were found to be benign.

Wiping away the condensation from the bathroom mirror with a towel, she stepped back and studied herself. As far as she could determine, there were no discernible changes in the shape of her breasts but, when she pressed deeper into the skin in a circular motion, the lump became impossible to ignore. Keeping a cool head, she called Hugo into the bathroom to seek his opinion.

After some gentle probing, the concern on his face spoke volumes. "I'll book an emergency appointment with a private doctor today," he said reassuringly. "We need to get this looked at."

"Really, it's probably nothing," she said with a

shrug.

Hugo towelled her dry. "Perhaps. But it's best that we find out sooner rather than later."

*

They cancelled all their engagements, including a lunch date with General Contento and Josefina at the Hotel Geneve. Though Sofia's stomach was in knots, she remained upbeat and cheerful, engaging Hugo in small talk as he drove her to a highly rated hospital under the bluest of skies.

The couple's first impressions of the facility were favourable. It resembled a luxury hotel, with white-painted concrete walls and a glass façade. The concourse was fringed with palm trees and a selection of international flags hung limply in the afternoon heat.

As medical oncologists weren't yet prevalent, Sofia was concerned that the hospital's methods would be hopelessly outdated, especially as there had been some incredible advancements in cancer treatments since the 1970s. She was annoyed with herself for even thinking it, but this was the first time in her two years of living with Hugo in Mexico City that she had contemplated a return to the future.

Her fears were exacerbated by a soulless physician who, after a brief physical examination, confirmed the existence of cancerous cells with nothing more than professional guesswork to corroborate his diagnosis.

He went on to discuss mastectomies with an

insensitivity that beggared belief. "But, I am getting ahead of myself. First I will book you in for a mammogram," he said cursorily, while an attending nurse took notes.

A fierce indignation rose in Sofia's eyes as she buttoned her blouse. "Now wait for just one minute," she snapped. "All you have done is confirm that there's a lump, and suddenly you're talking about removing my entire breast as if it means no more to you than an ingrowing toenail."

The doctor gave her a look of disdain that had taken him a lifetime to perfect. "In my experience, señora Ustinova, if we don't cut enough away, the cancer will return."

"In your experience!" she huffed. "Your experience is rudimentary. You have the experience of a novice. What about anti-oestrogen drugs? What about lumpectomies?"

"I … um … er…"

"See! You don't have a clue!"

The doctor's mouth hung open like that of a landed fish but not one word fell out. The nurse, meanwhile, had retreated two paces and was trying to shrink into herself.

Sofia grabbed her handbag, hurled an insult, then left the room. Hugo, who had been reading a magazine in the foyer, looked up when he heard the rapid click-clack of her stilettos on the ceramic floor. Knowing that this wasn't the time for words, he followed her to the glazed entrance doors.

Once outside, he wrapped her in his arms at which point she burst into tears. "Darling, what did the doctor say?" he asked, fearing the worst.

"I was hoping he would tell me that it was nothing to worry about," she sobbed. "But he did the opposite."

Hugo looked deep into her wet eyes and thumbed away her tears. "We will get through this, Sofia. Whatever it takes, we will get through this. So what happens next?"

"Next, I will ask for a biopsy and a second opinion. That idiot should be working in a butcher's shop, not a hospital."

Hugo looked back towards the entrance, aware that a nurse was trying to attract their attention. "Wait here, darling, I'll see what she wants. It might be something important."

The nurse was half in the glass door and half out, her expression contrite.

"Yes? What is it?" he asked.

"Señor, I am so sorry, but you have forgotten to pay the bill."

After visiting another, more empathetic, physician in a different hospital, it took eight nail-biting days for Dr Ustinova to receive a pathology report in the post. Hugo took a deep breath and opened the envelope while they sat together in the fountain courtyard. Cruelly and unequivocally, the tests confirmed the presence of cancer cells.

While Hugo was stabbed by the thought of losing

the love of his life to the disease, Sofia was determined to beat it. "We both know that there is only one solution to this problem," she declared defiantly. "We return to the future where the medical know-how is more advanced and where my chances of survival are greatly increased."

"And where a Russian hit squad is going to come looking for you—"

"To hell with them! We're not scared of those bastards, are we, darling?"

"No, we're not," said Hugo with a grand smile.

Later in the day, Sofia and Hugo privately apprised Vincent of their need to return to the year 2020, and asked him to inform the household that they had simply flown to England on an important business matter.

The Irishman, cognisant of the fact that they would be putting themselves in harm's way, couldn't disguise his trepidation. "Why 2020? Why not 2019? Why not any other time and date?" he fretted. "It will be impossible for you to avoid enemy detection while you're both going backwards and forwards to a hospital."

"We don't necessarily have any say in the time and destination of our journey," said Sofia, seeking to reassure him. "It's mostly in the hands of our friends above."

"Jesus, I know you're stuck between a rock and a hard place, but the Russians will stop at nothing to find either of you. I just wish there were some other way."

"I will find a way, Vincent," said Hugo with calm authority. "I always do."

In the event of their plans taking a disastrous turn, Sofia and Hugo had expeditiously drafted a power of attorney through which Vincent was given control of their finances and authorised to make business decisions on their behalf. They knew that his commitment to Luna and Pablo and to the running of the orphanage was as solid as their own.

Once Sofia and Hugo's affairs were in order, and when it was time for them to prepare for departure, O'Toole wore his sadness like a cloak. "I'll miss you both. I'll miss you terribly."

Sofia held his gigantic hands in hers. "Darling man, no matter how long we are gone, we will return in the blink of an eye due to the miracle of time dilation. Really, you will barely notice our absence."

"I will notice it *here*," replied Vincent, touching his chest and fighting to control his emotions.

"We'll be fine," soothed Hugo, patting his friend on the shoulder. "We need to do this on our own. Your time and place is here with María."

"Now don't you start all that stiff upper lip nonsense with me, you useless article," said the Irishman. "Go on, pack what you need and we'll meet up later."

*

Later, they reconvened by the cellar door, where Vincent was still putting on a brave face. "I'll bring Luna up to speed, sure enough," he reasoned, "but how am I supposed to explain the hellish noise of that contraption to the others when it starts up?"

"I'm sure you'll think of something," said Hugo.

There followed an ebb and flow of hugs and tearful kisses. The couple had intended to leave quietly without any fuss, but at that moment Luna, as if summoned by a bell, ghosted in from nowhere with a hurt look on her face. "You're both leaving without saying goodbye?"

"We're not leaving for good, darling," reassured Sofia. "We'll only be gone for a very short while and will be back before you know it."

"But you won't be back," said Luna, her bottom lip trembling. "I've already seen in a vision what happens."

"Seen what?" sputtered Vincent. "Jesus, Luna."

"I saw them leaving in the time machine but it never returned."

Sofia looked at Hugo with alarm in her eyes, then tried to dispel Luna's fears. "My darling girl, we would never abandon you. I have to make this trip because my life depends on it. Vincent will furnish you with all the details."

"Your life depends on it!" Luna snapped. "What could be so important that your life depends on it? A little melodramatic, don't you think?"

Sofia took a deep breath. "I have a cancer, darling.

A cancer that could kill me if I don't act quickly."

Luna's strings were cut. Nothing in her life had prepared her for this. "Then promise me you will come back," she exhorted, her eyes reddening. "Promise me right now. You two are my everything."

"I promise, darling."

"We both promise," said Hugo feeling his heart breaking.

Tears cascaded down Luna's face as she continued. "All that I have, and everything I am is because of you. I cannot bear to lose you. Please, take me with you. Please."

"You can't come with us," replied Hugo. "It's too dangerous."

"I don't fear danger," said Luna bitterly. "Take me with you."

"We have to go," said Sofia with as much detachment as she could summon. "We want to see you and Pablo shine, Luna. Never forget that we love you."

"Please!" urged Luna, sending Sofia into a world of torment.

Vincent, knowing that he had to break the impasse, hustled Sofia and Hugo through the door and, with a heavy heart, locked it behind them. While Luna remained frantic with despair, he dropped to his knees in prayer. "Merciful Jesus, please watch over Sofia and Hugo and shield them from harm," he entreated, resting his forehead against the door. "And yes, I know that Hugo is riddled with sin, but he is still more deserving than most."

The couple entered the cabin of the time machine wet-eyed and with just two suitcases between them. Shell-shocked, they were lost in each other's arms and took a minute to regroup.

"My God, that was hard," Sofia faltered.

"Really hard," said Hugo.

"Tell me honestly, darling, are we doing the right thing?"

Hugo gave her a comforting smile. "Of course we're doing the right thing. And anyway, in their timespan we'll only be gone for a short while, right?"

"Correct."

Resorting to stoicism, Sofia dabbed her eyes and slipped a clinical face mask into Hugo's trouser pocket. "We'll be needing these where we're going."

Hugo opened his linen jacket to reveal his shoulder holster and loaded handgun. "And I'll be needing this."

Sofia pressed her palm against the authentication handprint, prompting the control panel to appear. Unexpectedly, the console displayed a set of coordinates that were completely unknown to her. "Oh!" she exclaimed, stepping back from the interface, at which point the air came alive with a symposium of intergalactic mutterings.

"What is it?" asked Hugo.

"I'm not familiar with these coordinates. That said, I trust my extraterrestrial friends implicitly."

The murmurings grew louder, perhaps even

cheerier, as if she had made a favourable impression on her imponderable audience.

Hugo studied the hologrammatic screen with keen interest. "I know these coordinates."

"You do?"

"They're the ones for my Stoat Manor Estate."

*

England, 2020

Watched only by a constellation of stars, the estate's grain barn pulsed with a candescent light and shrieked at the moon before returning to silence and darkness. No sooner had the time machine burred to a standstill than Sofia and Hugo's phones began to ping back to life.

"Stay there," Hugo directed as he stepped from the craft with his gun drawn. He crossed the barn and took a door key from its hook, while Sofia wasted no time in scrutinising her phone.

Stepping into the beam of a security light, the Englishman's breath smoked in the frosty night air. He scouted around the barn's perimeter looking for any signs of unusual activity, then returned to find Sofia still preoccupied with her device.

"At first glance all seems fine," he reported. "Once you're settled, I'll make you a cup of tea and give you the grand tour."

Sofia didn't catch a word he'd said. The phone had her undivided attention. "Oh, how wonderful!" she exclaimed, abruptly breaking from her trance.

"What is it?"

With joyful tears running down her cheeks, she showed Hugo a 360-degree image. "The orphanage, darling. To this day, it still exists."

CHAPTER THIRTY-FOUR

Luna and Vincent's concern was heightened by the fact that Sofia and Hugo hadn't returned two days after their departure. By the time a week had elapsed, the silence of the couple's absence had become deafening. It didn't help matters that other members of the household had picked up on Luna and Vincent's unease and kept interrogating them as to what was really going on.

"You said that they would be flying back from England within a few days," said María to Vincent as he helped her to defrost the refrigerator. "They should have called us on the telephone by now. I am worried sick, and so is Pablo."

"Perhaps they've been too busy," Vincent replied, fiddling with his wedding ring and hating the fact that he was having to lie to his wife.

"Too busy to let us know that they are okay? Then this must be the mother of all business trips. I will give those two a piece of my mind when they do decide to call."

*

After two weeks had ticked by without any comm-unication from either absconder, Luna and Vincent agreed that they could no longer hide the truth from María and Pablo.

"But not *all* of the truth," cautioned Luna, leaning back to gaze up at the Irishman as he towered over her. "I don't want either of them knowing what I am."

"Jesus, Luna. I don't know what you are, myself. And anyway, they are going to think that we are entirely mad as it is."

Sitting at the kitchen table, it transpired that María and Pablo did think that the little Dane and the big Irishman were entirely mad. They stared at them with incredulity as each sought to explain how they had travelled from the future.

"Jesus, would you listen to us?" said Vincent to his accomplice. "I wouldn't believe the nonsense that's coming out of our mouths either."

"But why would we make this up?" Luna asked of the two disbelievers.

Vincent produced his mobile phone and slid it across the tabletop. "Now then, this'll win you over. Would you check this little beauty out? Have you ever seen anything like it in your entire lives?"

Pablo held the device in his hand and examined it. "What is it?"

"It's a phone from the future," said Vincent triumphantly, giving Luna a comradely wink. "You can carry it around with you and make phone calls whenever you feel like it."

"Wow! Could you make a call now?" said Pablo, gesturing to the rotary phone on the kitchen wall.

"Gah! No I can't," said the Irishman through gritted teeth. "Because the damn thing won't work in 1972."

"Oh," replied Pablo, passing the phone to María as Javier Solís sang out from the kitchen radio.

Just as Luna and Vincent had begun to run out of ideas, a deafening noise tore through the house, rattling its windows and shaking its walls.

"Bah! It is air in the stupid water pipes again!" grumbled María.

"Ahah!" shouted the Irishman raising a revelatory finger and waggling his eyebrows as the din enveloped them. "Our heroes have returned in the aforementioned time machine. Fetch the cellar key, Luna!"

"No need. I wear it around my neck!" she yelled, scampering out of the kitchen door with joy in her heart, delighted that her premonition had proved to be imprecise and that Sofia and Hugo had returned safely.

While the racket continued, the others followed Luna into the hallway. An intense light ebbed and flowed through the cracks around the cellar door as she hurried to open it.

"I cannot wait for you two to see this thing," said Vincent excitedly, while Pablo and María looked on in a daze.

The noise ceased as Luna flung open the door. She scuttled down the concrete steps during which time the previously doubtful duo gazed down at the machine in astonishment.

Luna disappeared through the skin of the craft, as if stepping into a cloud, but promptly reappeared with a crestfallen look on her face. "They're not there," she said as the first of her tears began to fall. "They haven't come home."

CHAPTER THIRTY-FIVE

Nine months later

The time machine stayed put in the basement, inanimate and entirely unresponsive. Needless to say, Sofia and Hugo's absence was felt deeply by everyone in the house. The couple had, after all, been the guiding lights that steered everyone in the right direction, bringing each of them to the point and place in which they needed to be.

Copernicus missed Sofia's company to such an extent that he was off his food for several weeks and kept a daily vigil by the cellar door, not wanting to miss her long-awaited return.

To take his mind off the hollow pain he was feeling, Vincent immersed himself in the day-to-day running of the orphanage, playing a supporting role to the best of his ability. Pablo and Luna, extinguishing the last lingering lights of adolescence, had, meanwhile, reached the age of nineteen.

Pablo, less boyish now and invariably with the faintest trace of a five o'clock shadow on his chin, spent almost every day ensconced in his art studio, his fabulist paintings continuing to draw wide acclaim from the city's usually fastidious art critics.

Luna, under the auspices of Professor Boros, had been fast-tracked onto a master's degree course at the institute. But, irrespective of how well things were going, and despite María and Verónica endeavouring to lift everyone's spirits with good food and terrible renditions of Mexican folk songs, a mood of despondency prevailed throughout the year.

*

Time proved to be a passable healer rather than the great one it was purported to be. Luna found her niche in the lecture rooms, libraries and laboratories of the physics institute where her scientific foresight was the envy of everyone who came to know her. With colleagues hanging on her every word, she predicted an Orwellian future where household appliances would routinely respond to voice commands, where computers could be worn on wrists, and where motor vehicles would be able to drive from one place to the next all by themselves.

Luna herself was fascinated by a young American female researcher who was two years older and several inches taller, and whose parents had recently relocated to the city. Katie Gilroy was a social butterfly who seemed to flitter through life with the greatest of ease. An eye-catching, self-possessed young woman with sooty eyelashes, she had the male researchers panting in her presence and the females eating out of her hands.

Despite Luna possessing only a smidgen of sociability, they struck up a friendship. Katie saw a uniqueness in Luna that she found intoxicating. On the final day before the Christmas break, they were the last two in one of the laboratories after everyone else had set off home to enjoy the season's festivities with their families.

Katie, uninhibited after imbibing boozy fruit punch all afternoon with the rest of the team, made a beeline for Luna while the Dane was busily pressing buttons on a thermal evaporator. "Hey, Luna, what's up?"

"One moment, Katie, I'm almost done."

While she waited for Luna to finish, Katie removed her lab coat to reveal a mini-skirted dress and a chain which looped across her hips.

"There, I'm done," said Luna switching off the device only to find that Katie, for some strange reason, seemed to be undressing her with her eyes.

"I'm mightily intrigued by you, Luna," announced the American with a villainous smile.

"How so?"

"Because you're, like, a total genius and super cute with it."

"Thank you."

Katie arched one eyebrow in a vampish fashion. "So, what are you *really* into?" she purred. "Because I'm keen to know."

"Oh, books, nature, chess, archaeology—"

The American's smile flowed into a laugh. "I guess what I really meant to say was who do you dig more, guys or chicks?"

Luna looked at Katie enquiringly. "Dig?"

"Yeah, as in what is your type?"

"I'm unmoved by either."

Katie narrowed her eyes and circled a finger in Luna's direction. "Oh, you would definitely be moved if I were to kiss you, honey."

"I doubt it," said Luna pulling a face.

"Wanna try me?"

"What?"

"You wanna try me, right here, right now? Because I sure wanna try you, honey."

To her complete surprise, Katie's unanticipated advances lit a fire in Luna. Though she'd never considered it before, the thought of kissing another woman instantly thrilled her. "But someone might walk in," she said, allowing herself an impish smile.

"Pffft! Who cares? That's half the fun."

In a rare moment of spontaneity, Luna unbuttoned her lab coat and leant back against a filing cabinet. She was a late bloomer and it was only in the past year that modest curves had begun to augment her elfin body. "I suppose you *could* try me," she said coolly. "But there's no guarantee that I would like it."

The moment was charged with intimacy. Katie's eyes were filled with desire and she could barely restrain herself. "Are you sure about this?"

"I'm sure."

Katie moved in close and began to kiss Luna passionately. Luna allowed her wrists to be pinned against the metal cabinet as the American pressed against her crotch and whispered profanities in her ear.

After another feverish bout of kissing and fondling, Katie broke away with a wicked grin on her face. "So tell me you weren't moved by that," she said breathlessly.

"I did enjoy it," replied Luna, her face flushed and eyes gleaming with a crystalline brightness. "I enjoyed it very much. But I'm not so sure that I would want to do it again."

Katie's grin grew wider as she stood with her hands on her hips. "Then I would say with a great degree of certainty that you are into guys, honey."

*

On her cab ride home, Luna couldn't escape the rush of excitement that Katie had aroused in her. It had been an awakening of sorts, one that she was keen to explore. After paying the fare, she entered the house via the courtyard and was surprised, if not a little dismayed, to find Pablo sitting at the kitchen table in the company of a very pretty girl.

He was immediately out of his chair making introductions. "Luna, this is my friend, Angélica."

Angélica shifted in her seat and offered her hand. Luna took in her cognac-coloured eyes and convivial smile. "*Buenas tardes*, Luna. Pablo has told me so much about you."

"And yet he has told me nothing about you," replied Luna, staring at Pablo a little more reproachfully than she had intended. She wondered why she was so resentful of this personable young lady and came to the realisation that she was jealous for the first time in her life.

The awkwardness in the room was palpable. Pablo, in his nervousness, rubbed the back of his neck. "Um, Angélica kindly sat for me today," he faltered. "Her parents, they want her to have a portrait for her eighteenth birthday."

Luna managed to recover some decorum. She was annoyed with herself for showing a failing that she hadn't previously possessed. "It is a pleasure to meet you, Angélica. I hope that you are very happy with the painting."

"I am sure to be!" Angélica gushed, her eyes as big as saucers. "Pablo is my favourite artist. I love his paintings so much."

"Then we share the same love," said Luna as she left the kitchen.

Luna went directly to her bedroom where she kept a hardback copy of a highly publicised sex manual titled *Everything You Always Wanted to Know About Sex* (*But Were Afraid to Ask)*. The book was written by David Reuben, an American physician. She had bought it out of casual curiosity but hadn't looked at it since the day she'd carried it home. Now, because of her sexual awakening, she was inordinately keen to unlock its secrets.

That night, and over the course of the weekend, Luna left no stone unturned in her quest to find out more. The book portrayed sex as a divine art form, and she delighted in discovering words that were almost operatic in their enunciation: Latin words, such as *gamahuche*, *fututio* and *fellatio*. By the time she had read the manual from its first page to its last, her spirit of enquiry had drifted from the cerebral and was heading for the physical.

Luna started to sleep fitfully, surrendering to a succession of torrid dreams in which Pablo would pin her against a filing cabinet in the middle of a forest and kiss her lustfully. She would wake abruptly, annoyed that she couldn't participate in whatever should happen next. Pablo had, without realising it, untangled the briars in her heart.

Unbeknown to her, he was experiencing the exact same dreams.

CHAPTER THIRTY-SIX

Mexico City's Christmas Eve celebrations were as flamboyant as ever: a towering pine tree had been erected in the Zócalo and lit up with an extravagance of bulbs. Carols were sung in every corner of the main square, and gargantuan tinselled decorations in the shapes of bells, poinsettias, stars and giant candles adorned the façades of the buildings. Processions of candlelit worshippers streamed through the city's streets re-enacting the scene of Mary and Joseph going from door to door in Nazareth, seeking shelter while Mary was about to give birth to the baby Jesus.

Meanwhile, a smaller evening celebration was held at the orphanage. A profusion of Christmas lights had been strung across the building's exterior and a giant-sized Nativity scene had been set up on the floodlit basketball court. Before the festivities could begin, those in attendance were asked to observe a minute's silence to honour the life of Magdalena Velázquez, who had died peacefully in her sleep just one month after her rousing speech at the orphanage's opening ceremony.

Trestle tables almost buckled under the weight of buffet food provided by María, who had been ably assisted in its preparation by Mercedes and many of the orphans. On offer was an abundance of traditional festive foods, such as *tamales, romeritos, churros,* all washed down with steaming mugs of *champurrado* and glasses of Mexican eggnog. Ex-teachers and pupils, together with adoptive parents and members of the local community, gathered together to eat, drink and socialise, while the children bashed the living daylights out of several candy-filled *piñatas.*

Magic Miguel, to whom Pablo was paying a monthly retainer so that he no longer had to beg for a living, could not have been more appreciative of his friend's philanthropy. He spent much of the evening trying to demonstrate his gratitude. "Thank you for everything, Pablo. God has sent me the best friend that a fellow could hope for," he croaked, as fireworks whistled and exploded in the night sky. "I do not deserve the kindness you have shown me."

"My dear Miguel, you can thank me by continuing to attend the day classes at the orphanage. This is very important for your future. You were always there for me when I had no money, so God has sent me a best friend also."

During the course of the evening, Luna was never far from Pablo's thoughts. She was present at the party but had barely said a word to him since leaving the house. Earlier he had been thunderstruck by an unprecedented change in her appearance. Firstly, she was wearing a black cocktail dress that Sofia had bought for her eighteenth birthday, only for it to languish in the box it came in for the best part of a year. Secondly, she was wearing mascara, a custom he hadn't imagined her adopting either in this lifetime or the next. Even so, she seemed perfectly comfortable in her surroundings, chatting cordially to whoever approached her and enjoying the occasional cigar.

He stared at her, perhaps more often than he meant to. Occasionally she gazed back with the same look in her eyes that he'd seen in his hot-blooded dreams. Pablo was drawn to Luna as a moth is to a flame, captivated by her mystique. Once the guests had begun to thin out, he plucked up the courage to approach her. He wished he had the conviction to tell her that the mascara brought out the prettiness in her eyes, and that he couldn't stop thinking about her, but instead he plumped for, "Your dress, it is beautiful, Luna."

"It's black, like my heart," she replied, charmed by his awkwardness.

Love had taken possession of Pablo's soul, the kind of love that gnaws away at a person's rationality, that has them stumbling over their words and leaves them frantic with desire.

With his heart in his mouth, Pablo was all set to declare his love for Luna. He had just uttered the first syllable when María unwittingly closed his window of opportunity by joining them. "It warms my soul to see you two getting on so well," she cooed, wrapping them both in her arms.

At the party's end, after a mass tidy-up and with the children sent to their beds brimming with happiness, Vincent swung the Batmobile round to the orphanage's main gate. María, Luna and Pablo clambered in, María in the front passenger seat and the youngsters in the back. Because the prevailing mood was so buoyant, and because he had been told off by his wife umpteen times already, Vincent refrained from mentioning how sad it was that Sofia and Hugo weren't there to join in the celebrations.

The car's momentum as it turned right into Avenida Destino seemingly caused Luna's fingertips to slide across the leather seat onto Pablo's hand. Thrillingly, her fingers rested there, leaving him rigid in his seat, not daring to move a muscle. He surreptitiously stared down at her digits and wondered if she was even certain of their whereabouts. His hand, he reasoned, most likely felt the same as the padded leather of the car seat. In any event, he liked Luna's fingers being there and left it up to her to decide what she wanted to do with them.

Even when Vincent pulled up to the house, Luna's hand lingered on top of Pablo's for a moment longer than he expected. He summoned the courage to glance at her and, much to his delight, she gifted him a meaningful look before climbing out of the vehicle.

Once indoors, they withdrew to the living room where Vincent ceremoniously opened a bottle of

Champagne and poured four glasses. "*Feliz Navidad!*" he shouted, hoisting his glass to the ceiling.

"*Feliz Navidad!*" the others responded. Faithfully recalling one of Hugo's many etiquette guidelines, Luna and Pablo were careful to hold their glasses by the stems.

With Christmas tree lights twinkling behind her, María raised her glass. "May all of your dreams come true, Luna and Pablo. We are very proud of you."

"Hear! Hear!" roared Vincent, trying to hide the fact that he was becoming misty-eyed and emotional.

"Wraow! Wraow!" cheered Copernicus from Luna's lap.

Vincent regaled everyone with roguish stories of his childhood in Ireland, describing his father as being 'slippery as a buttered eel' and his sainted mother as 'a dove among crows'. He revisited memories of himself aged fourteen, working on his father's dray in the lead up to Christmas, rolling barrels of Guinness into the cellars of some of Dublin's busiest pubs.

"Only when my parents were gone from this world did I understand the true imperishable love that I had for them," he said with a rueful shake of his head. "May God continue to keep them in the palm of His hand."

"Oh, stop it, Vincent. You are making us all sad with such talk," María scolded. "And this is supposed to be a happy time. Perhaps you can tell Luna and Pablo the story of the long conversation you had with señor Elvis Presley on our honeymoon in Las Vegas—"

"God, yes," said Vincent with a shake of the head and a throaty chuckle. "I'd been knocking back whisky in the hotel bar like it was going out of fashion and suddenly there was the great man himself, in all his finery, posing for photographs and wearing fecking sunglasses indoors."

Luna and Pablo edged forward on the sofa they were occupying and listened with keen anticipation.

"So naturally, I struck up a conversation with Mr Presley. Told him how much I enjoyed the show. Even told him that he was shorter and fatter than he looked on the stage—"

"Oh, no—" gasped Luna seeing where this was heading.

"You've got it," the Irishman continued. "It was only after I'd asked for his autograph and wished him good luck for the rest of the tour that María told me he was one of those Elvis impersonators!"

In a rare moment of good humour, Luna burst out laughing, as did Pablo.

Vincent rose slowly from his armchair with a huge grin beneath his splendid moustache. "And on that bombshell, María and I will bid you youngsters goodnight. But, before we do, I would like to make one last, very important, toast." He hoisted a filled whisky glass and at the same time tried to keep his heartache at bay. "To absent friends!"

"To absent friends!" cheered all.

"I wanted to leave those two alone because there's a little something going on there," said Vincent to María as they ascended the stairs. "Love is in the air tonight. You can see it in their eyes."

"I don't think so," she scoffed. "They are only like brother and sister."

"Hardly," replied Vincent. "They were born six thousand miles and sixteen years apart."

"Well, if they do fall in love," said his wife, "they have my blessing."

Vincent produced a sprig of mistletoe, seemingly from nowhere, and held it above María's head. "How about a Christmas kiss, my little darlin'?"

Though they shared the same sofa, an uncomfortable silence existed between the teenagers. Words landed on the very tip of Pablo's tongue but flew away before he had the conviction to speak them. Then, much to his surprise, Luna threw him a compliment; told him that he looked very smart in his beige slacks and navy-blue shirt.

"Why do you sit so far away, shoeshine boy?" she said, with a rebellious glint in her eye, patting the cushion next to her. "You can move nearer to me, if you like."

Tingling with anticipation, Pablo shifted along the sofa and came to rest within touching distance of his soulmate. His compulsion to kiss her was extraordinarily strong. Again, Luna slipped her hand over his, only this time there was no ambiguity in its intention.

"I noticed that you didn't move your hand away when I touched it in the car," she said in a measured tone.

Pablo could feel her glittering eyes boring into him but was too shy to look her directly in the face. "I thought that maybe you had touched me only by accident," he replied, casting his gaze down at the black army boots she'd paired with her cocktail dress.

Luna's hand remained determinedly upon his. "So would you like me to touch you anywhere else?" she enquired, adopting the direct approach that had worked so well for Katie Gilroy.

This triggered a fluster of hot excitement in Pablo and caused his pants to tighten. He dared to look up and caught the come-hither look on Luna's face. Drawn to her gravitational field, he began to make his move, but she had already taken the initiative. Unable to contain herself any longer, Luna let out a low growl and pulled Pablo onto her. They kissed fervidly for a short while until, for no apparent reason, she pushed him away.

"Oh, did I make a mistake?" he asked, raising his hands as if she had him at gunpoint.

In a confusing about-turn, Luna threw him a sullen look. "You know only too well that you shouldn't be kissing me when you are dating someone."

Pablo was baffled. "Dating someone?"

"Angélica." Luna spat out the girl's name as if it were anathema to her.

Pablo was quick to untangle her misunderstanding. "You are wrong, Luna. Angélica is not my girlfriend. She is just a friend." Here he found the perfect opportunity to declare his love. "I do not look to other girls. I only ever think of you, in my head, in my dreams, and of course in my heart."

An irrepressible surge of desire coursed through Luna's veins and set her heart racing. Pablo's body was a little more muscled now, thanks to Charles Atlas's Dynamic Tension Program, and she longed to feel it pressed hard and naked against her.

"Pablo, have you ever had sex?" she asked without preamble, holding his gaze.

"Of course not," he replied, shocked by her candour.

"Then we can find out together. Stay here for a while, then come up to my bedroom in fifteen minutes. I will be waiting for you."

At this point, Luna remembered that the framed print of one of Pablo's paintings was hanging in plain sight so immediately resolved to do something about it. She rose from the sofa, downed the half-glass of whisky that Vincent had left behind and headed for the door, leaving Pablo in a high state of bewilderment and excitement.

Pablo kept an eye on the minute hand of the antique mantel clock for precisely fifteen minutes, then switched off the downstairs lights and also the ones on the Christmas tree. In the half-darkness he took the stairs two at a time and hastened along the landing.

Guided by a procession of lit tealights Luna had placed on alternate steps, he ascended the creaky staircase to her room and stood at the top with his heart beating against his ribcage.

Luna, who was now freshly soaped and perfumed, saw his shadow quivering in the light under the door and heard his hesitant knock.

"It is me," he whispered through the door.

"Who else would you be?" she teased. "Come in."

Pablo tentatively opened the door and was met by the sight of Luna sitting on the edge of her bed, almost spectral in the moonlight. She was barefoot, having removed all but her black cocktail dress. A red flower sat behind her ear. In the dim light, Pablo noticed that she had, for some reason, draped a towel over what he assumed to be a picture on a far wall.

Luna studied him and picked her words carefully; she needed to make sure that her special night wouldn't end in ignominy. "Tell me honestly, Pablo, do you really like what you see?" she enquired, leaning back. "Do I move you? Do you desire me?"

"Of course! How can you doubt it?"

"Because you might not have such feelings if you really knew me."

"But I do know you."

With that, Luna rose from the bed and turned her back to him. "Unzip my dress. Then you will see."

Pablo stepped forward and pulled on the zip. The dress peeled away to reveal a bark-like column of skin that ran almost the entire length of her backbone.

"See? I am not of this world," she said softly.

"I do not care," he replied, planting soft kisses all along the rough line of husk. "I already knew."

Luna turned abruptly, holding her dress up with one hand. "You knew?"

"I saw you one day when you thought no one was watching. You moved down the staircase like it was a hill made of ice. Your feet did not touch the floor. So I knew."

Luna was delighted to have been caught unawares in such a way. "I could grow to love a man like you," she whispered.

"I fell in love with you before I knew you," he replied.

In an instant, Luna was off her feet, wrapping her legs around Pablo's waist and kissing him feverishly. Pablo returned her kisses as he lifted her onto the bed. Her mouth tasted of whisky and cigars, and the air around them was charged with static.

In her eagerness to unbutton his shirt, Luna's dress fell to her waist to reveal a slightly built body and emergent breasts. She hastily unbuckled his belt and unzipped his trousers, sliding her hand inside to feel his tumescence. No longer a shy teenager, Pablo divested himself of his shirt, shoes and trousers and removed his Y-fronts to reveal an impressively erect penis.

Luna had never seen one in the flesh before, apart from when a tramp in the park had felt the need to pleasure himself openly one sunny afternoon. In any event, the vagrant's gobbet of gristle really wasn't much to write home about, as far as she could tell. By way of contrast, Pablo's was a handsome creation, impressively upright and slightly threatening. And it hadn't escaped her notice that he seemed especially keen to show it off.

Pablo removed Luna's dress entirely and peppered her with kisses all the way down to her stomach. She gasped loudly when he burrowed his mouth between her parted legs. He enjoyed the sharp taste of her and delighted in hearing the soft moans that escaped the back of her throat. Though uneducated in the ways of love, it transpired that pleasuring a female came naturally to him.

"God of Thunder!" Luna gasped, throwing back her arms. "You were born to do this, Pablo."

The shudder of her orgasm, when it came, was profound and unexpected, and it took her almost a minute to recover from it. "I want you," she urged when revived, pulling hard on his hair.

Pablo gazed down at her with unveiled adoration. Moonlight hugged the contours of her naked body, her skin as white as the sheets she lay upon. The promise of her thrilled and worried him in equal measure. "Are you sure?" he asked, his *membrum virile* still standing to attention.

"Of course I'm sure," she said impatiently. "But you must stop at some point. I'm sure you know why."

"Yes, I understand."

A black cloud obscured the moon and threw a dark

shadow across Luna's face, making her eyes glow green like those of a cat caught in headlights. She began to hover parallel to the mattress, allowing Pablo easier access. He made love to her with a sensuality seldom seen in one so inexperienced. They moved in perfect harmony and together experienced a pleasure far greater than each had ever known.

"You are my god!" growled Luna, biting his ear. "Don't stop."

"But I have to stop," Pablo gasped.

"Then I will help you when you do."

Once sated, they floated together in their own private biosphere, their world reduced to the softest of kisses and the gentlest of caresses.

The moon reappeared in a raven sky. Through the window it cast its light upon Luna's smiling face and on the gloss of Pablo's black hair.

"Luna, you are an angel who has fallen to Earth," he grinned. "I love you without fear and I love you with all of my heart. It is as simple as that."

Not quite believing what she was about to say, Luna gazed into his trusting eyes. "I love you too, Pablo. Perhaps I always will."

The Mexican, at that moment, was struck by a flash of inspiration. "Luna, I will paint a picture of you in your honour. It will be the first of many."

*

As soon as the Christmas festivities had finished, Pablo closed the door to his studio and set about creating a painting to commemorate his first night with his sweetheart. Once completed, he framed it himself and presented it to Luna in her bedroom. It depicted her barefoot and floating above rooftops in a starry sky wearing the same black dress she had worn to the party. In the bottom-right corner, in red paint strokes, he'd scrawled his name and the year.

"I have simply called it 'Luna'," he announced proudly.

Luna, with a playful look on her face, readied herself to ceremoniously remove the towel she'd draped over the picture on her wall. She had thought long and hard about whether or not she should reveal it to him, but he already knew that she had travelled from the future so the cat was out of the bag anyway.

She gripped the edge of the towel and threw him a puckish smile. "Pablo. Prepare yourself for this, because you will not believe your eyes."

CHAPTER THIRTY-SEVEN

April, 1975

In the three years since Sofia and Hugo's disappearance, everyone in the house had resigned themselves to the prospect of never seeing them again. Casual friends and acquaintances of the missing couple, imagining a scandal of some description, had stopped asking after them and simply carried on with their lives. The very best of their friends, couples such as Eduardo Volante and Rafa, General Contento and Josefina, stayed in touch with Vincent and María and met up with them as often as possible.

"Good friends are like a winning lottery ticket," said Vincent to Contento as they reclined on sun loungers by the general's outdoor swimming pool. "Wonderful to have but painful to lose."

"Whereas bad friends are painful to have and wonderful to lose," asserted the general with a roguish wink.

As a way to circumnavigate any awkward questions, O'Toole had previously confided in the general that Hugo was working for the British Secret Service, which accounted for why he and Sofia hadn't been able to stay in contact.

"I hear that Pablo and Luna are doing very well in life," said Contento as his butler approached with two glasses of cold beer on a silver platter.

"They're doing grand," replied Vincent, fanning himself with a straw hat. "There's talk of some art expert from San Francisco coming down to look at Pablo's paintings. Luna made her master's degree look like child's play and already has universities such as Oxford and Harvard making overtures."

O'Toole thanked the butler as he took one of the glasses and clinked it against the general's. "*Sláinte*, Ricardo!"

"*Salud*, Vincent!"

Vincent took a generous swig of beer and gazed languidly at the sun's glittering dance on the surface of the pool. "Oh, there is one more piece of news about Luna and Pablo," he remembered suddenly.

"And what is that?" asked the general, cleaning his sunglasses on the hem of his Hawaiian shirt.

"They're getting married."

*

Luna and Pablo thought about Sofia and Hugo often, either speculating as to what they might be doing or conceding with great sadness that they might not be alive. As if to punctuate their absence, the time machine vanished one day without making the slightest sound, leaving no trace as if it had never existed.

"It's remarkable to think," said Luna to Pablo while they reminisced about the missing couple, "that, strictly speaking, Sofia and Hugo haven't even been born yet."

The couple's sense of loss was profound. They missed their guardians' unstinting love, their pragmatism, the reassurance of their protection and mostly their natural warmth. They pined for the smell of their perfume, their smiles, their winks, their hugs and late-night conversations. They wished that they could enjoy just one more family meal together, or for the house to resonate again to the pleasant sound of Sofia playing on her grand piano.

The youngsters, each twenty-one years old and approaching twenty-two, were soon to be married. Their engagement had come about after Pablo had asked María to tell him the instant she caught sight of Luna shinning up her favourite tree in the courtyard. Only two days later, the cook had witnessed Luna doing just that from her vantage point in the kitchen.

Once tipped off, Pablo downed his paintbrushes and ventured outside bearing a wooden ladder that he propped against the tree. From one of its highest rungs, he held out an engagement ring and proposed to Luna as she rested on a bough with her squirrel friend for company.

Pablo treasured every bit of her, body and soul. In turn, she considered herself fortunate to have him as her husband-to-be. Much of the inherent goodness that shone through everything he said or did rubbed off on Luna and made her a more complete person. With Pablo by her side, she felt that anything was possible.

*

Although a staunch non-believer in Christianity, but knowing how much it would mean to him, Luna acceded to Pablo's plan to get married in the Church of the Wounded Angel. In order to do so, she would first have to participate in an assessment of her readiness for sacramental marriage conducted by Father Pedroza. The priest, though he would have preferred Pablo to marry a Catholic girl, and ideally a Mexican one, was nevertheless looking forward to presiding over the ceremony.

"Pablo, it's Father Pedroza," said the padre one evening over the telephone. "If it's OK with you, the new bishop would like to accompany me when I visit tomorrow morning. He, as do I, needs to ensure that you both understand your moral obligations within the arms of the Catholic faith."

"It will be an honour," replied Pablo with feigned enthusiasm, secretly unnerved that someone as illustrious as a bishop would be getting involved. "Is there anything else we need to do beforehand, Father?"

"No, just have all the necessary documents to hand and see to it that Luna puts her best foot forward. I have yet to meet him but by all accounts my new boss is a very reasonable fellow, so this should be an easy ride."

"That is very good to hear," said Pablo, mightily relieved. "We will see you tomorrow, Father."

*

Pablo was weak at the knees and in a high state of nervousness the next morning as he awaited the arrival of the clergymen. María had baked a Victoria sponge specially for the occasion and Vincent had been instructed to make himself scarce.

Pablo's heart performed a somersault when the doorbell sounded on the stroke of ten-thirty and he suffered a last-second panic attack before setting off for the hallway. He stood at the front door as if about to face a firing squad and took more than a moment to compose himself.

After wiping his sweaty palms on his shirt, he took a deep breath and pulled open the door. Squinting into the light, the first person he saw was Father Pedroza who was dressed in his usual black cassock and barely more than a silhouette with the sun behind him. "Please come in," greeted Pablo, stepping to one side to receive the two men. But then, as he became accustomed to the sun's glare, he was startled to see a very familiar, and most unwelcome, face coming towards him.

The clergymen stepped into the cool of the hallway. The bishop was a thin man with a cerise skull cap atop his greying hair. A chunky gold crucifix and chain hung over his flowing robes and clerical collar.

Father Pedroza wondered why Pablo was rooted to

the spot, his eyes big as oysters, as if he had seen a ghost. "Pablo ... Pablo," said the padre, resisting the urge to snap his fingers. "Please be introduced to His Excellency, Bishop Severiano Salazar."

The bishop offered his bony hand to the stupefied youngster. "It is a genuine pleasure to finally meet you, Pablo," he said with the kindest of smiles. "Father Pedroza has spoken of you in glowing terms."

"B-but we already know each other," stuttered Pablo, keeping his distance. "You used to work here."

Both the priest and the bishop looked at each other with incredulity.

"I used to work here?" enquired His Excellency in an amused tone. "In which capacity, might I ask?"

Pablo knitted his brow, not sure whether to be annoyed or embarrassed. "You know in which capacity," he retorted. "You were our butler!"

"Me? A butler?" sputtered the bishop, thrown into a state of confusion by the lad's irrationality. "But I have served the church all my adult life."

Luna, who had been earwigging from the living room, had swiftly unpicked the cosmic conundrum and promptly flew to Pablo's rescue. "Hello, I'm Luna. Pleased to meet you both," she schmoozed, briskly shaking hands and casting Pablo a stern glance. "I think that what my fiancé was trying to say, Your Excellency, is that you look remarkably like a butler we once employed."

"Ahah! So that's it!" exclaimed the bishop, throwing back his head and chuckling to himself. "A doppelgänger, eh? Hopefully I am the more handsome one?"

"Oh, undoubtedly!" replied Luna, taking Salazar by the arm and leading him to the kitchen. "Would you like coffee and some home-made cake before we get down to business, Your Excellency?"

"Please, call me Severiano," said the bishop with a twinkle in his eye.

Following on behind, Father Pedroza, delighted at the way in which things were progressing after such a shaky start, gave Pablo a secret thumbs-up.

CHAPTER THIRTY-EIGHT

The day of the wedding.

Sofia and Hugo stood before the monastery-style front door of their former home on Avenida Destino and rehearsed greetings under their breath. Feeling extremely fortunate to have been given the chance to return to Mexico City on such a precious occasion, they paused to enjoy their surroundings and further contemplated the mysteries of the Universe.

Auspiciously, the setting was perfect for a wedding. Overhead, citadels of white clouds floated in a majestic sky and the bells of the Church of the Wounded Angel rang out in celebration of Luna and Pablo's big day.

"I do wish we had been given the opportunity to dress a little smarter," said Sofia, casting a critical eye over Hugo's crumpled linen jacket and his open-necked shirt. "It would have been nice if I could have at least worn a fabulous hat."

"It couldn't be avoided," Hugo reasoned, breaking into a smile. "We had no option but to come as we were."

With a disapproving look, Sofia prodded the

shoulder holster that was hidden by his jacket. "And, darling, who brings a gun to a wedding?" she huffed.

"I was wearing it when we were summoned," he said. "And anyway, everyone will be delighted to see us no matter how we look or act."

With one hand on the cast-iron door pull, Hugo asked Sofia if she was ready. She smoothed her skirt and took a deep breath. "I'm ready."

"Nervous?"

"Very."

The Englishman yanked sturdily on the handle and heard the bell clanging uproariously on the other side of the door. The couple each took a step back and exchanged excited glances.

*

Luna was descending the grand staircase, her hair in a Scandinavian braid and her wedding dress floating about her like a cloud, when the doorbell sounded.

"Pablo! There is someone at the door!" she cried. "I don't want anyone to see me until I am absolutely ready!"

Her husband-to-be, stylishly dressed in a velvet suit and bulky bow tie, was already on his way. "Do not worry, my love!" he replied, mindful not to look up the staircase. "I will ask them to close their eyes!"

As he pulled open the door, Sofia and Hugo beamed at him with extravagant delight. "Surprise!" they cheered in unison.

Pablo blinked into the light. Naturally, he had

expected to see someone standing there but even when he craned his neck to look left and right the sidewalk was peculiarly empty. "There is no one here!" he yelled to Luna.

*

Following their first night together at Stoat Manor, Hugo had served Sofia breakfast in bed. Afterwards he introduced her to his stable hands and also to the team of horses he had missed deeply whilst he was away.

It was bitterly cold that morning and Sofia hadn't thought to pack a winter coat, so Hugo elected to drive her to Henley-on-Thames to buy one. For convenience, they wore the same clothes they'd travelled in and hurried towards his Range Rover through a frantic blizzard of snowflakes.

Hugo didn't know that two Russian spies, under the cover of darkness, had sprayed a military-grade nerve agent onto the door handles of his vehicle. Neither had he foreseen that he and Sofia would later be found on a country road unconscious in their car seats. Despite the best efforts of a critical-care team, they never regained consciousness and were pronounced dead four days later.

*

As Pablo closed the front door, he imagined he caught a waft of perfume, a scent familiar enough to stop him in his tracks. Nevertheless, conscious of the fact that Luna was still glaring at him from halfway up the staircase, he lowered his head and headed for the courtyard.

With the wind taken out of their sails, Sofia and Hugo stood in the hallway and accepted their situation with calm stoicism. No man is ever free from his own history reflected Hugo, thinking of the lives he'd taken and those he had left bereft of a husband, a father, a brother or a son.

Their spirits were lifted by the sight of Luna descending the stairs, raising the hem of her dress as she did so. She swished past Sofia and Hugo, completely oblivious to their spectral presence, but then stopped abruptly to loudly sniff the air around them as she detected strong notes of Chanel Nº5 and Old Spice.

"Are you here?" she whispered excitedly through the sheer white veil that covered her face. "If you are, know that I love you both with all of my heart and I always will." With that, she blew kisses in their general direction and bustled towards the living room, casting a backward glance as she disappeared from view.

The couple ghosted along the hallway and paused at the living-room doorway to witness María trying to wrestle a pair of satin pumps onto Luna's feet. Accompanied by Copernicus, who seemed to be the only living thing that could see them, they proceeded to the fountain courtyard where Pablo was now standing by the back gate alongside his best man, Magic Miguel. Beyond the gate, dressed in the orphanage's school uniform, was a buoyant crowd of girls and boys, none of whom could contain their excitement.

The midday sun was leopardskin-dappled through the trees, painting a translucent rainbow in the fountain's mist and highlighting veined patterns on the wings of butterflies. The church bells, relentless in their refrain, continued to peal for all to hear, their resonance bouncing off walls and rooftops. Waiting expectantly in the church was a large congregation of staunch friends and thrilled associates.

Vincent breezed past Sofia and Hugo. Upon his signal, Pablo opened the gate and a tide of excited orphans spilled into the courtyard, filling it entirely. To mark the occasion Madame Díaz-Zorita sang *Ave Maria* from her balcony, and the church bells seemed to clang even more cheerfully at the sound of her magnificent voice.

Sofia and Hugo were joined unexpectedly by Pablo's parents, Rosa and Gerardo, and the four exchanged hugs and kisses, delighted to be in each other's company. At about the same time, Hugo felt certain he saw two chalk-skinned beings, one male, one female, moving stealthily along the branches of Luna's favourite tree.

The bride, accompanied by bridesmaids María and Verónica, looked resplendent in her beautiful wedding dress. When she appeared in the courtyard, the orphans were sent into a fit of unrestrained rapture that threatened to drown out the sound of the church bells.

Vincent, who would soon be walking Luna down the aisle, grabbed everyone's attention by clapping his huge hands together and raising his voice in a commanding fashion. "Hey, listen up! If everyone is ready, let's form an orderly line and proceed to the church!"

Nonplussed, almost all of the orphans looked to Pablo for a translation. "*Si todos están listos, hagan fila para ir a la iglesia!*" he shouted, gesturing in the church's direction and positioning himself to lead the jubilant procession.

Sofia and Hugo delighted in the smiles of those they loved and those whom they had helped to gain a foothold in this life. They were safe in the knowledge that Luna would go on to become an acclaimed physicist and climate-change activist, and that Pablo's artwork would be enjoyed by millions around the globe.

Hugo took Sofia by the hand and threw her his invincible smile. "All told, we did some good in this world, didn't we?"

Sofia held him close and kissed him on the cheek. "We were amazing, darling."

"Writers are only ever as good as their readers."

Kevin Ansbro

ACKNOWLEDGMENTS

Thank you, dear reader, for choosing to cast your eyes over the pages in my book. The fact that you've reached this point at least reassures me that you haven't hurled it at a wall, thrown it onto a bonfire or put it through a macerator.

I would also like to thank the following: Julie, my wife, for editing my first draft – often with a virtuosity that makes me wonder if she should be the one doing the writing; Karen 'Genghis' Holmes, my actual editor, and Catherine Cousins, who are both totally amazing; Gabriel García Márquez and Salman Rushdie for introducing me to a linguistically playful way of writing; my Mexican friend, Kita Huerta, for her local knowledge and guidance; my good friend, Lars Dradrach, for his help with Danish dialogue translation; Ian Fleming for starting a tradition of fictional (and highly improbable) secret agents; Albert Einstein for transforming our understanding of time and space; Nicolaus Copernicus for gifting me a great name for a cat, and Johannes Gutenberg for inventing the printing press.

Lastly, but certainly not least, I would like to offer my gratitude to our wonderful National Health Service staff and to everyone around the world who has worked tirelessly on the frontline in the midst of a global pandemic.

Big love to you all!
Kevin

BY THE SAME AUTHOR

Kinnara

(Paperback and eBook)

The Angel in my Well

(eBook)

The Fish That Climbed a Tree

(Paperback and eBook)

The Minotaur's Son

& other wild tales

(Paperback and eBook)

An excerpt from
Kinnara

Jao, understanding the need to make the trip more memorable, issued a sporting dare. Sawat loved a challenge and this instantly made him forget his disappointment at not seeing the dolphins. His uncle asked if he was capable of diving down and touching the sea bed: he remembered doing the exact same thing when he was a teenager. Hoping to turn it into an exciting escapade for the boy, he even teased him about the sea spirits who lived beneath the waves. Returning with one stone, a shell or even a clump of seaweed, would offer proof of his success.

Sawat couldn't wait to make his attempt; he was a strong swimmer and could hold his breath for a considerable length of time. Plus, he wanted to impress his uncle who was his only paternal influence since the death of his father.

Jao ensured his nephew donned a wetsuit. Despite the surface temperature being comfortable on such a hot day, the water was a great deal colder the further down you went. Sawat dropped into the sea, clutching a dive torch. He took three shallow breaths then, on the fourth, inhaled as much air as his lungs could manage and disappeared beneath the surface. He found it incredibly easy at first and the seabed soon appeared in the torch's bright beam. Going further, though, was more of a struggle; his ears were collecting unfamiliar sounds and the depths buoyed his body, resisting it with a hostile determination. *Perhaps it's the sea spirits pushing back at me,* he imagined nervously. His fingertips had almost reached the bottom, when, unbelievably, he saw something large move. Sawat redirected the torch: He hadn't imagined it; sitting on the sand was one of the spirits his uncle had warned him about, only this one seemed to be half-human, and half-bird! He had never been so scared in all of his life. Sawat yelped in terror, but only a bubble ballooned from his noiseless mouth. He recoiled and twisted his body so that he could return to the safety of the boat. The water roared against his eardrums. His uncle, meanwhile, was beginning to worry whether he should have issued the challenge in the first place. Sawat seemed to be underwater for a disquieting amount of time. Jao was about to dive into the sea himself, when his nephew burst through the surface with cold fear in his eyes. The boy was shouting and babbling incoherently. Jao dragged him from the water, fearing that some damage may have occurred or that he had been stung by jellyfish.

"Uncle, I saw the sea spirit! I saw the sea spirit!"

Jao was hugely relieved, realising that the kid had

simply let his imagination get the better of him. He turned the ignition and allowed the engine to idle. Sawat, though, was still babbling incoherently…

An excerpt from
The Angel in my Well

It was blackboard-dark as I arrived home on Friday evening. Gentle flurries of snow embellished the frigid air and dissolved on my face. I carried a flimsy supermarket bag, filled with cleaning products, which I held between my teeth as I fumbled for the door key. A bottle of Australian Shiraz, tucked under one armpit, threatened to smash to the ground any second.

After spreading my goods like budget raffle prizes across a worktop, I walked into the hallway and clicked the central heating on. Sifting through my burgeoning pile of takeaway menus, the *Royal Bengal* this time, I sat down to make some choices. I really don't know why I do this, because I'm a creature of habit. I invariably select the same dishes, and those dishes already have their numbers heavily ringed in ballpoint pen.

Just as my anticipation of delicious comfort food was causing a Pavlovian reflex, I was aware of a strange caterwauling noise coming from outside the cottage. I padded over to the kitchen window expecting to see a fox, or some similar nocturnal creature, but didn't see anything out of the ordinary.

The sound continued: there most definitely *was* a sound, but despite craning my neck close to the glass, there was nothing in view, just the stand-still silhouette of hostile trees that loomed like spectres. This extraordinary noise seemed to grow louder and sounded like no animal that I could ever imagine. Transfixed, but also fearful, I opened the front door and stepped out into the chilled night air. The sky was crow-black, softened by some lithium clouds that had nestled down for the night. And there it was again, the echo of a nearby voice, almost *human*. But all around me was just the eerie emptiness of my front garden and the wispy blossoms of snow that fell silently from the darkness.

Becoming ever more anxious, I could hear the sound of frantic splashing coming from the direction of the well. Instinct overcame dread and I sprinted across the lawn. I then recoiled in horror at what I saw...

An excerpt from
The Fish That Climbed a Tree

L ondon was under a canopy of darkness by the time the Body Snatcher prepared to leave the warehouse. He punched in the key code, his grisly cargo already bagged up and thrown into the back of his van. Yuri and Pascal trusted him enough to lock up and had earlier taken their leave after paying him the agreed sum of cash.

Under a thin crescent moon that hung like a toenail clipping in the night sky, the man was relieved to rinse his lungs with the damp, brackish air that drifted in from the Thames. He wasn't best pleased that his nostrils, skin and clothes were polluted by the smoky, charcoaled climate of the warehouse; it was an unnecessary add-on to the precise list of things that he had to deal with. As a phlegmatic man, predisposed to discipline and diligence, he was less than enamoured by the African's incautious method of execution. Setting fire to a victim was as messy as it was inefficient; in his view, a loose cannon such as Pascal was a serious liability in his line of work. Yuri, on the other hand, was more measured and clinical, a person that the Body Snatcher could at least do business with. In truth he intensely disliked both men but the risk-to-reward ratio was weighted solidly in his favour.

Those two donkeys would've probably dumped the body in the river, he thought as he drove towards Tower Bridge against a glimmer of luxury wharfside apartment blocks lit up like cruise ships above the black mirror of the Thames.

An excerpt from
The Minotaur's Son

It was with much fanfare, banging of drums and blowing of whistles that the Circus Extraordinario descended on the remote Colombian village of Agua Mala one cloudless afternoon. Because Agua Mala was a three-day dirt-road drive from civilisation, its population of just 178 people were naturally astonished that their modest outpost would be graced by such a thrilling event.

The village comprised forty-three adobe houses, a rustic church, a makeshift school and a bar that doubled as a whorehouse. Its inhabitants kept pigs, goats and chickens and farmed a field of coca solely to keep the drug traffickers from razing their homes to the ground while they slept.

The locals weren't to know that Esteban Ortiz, a crooked businessman and founder of the circus, was drawn primarily to their blot on the landscape by fanciful folktales of Isidora, the winged nymph who was said to bathe in the river's malodorous water. A photograph showing her to be the size of a young child had recently been handed to the entrepreneur, providing him with unequivocal evidence of her existence. He knew only too well that such a remarkable specimen would make a very welcome addition to his troupe, should he be able to capture and groom her.

From a fleet of trucks and caravans there appeared a succession of circus performers, most noticeably a bearded lady and a three-legged Cossack. After spreading canvas sheets across a jungle clearing and erecting a metal frame, the ensemble worked as one to winch their grimy circus tent to its full height. And then, as trees reverberated to the sound of mallets driving stakes into the ground, the star of the show, the legendary Minotaur, made his much-anticipated appearance. After a swish of his tail and much flexing of muscles, he acknowledged the cheers of the locals who had cancelled a day's farming to catch a glimpse of his fabled animalism.

www.kevinansbro.co.uk

Twitter: @kevinansbro

Goodreads: Kevin Ansbro

CPSIA information can be obtained
at www.ICGtesting.com
Printed in the USA
BVHW032043250821
615213BV00005B/101